SHADOW POINT

BY

AMY BRIANT

Bella
BOOKS

2010

Bella Books, Inc.
P.O. Box 10543
Tallahassee, FL 32302

Printed in the United States of America on acid-free paper.

First Edition Bella Books 2010

Editor: Katherine V. Forrest
Cover designer: Judith Fellows

ISBN-13: 978-1-59493-216-8

About the Author

Amy Briant is a native Californian. She grew up in a part of San Diego called Point Loma, which greatly resembles Shadow Point except for the malevolent phantom. This is her first novel. She lives in the San Francisco Bay area. Find out more at www.amybriant.com.

Dedication

For my mother, who gave me her love of books;
And my father, who gave me his love of music.

Acknowledgments

My thanks to editorial director Karin Kallmaker, editor Katherine V. Forrest and the rest of the Bella Books team.

Prologue

They found my brother's body by the tide pools. Some small, probably squishy, sea creature had stung him with a virulence that could not be denied. The resulting anaphylactic shock was the end of James. With no one else around, he had no chance of making it back to a phone before his cold little heart stopped for the last time.

They said it was sunset when they found him. The tide was trying to take him out, but his shirt snagged on a rock.

They told me all this later, of course. I wasn't there. I was in Boston, getting fired.

All in all, it was really inconsiderate of James to go and die on us like that, leaving his only child an orphan and turning my life upside down. Served me right, he would have said.

Chapter 1

Well, not totally fired. But there was a lot of yelling and gesturing and finally, a suggestion from the boss—an order, really—to take at least three weeks off starting immediately.

Increasingly erratic and hostile, they said I'd become. Inappropriate behavior. Unproductive. Disrespectful. Poor attitude. One final warning, one final chance. But first go away for three weeks.

Go where? I thought, sitting on my couch in my apartment. Three weeks stretched out before me like an uncrossable desert. I'd never taken more than a week off in my entire life. Which was only twenty-eight years, of course. James was five years older.

My apartment looked weird to me in the stark light of a Thursday afternoon. I was hardly ever home, period and never willingly both home and conscious in the daylight hours of a weekday. The living room smelled of dust. My suitcase was still by the front door, where I'd left it when I'd gotten home late the night before from my most recent training trip to one of the regional offices. Atlanta? Chicago? I'd already forgotten.

Three nineteen p.m. and I was trying to think what was good about my life. I was drawing a blank, so I lay down on the couch to facilitate the process. Sternly telling myself it was way too early for a drink. And that I definitely would not, could not, call Isabel.

I was still lying there when the phone rang at 5:07. That was odd. Nobody ever called me at home. I was never there. Anybody who knew me at all called my cell. I rolled off the couch with a groan and answered it with no premonition whatsoever. The message light was blinking—I hadn't noticed that the night before. Hadn't bothered to check. And that morning, I'd been in my usual high-speed-rush-out-the-door mode, so I hadn't thought to check then either. Nobody ever called me at home.

"May I speak to Madison McPeake, please?" A man's voice, but not one I knew.

"Speaking."

"Ms. McPeake, this is Lieutenant Delgado with the United States Navy in San Diego. I'm very sorry, ma'am, I have some bad news for you."

He didn't sound sorry. He sounded entirely matter-of-fact. I had no idea what the hell he was talking about.

"Um…I'm sorry, are you sure you've got the right person?" Even as I said it, I thought: James. James might be in San Diego.

"It's about your brother, ma'am—Dr. James McPeake?"

"Oh." Pause for me to take in some air. "What…what's happened?"

"I'm sorry, ma'am. There's been an accident. Your brother is dead."

3

Chapter 2

The next flight to San Diego with a seat available wasn't until the next day. My job required constant travel, but neither my platinum nor my bereaved status could shake loose a seat any sooner. Even my chances at standby on the red-eye were slim and none, per the agent, since thunderstorms in Dallas had delayed so many other flights earlier in the day. So, I numbly unpacked my suitcase, threw that stuff in the wash and repacked with more casual clothes. And a black suit, black shoes, black hose, black silk shell. Pearls. I hadn't noticed before how my professional wardrobe was also perfect for funerals. All purpose for every occasion.

James and I were not close, to put it mildly. Somewhere in his high school years, he'd started going to church, falling in with right-wing Christian fundamentalists. Overnight, it seemed, he'd grown from a normal teenage boy (whatever that means) into a rigidly conservative adult. Meanwhile, my adulthood had taken me into sex, booze and capitalism—not necessarily in that order. I hadn't even talked to him for several years. But we had no other siblings and our parents were both dead, so I guess I still got "next of kin" in the little box on the form. Our father had died from emphysema six years prior and our mother from an accumulation of problems when we were young. James's own wife had died giving birth to their only child.

The only time I'd ever met the wife was at their wedding. I was in my final year of college. James had recently earned his doctorate in marine biology. The ceremony took place at the small offshoot church she'd attended since childhood, about an hour from my school in San Francisco. I was the only relative present from our family, as Dad had passed away the previous January. I hadn't seen much of my brother since he'd left home, but was glad he'd invited me to the wedding. At least there was that much of a connection still left. Having never met the bride, I didn't know any of her family, or any of James's friends either, all of whom seemed to be fellow members of the Church of the Benevolent Fount. I felt completely out of place. I really didn't want to be there, but I felt I couldn't reject the olive branch of the wedding invitation. At least I wasn't in the wedding party, thank God.

The nuptials followed the lengthy service that Sunday morning. Thankfully, the ceremony itself wasn't too long. I was already freaked out because I'd committed no fewer than four of the sins cited by the preacher in his interminable and agitated sermon that very morning. And that didn't even count speeding, chewing gum on Sundays and listening to devil music, all of which I'd further accomplished on the drive to the church.

Chloe, the bride, was pale and thin, nervous and birdlike. When she clasped my hands tightly in the receiving line, hers were as cold as ice. But her eyes burned with a fever beyond the normal wedding day excitement. With minimal eye contact, she mumbled something to me—some quote from scripture, I think. James extricated me from her grasp and wordlessly handed me off to one of his friends, who walked me down to the church basement for the reception (no alcohol or music, of course). While his friend asked me if I'd accepted Jesus Christ as my personal savior, I glanced back over my shoulder at James. He was smiling at the minister, but he looked tense. There was something else in his expression too—resignation to his fate, perhaps? I wondered why he was marrying her. She had a frail prettiness, I guess, but she struck me as a complete whack job. The baby's arrival seven months later seemed to answer the question.

But I didn't know about the baby or his wife's death. I'd hoped my attendance at the wedding would spark some kind of renewed contact between James and myself, but I didn't hear from him after the wedding. I wasn't even too sure where they were living. There'd been some talk at the reception of him accepting a job back east somewhere. Finally, I got a Christmas card at the end of that year. I was thrilled to find a baby picture enclosed, but that was soon tempered by the news of Chloe's death. The return address was a university in Maine. He said he'd be passing through San Francisco on business soon and hoped to see me then, but didn't say when.

I don't know if he got my letter in reply, giving him my phone number. He never did call, but instead showed up unannounced one rainy evening at the run-down Victorian house where my girlfriend and I shared a small apartment on the top floor. Maybe he thought we could go out to dinner. Maybe he thought it would be a nice surprise. Yeah, too bad he didn't call first. I can still imagine him standing out in the dimly lit hallway, both the rain on the rooftop and the music blaring from our stereo drowning out his knock. When that went unanswered, he tried the knob and opened the door on a naked Isabel, rather enthusiastically going down on me on the living room floor.

Hadn't heard from him since. No phone calls, no e-mails, no more Christmas cards. If I'd been waiting for him to be the first to reach out, well, my wait was over.

And now, as next of and only kin, I had no choice but to haul myself out to California and deal with it. Good thing I had all that time off.

6

Chapter 3

So that was Thursday. I woke up late on Friday morning to the obnoxious squawking of one alarm clock by the bed and another in the bathroom. You drink enough, you learn these tricks, so you still show up on time even though you feel like shit.

I felt like shit.

But I got myself to Logan on time for the flight.

The first drink the day before had seen me through the remainder of the conversation with Lieutenant Delgado. Turned out there were three messages on my home voice mail, one very late on Wednesday night and one on Thursday morning from him. The other message was just a hang-up, but also from a San Diego number. Caller unknown.

It was Wednesday when they found James. The second drink got me through the airline reservation. A few more covered laundry and packing. And there were conversations that had to be gotten through with child protective services, the coroner's office, a funeral home… It was all a bit of a blur.

In the cab on the way to the airport, I sucked down some aspirin and a Coke. I then suffered a spurt of panic when I couldn't remember if I'd made any other phone calls the night before. My heartbeat calmed when I checked the cell—nope, no outgoing calls to Isabel or anybody else, except the airline and the San Diego numbers. I cracked the window and fired up a cigarette, not bothering to ask the cabbie if it was okay with him. I figured it could only improve the funk of the taxi anyway. He flicked me a glance in the mirror, but didn't say anything.

And who was there to call anyway? No one. Work didn't care. My boss had emphatically banned me from speaking to him for the next three weeks. No family left, except an unknown five-year-old waiting for me in California. Gulp. No significant other. No friends to speak of these days. I'd drifted apart from college and childhood friends with the move to Boston. They'd all seemed to get married to the first guy who'd shown the slightest interest and be immediately caught up in producing children oddly similar to each other, with little concern for my progress. Not to mention the two "close" friends I'd lost upon coming out.

Fuck 'em all.

I overtipped the cabbie since he hadn't bitched about my smoking and looked forward to the screwdrivers awaiting me in first class. A hot flight attendant wouldn't hurt either.

Getting through security was the usual ordeal, but I did my best to summon up my Zen travel mode. At the head of the queue, I handed my driver's license and boarding pass to a very large TSA employee. She looked me up and down, clearly unimpressed.

Comparing me to my license for the second time, she said doubtfully, "This is you?"

I assured her it was. She looked skeptical, but shrugged and passed me through. I looked at my license before putting it away. Wasn't that bad a picture. What had she seen? Five foot seven, one hundred and twenty-five pounds, long dark Blonde hair, green eyes. I checked myself in the little mirror I kept in my purse. I looked all right to me, or at least no worse than usual. All right, maybe a little haggard. That was good, actually, since it would keep guys on the plane from hitting on me. First class is always teeming with excruciatingly boring salesmen from places like Dayton and San Bernardino who are overjoyed to find a Lovely Young Lady seated next to them. If they only knew I had my eye on their girlfriends and sisters...tee hee.

In my seat on the plane before takeoff, I checked my cell phone voice mail. Reflex, really. No messages. Clearly, everybody at work had gotten the persona non grata memo. I'd thought maybe one or two of my buddies might call and offer their sympathy and support... But I guess their distancing themselves wasn't a huge surprise. Career comes first.

They tell you not to let yourself get too tired, too sad, too lonely. Good luck with that, Jack. I guess I had let myself get a little...a little too Madison, at any rate. Too Madison for my boss, clearly. Maybe I had gotten a little "erratic." Probably should keep my opinions to myself in staff meetings, but why the hell did they invite me to those things if I wasn't supposed to participate? And there was that one time I hadn't come back from lunch. And it's true I had been showing up later and later, although it didn't seem like anybody noticed.

In the midst of my confused and conflicted feelings about James and my moderately vicious hangover, I confess I was a little happy to not be at work. Bastards.

I wrestled my purse out from under the seat in front of me. I had a picture of the kid in there, the one from the Christmas card. Katie. Katherine Lily McPeake, my own flesh and blood, named for my mother. The snapshot was a blurry image of a generic, chubby, more or less McPeakey-looking baby staring off camera, clutching a little stuffed animal. A pink walrus, upon closer inspection.

Blonde baby hair, blue baby eyes, that wise old geezer look some babies have. She was five now. I had no other pictures. And

I was now responsible for this small person, who I had never met. James had a lot of faith in his Creator, but this seemed like a pretty bad plan, even to me.

The flight attendant was so not hot. She leaned in to reclaim my glass as we were preparing for takeoff. There were only ice cubes left anyhow. Her name tag proclaimed her to be ANGELA. Fifties, gray hair, half-glasses on a chain, deep gravelly voice. Not quite the angel I was in need of.

But she kept the screwdrivers coming as we raced through the heavens toward the other horizon.

I'd bought some reading material in the Boston airport— the San Diego newspaper, plus a copy of good old Dr. Spock. Hey, I needed the advice. What did I know about kids? A single gay workaholic? Without even a sister of my own? The only thing I was sure of was that I was a piss-poor choice for instant parenthood.

The book unopened on my lap, I kept looking at the snapshot, even though I knew the kid must look nothing like the baby now. She'd be walking, talking, probably have strong opinions and bad habits. All the same disagreeable things I dislike about grown-up people. Plus, be prone to the high-pitched noises and overall stickiness I associate with small children. If she'd heard anything at all about me from her dad, it couldn't have been very good.

Yeah, kid, your aunt's going to hell for sure. Now eat your vegetables.

Where exactly had James gone wrong? I had asked myself that question more than a few times over the years. We had been good friends as children, even with the five year age difference. At least, I thought we had. Isabel had once suggested to me that maybe James was always jealous of me, that I was the baby who'd come along to steal all the attention away from him after five glorious years of being the only child. Maybe... Maybe he loved me and he hated me. The older I got, the more I saw that in people—the ability to harbor two completely conflicting emotions with no conflict. I don't get that. I'm probably stupid.

My brother and I had grown up in San Francisco, playing hide-and-go-seek and riding our bikes with the neighborhood kids when it wasn't too foggy and board games when it was. He was the protective big brother and I was the adoring little sister following him around like a puppy. But somewhere in our teens, some crack in the foundation of our relationship had developed and deepened, like cold, rank water seeping into the cellar, unnoticed by the residents. And it wasn't just me. He was constantly fighting with our father too, although the old man admittedly was not the easiest person in the world to get along with. The two of them were always battling over something—homework, chores, money, James's newfound religious beliefs... By the time I'd finished high school, James had all but estranged himself from us. Seemed like he spent all his time either studying or in church. He'd moved out after a huge blowup with both me and Dad, where he'd told the old man he hated him and told me I'd ruined his life, that I'd been persecuting him since I was five years old. Yeah, right, maybe back when we lived in Crazy Town. The irrational invective was bad enough (not to mention the spit spraying my face on "PERsecuting"), but my dad's despairing, hurt look as James stormed out was the worst. I still couldn't forgive my brother for turning on a sick old man like that. Ten years later, it still seemed hateful. Wasteful.

Our parents weren't particularly religious and certainly weren't regular churchgoers. Both sets of grandparents were—one Catholic, one Protestant. Maybe these things skip a generation. In any event, whatever James was looking for, he seemed to find it within the structure of his church.

I was still looking. Religion was definitely not the answer for me, seeing as how all the church people I knew skipped right over the "love thy neighbor" stuff to get right down to the "let's stone her in the village square" stuff. God Bless America.

I'd hoped James would find some way to be okay with me being gay, but I hadn't found a way to talk to him about it before that debacle at the apartment. I still held dear those memories of childhood games and secrets, but I guess he didn't. His rejection of me was total. And that hurt.

But now he was dead.

And the photograph of Katie was all I had to connect me to what was waiting at the other end of the journey.

Chapter 4

I should have arrived in San Diego around two p.m. Pacific time, but more thunderstorms in Dallas delayed the takeoff of my connecting plane. I fell asleep for the last hour of that flight, pages two and three of Dr. Spock facedown in my lap. I groggily awoke when we touched down in San Diego around four thirty p.m. local time. I got my suitcase from baggage claim and made my way to the rental car office. A Coke from the vending machine there overrode the nasty taste in my mouth and some of the cobwebs in my brain.

In the crowded terminal, for just a split second, I thought I'd seen the back of James's head going down a long corridor in front of me. Of course, it wasn't him. I knew that. My mind had played that trick on me before when I'd lost someone. You start seeing the dearly departed everywhere you go. On the street, in the store, in a passing car...I hate that. First the millisecond of joy, then the brutal face plant of reality's return. It may not always look like much from the outside, but grief is awful. And your brain is no help whatsoever. But after all, how do we expect our brains to assimilate the fact that someone we've known all our lives is gone? Forever. Just like that. Just gone. How does that even work?

I don't know. I wrenched my mind back to the immediate present and my next problem to solve, namely, renting a car. Lieutenant Delgado had warned me that the Navy facility was remote and difficult to reach, so I knew enough to get a four-wheel drive vehicle. With a child seat. James's own SUV (a Ford Explorer) was still parked down there by his cabin, but it seemed prudent to get my own since Delgado said the Explorer was locked and there was no sign of the key. James always drove Fords, my brain thought disconnectedly. Maybe it was in the Bible somewhere.

After putting the top down on the Jeep, I followed the directions Delgado had given me and steered it southwest toward Shadow Point, a narrow peninsula separating the ocean from the bay. I could see it as I headed out from the airport—an imposing, almost mountainous presence rising above the sparkling waters of the bay. A dark fog bank was just climbing over the summit from the ocean side, threatening to blot out the San Diego sunshine. But down here, the temperature was still in the seventies and the light breeze in my face off the water was refreshing after the hours on the plane. My lone suitcase rode in solitary splendor in the cramped rear, strapped in next to the child seat. The rental car guy, thank goodness, had put that in since I had no idea how it worked. Guess I'd be figuring that out pretty quick.

The real estate section of the San Diego newspaper had backed up my own Internet research from the day before (before the zinfandel completely took over). Shadow Point was known for its pricey residential real estate and exclusive water view neighborhoods, but in truth, eighty percent of the peninsula was owned by the Navy and closed to the public. A dotted line on the map separated the homes from government property, as did security kiosks staffed by armed sailors. Only Delgado's prior approval, my ID and my name on a clipboard would allow me to pass when I reached those checkpoints.

I drove up the aptly named Hill Street to find that commerce on the Point was almost nil and appeared to be limited to a general store, a tiny barbershop and an even tinier realtor's office, all ensconced in a one-story, gray frame building with an inordinately large parking lot. This was all about a half mile down from Uncle Sam's demarcation line. Residents had to head farther down the hill to get gas, visit the ATM, see a doctor or otherwise take care of business. Pulling into the parking lot, I noticed one more commercial enterprise on the far side of the football field-sized space. A dingy, gray warehouse squatted over there like an enormous toad. The letters "CBF" were prominently painted in faded black on its garage doors (of a size to accommodate eighteen wheelers) and a smaller sign by what must have been the office was marked "Conrad Bly Freight." It seemed an odd and isolated spot for a freight depot, but what did I know. A semi idled nearby, taking up several parking spaces. It too, had the big black CBF on its trailer. I saw no workers or other signs of industry. I parked the Jeep in a far corner, hoping the unsecured suitcase would be okay for a few minutes.

Forewarned by Delgado (again), I went into the store to pick up a few essentials. He'd told me to expect electricity and water at the cabin where James and Katie had been living, but not much else. My shopping list was short: booze, Coke, bottled water, fruit, toilet paper, trash bags and some Lean Cuisines. Plus a corkscrew, cigarettes and a box of animal crackers. For the kid. Right? Kids like animal crackers, right?

Like I had a clue.

The plumply pale teenage cashier at the Shadow Point General Store tallied up my items with only a quick, feral glance at my face and no conversation. Which suited me just fine. She was a Goth, her hair dyed an unnatural black, all black clothes, lots of piercings but only one visible tattoo—a large Maltese cross

15

on her right forearm, outlined in red. And blood red fingernail polish. Her nametag labeled her Dawn.

She seemed tongue-tied as I gathered my bags and she handed over my change. For a moment, I thought she was going to touch my arm, but she pulled back. Meeting my eyes for the first time, she said solemnly, "You be careful out there." Her eyes were dark, underscored by deep shadows and eyeliner. No smile.

I was startled, expecting something more conventional like "have a nice day" or "thanks for shopping with us."

"Okay," was my witless reply. She nodded once, as in affirmation. I headed toward the door with my purchases, glancing back as I exited, but she had turned away to talk to a co-worker.

My suitcase was still there, unharmed. I wedged the groceries in on the floor of the Jeep, then clambered back in to make the drive out to James's cabin. Despite the oversized proportions of the parking lot, there was only one way in and out. Annoyingly, another CBF semi was making its tortoise-like way into the parking lot just as I was trying to exit. The driver had misjudged the angle, so he had to keep backing it up, then trying again until he got it right. I impatiently sat well back of the entryway to give him plenty of room, then zipped up to the edge of the driveway and back out onto the surface street once he'd finally lumbered in. The driver quite unnecessarily honked his air horn at me as he passed. Jerk. Maybe CBF meant "can't be fast," I thought grumpily as I headed toward the Navy end of the Point.

The steely-eyed guys at the kiosk reluctantly let me pass after thoroughly checking me and the vehicle out. I thought the automatic weapons were a bit much, but who knew what the Navy had cooking out there. A large sign made it clear that the gates—both going in and coming out—closed half an hour before sundown and anybody out on the Point after that would be spending the night. Finally waving me through, one of the sailors told me to keep going for another five miles. There was only the one main road on and off the Navy installation, so at least I wouldn't get lost. The next security kiosk to block my passage would mark the entrance to the outermost labs. From there, I could take a rugged and rutted dirt track down to the small encampment where James and another marine biologist had been living and working.

I tried the radio, but couldn't get anything besides scratchy static and the occasional burst of Mexican music from a Tijuana station. It didn't really matter. The scenery was spectacular. I was driving south along the crest of a high hilltop which reached down on the left to San Diego Bay, with sailboats, cruise ships and a huge Navy aircraft carrier in motion and down on the right to the Pacific, where the sun was a few hours away from setting. I could see the fog bank about half a mile ahead, though and soon enough, tendrils of gray mist were creeping across the roadway. I wished I had pulled a jacket out of my suitcase back at the store. Or put the top up. The temperature had cooled rapidly and I shivered now inside the Jeep, trying to huddle down in my seat to conserve a little warmth. I turned the heater on, but no luck—it seemed to be broken. A faint smell of exhaust, but no warmth, emanated from the vents. I hoped I'd be at my destination pretty quick as I was already chilled to the bone.

The land was fenced with chain-link on both sides, with government No Trespassing signs posted every hundred yards. Scrub brush lined the open country inside the fences, but that soon gave way to white, wood frame buildings obscurely marked with signs like Building 13MZ and NOSC. None were accessible without passing through yet another security kiosk off to the left or right. As I sped around a slight curve, I caught a quick glimpse of a large pool of clear water down to the right, on the ocean side. A tall metal framework arched mysteriously over the pool, like something from a giant Erector Set. No pathway or entrance was visible from the road. My fast glance caught a guy in a wetsuit crouched down by the side of the pool, with a clipboard. I sensed they were big on clipboards out here. In that quick snapshot view as I whizzed past, I thought I saw something surface in the pool.

Fins, at least.

The buildings thinned out as I kept going and the view on both sides was eventually taken over by a low, whitewashed, adobe wall with well-manicured green grass beyond. White crosses marked gravesites, marching in a regular pattern down toward the edge of the cliffs on both bay and ocean sides. San Cerros National Cemetery, read a sign by a gated driveway.

The fog had thickened considerably. I slowed, but kept going. I hadn't seen one other vehicle since I entered government property. Surely, the end of the Point must be near. Besides the cold and wet of the fog, an unpleasant odor now punctuated the chill air. The cemetery ended and the scrub brush returned, as did the chain-link fence and the monotonous warning signs. Locked gates marked dirt driveways occasionally, but there was nothing indicating what lay beyond. The ground rose to my right, blocking the view of the ocean. Concrete emplacements had been built right into the side of the hill, marked with names like Battery Phoenix. I'd read on the 'net that these had been constructed during World War II, when a Japanese attack from the sea was anticipated. The entrance from the road supposedly led through tunnels to machine gun nests on the hillside overlooking the sea. Rumor was the facilities were currently used by the Navy for top secret research.

I wondered what kind of research James had been doing out here. I'd never really understood exactly what it was that he did. Delgado had mentioned he'd come to them from a job in Hawaii for some private foundation. From California to Maine to Hawaii, then back to California for this Navy job as a civilian contractor. His last stop.

Another quarter mile and I finally reached the kiosk. No less than three armed sailors awaited me there. Two were guys. The third, a young and sturdy Latina with her M16 cradled in her arms, stood at the rear of the vehicle and kept her eyes pinned on me as my ID was checked, the ubiquitous clipboard was consulted and phone calls were made to confirm the acceptance of my decidedly nonofficial presence. In the side mirror, my attempt at a smile looked weak and failed to reassure me, let alone her.

Ahead of me, the peninsula ended. A round white lighthouse perched on the brink, its bright beam swiveling around every few seconds. The foghorn bellowed periodically, sounding strangely muted in the mist, like a distant cow mooing for its lost calf. Once again, my Internet surfing from the day before had informed me this was a modern and fully functional lighthouse. There was an old lighthouse down at the base of the Point, but a fire had all but destroyed it. Only the ruins remained now. Which inspired the construction of the current lighthouse, built back in the late thirties but kept technologically up-to-date to continue serving a very real purpose.

The sailor inside the kiosk stepped back out. "You're to proceed to the administration building, ma'am. Lieutenant Delgado is waiting for you there."

I loved being called ma'am at twenty-eight.

"Where is that, exactly?"

"Just ahead, ma'am. You'll see the signs."

And indeed, there were boldly marked signs leading me the short distance to the Administration Building once they'd raised the barrier to let me through the security checkpoint. In the rearview mirror, I could see the Latina fingering her weapon as she watched me drive away.

Chapter 5

Lieutenant Delgado was dark-haired, dark-eyed and bespectacled. And impressively efficient. But chatty. Among other things in our first meeting, he informed me that the Portuguese had been the first European explorers to set foot on Shadow Point, that he himself was of Portuguese descent, as were many San Diegans living in the area and that the rumors about the old lighthouse being cursed and/or haunted were mostly untrue. Ha ha.

This failed to get a laugh out of me. It wasn't exactly the best time for a joke, which he belatedly seemed to sense.

This was after he'd assured me he was very sorry about my brother's untimely demise, offered me any assistance he and his staff could provide during this difficult time and gotten me to sign a whole stack of forms that basically said I would not sue the shit out of the U.S. government.

It took like an hour to go through that crap, but I signed. My employer had several large contracts with the federal government and my continuing employment depended on me maintaining a security clearance. I was making excellent money, so I was not too (?) worried about the financial burden of adding a child to my household. James no doubt had some life insurance too. Besides, a marine biologist gets stung by some of the biology he was studying—who was I going to sue? Mother Nature? In short, I wanted to get in and get out of there as soon as possible—to bury my brother and take my niece home—with the minimum hassle. So, I signed.

A sailor in a Navy truck followed my Jeep down the dirt road to the cabin where James had lived with his little daughter. Delgado insisted on accompanying me down, describing the road as treacherous for the first-time driver. In his office, before we left, he'd told me there were three cabins: one for James and Katie, one for the other marine biologist and a third that was vacant. The cabins had been put up in the fifties for some obscure naval reason and "weren't much" in Delgado's words. Power lines had been installed at some point. They arced down from the topside offices to provide the cabins with electricity and there was plumbing too, but no phones. The researchers used the phones in the office when they needed to—cell phones didn't work on the Navy end of Shadow Point. Some feature of the geography, or the atmosphere, or something, made the signal nonexistent. Maybe all the Navy communications equipment jacked up the transmission. I felt naked without a working cell phone within reach for the first time in years.

My hands gripped the steering wheel tightly. The dirt road *was* precarious, hardly better than a footpath. I could feel the tires slipping as I cautiously maneuvered down the steep grade, thick vegetation on both sides brushing the vehicle. Delgado had offered to drive, but I figured I might as well start practicing since I could hardly count on him or anybody else to ferry me in and out during my brief stay. The road serpentined back and forth along the hillside. No doubt a straight descent would have been dangerously precipitous, but all the curves made the journey that much longer and a lot more nauseating. The top of the hill didn't actually look that far away above us, but I was never good with distances. In any event, it was taking a good ten minutes or more to traverse to the bottom. I was concentrating so hard on not tipping us over that there was little opportunity for conversation, but I did manage one question.

"Does anybody ever just walk straight up through the bushes to topside?" I was already adopting their lingo.

Delgado shook his head, offering one completely sufficient word of explanation. "Snakes."

He was hanging on for dear life, probably questioning the sagacity of allowing a civilian female to take the wheel for this death ride. Besides the hazardous road conditions, the setting sun was nearly blinding us as we headed down to the sea.

Finally, near the bottom, the brush cleared out into an open area—a natural dell with three crappy looking cabins in a triangle around the open area and a couple of sad looking trees that provided a few scraps of shade. Oddly, the fog had cleared by the time we reached the foot of the hill. The air felt humid and charged. The sun was low in the sky, but there was still maybe a half hour or so of daylight left. An old, dented and raggedy looking dirty white International Harvester pickup truck was parked under the trees, next to (presumably) James's Explorer. His bumper was clean. The other car sported three weathered stickers: one said Hussong's, one was a blue and white decal with a seagull and the letters OB on it and the third urged us to Pray For Surf. I'll bet James had loved that one.

Delgado had said the cabins weren't much and he was right. All three were small, wood frame, ramshackle, gray paint peeling off in strips. A porch ran the width of each cabin with a wooden railing that had been painted white a long time ago to match the window frames. We pulled up with a scrunch of gravel in front of the center cabin. A few scraggly wisps of grass were trying their best to pass for a yard. Three ratty-looking aluminum chairs were clustered around an upended milk crate on the porch, taking up most of the room. On the ten feet of sidewalk leading up to the porch, a red tricycle was parked at an angle. My throat caught for a moment—it was just like the one I had when I was a little girl.

When the truck behind us had similarly parked, the stillness seemed absolute. No living thing moved in the landscape. The foul odor I'd noticed above was more pronounced down here, although it seemed to come and go, rotten eggs mingled with the salt smell of the sea.

After a moment, small sounds and movements began to reassert themselves. Wind chimes dangling on the porch jangled discordantly. I noticed the railings sported a collection of seashells. The roar of the surf was a constant, forceful murmur in the background, although I couldn't actually see the water from here. Seagulls shrieked overhead, winging toward the ocean. And the screen door on the cabin to the left was loosely swinging with a grating squeak and an occasional bang that made me long to tear it from its hinges. The screen itself was torn and hanging down like a dead frond on a palm tree.

Delgado jumped out, clearing his throat to catch my attention. "Shall we go in, ma'am?" The door from the truck behind me opened and then was slammed shut.

I was still in the driver's seat. After that bone-jolting ride down the hill, I needed a second to make sure all my internal organs were still in the right spots. I eased out and planted my feet on the ground, stretching and twisting to pop a few errant vertebrae back into place. During my final bend, I noticed the sailor behind me checking out my ass with a smirk. I glanced over the hood at Delgado, who was looking me right in the eye. Two points for Delgado. Or maybe he was gay. I must admit my gaydar is the worst gaydar ever. I have absolutely no idea who is straight and who is gay in this world. I must've been out that day (no pun intended). Which had led in recent years to a couple of truly mortifying conversations with attractive and, unfortunately, Totally Straight Women. Which, coupled with the whole Isabel thing, had led me to embrace celibacy as a positive life choice for the moment.

Not that I really believed that. But nothing else seemed to be working. Actually, nothing, period, seemed to be working at the moment.

It was almost like I was expecting the phone call that James was dead. Or at least expecting something else really shitty to go ahead and happen. Everything else was already fouled up.

Delgado spoke again—"Ready, ma'am?"

I nodded. I grabbed my purse from behind the driver's seat and we went in.

Chapter 6

"Child Protective Services, Mrs. Augustine speaking."

The day before, I had dialed the number given me by Delgado and navigated a frustrating telephone tree of press one for this county service, press two for that and finally found a real live person on the other end. Mrs. Augustine.

Delgado had told me how they'd found James on Wednesday evening. They sent a guy down to look after he didn't come to pick up Katie from the topside day care facility. The military police were called in after the body was found. And they then called SDPD, who called CPS when they realized the custody of a minor child was involved. Poor Katie had been whisked from the familiarity of day care to a county facility, then to a foster home, all in a matter of hours when no family member was available to take her in. Delgado said the other marine biologist, a Dr. Piper, who was well known to James, Katie, Delgado and the rest of their small community out on Shadow Point, had volunteered to take Katie in until I could be located and get there, but the county would not allow a non official, non family member to care for her.

Poor Katie. By the time I got the call on Thursday, she'd already spent the night in a foster home, awakening amongst strangers, with little idea what had happened to her daddy and waiting for an aunt she'd never met. Poor little kid.

And then I couldn't get there until Friday afternoon. I'd asked Mrs. Augustine if she could bring Katie to the airport and meet my flight, but apparently it didn't work that way. She seemed offended that I had even suggested it.

As she had asked, I called her number as soon as I landed in San Diego. Irritatingly, though, I got her voice mail. And again, when I called from the rental car office. And, again, sitting in the rental car, trying to figure out my next move. Should I wait for her to call me back on my cell phone at the airport? Or head out to Shadow Point? Delgado had advised me I needed to be at the final guard shack before sundown to gain access to James's cabin that day. I wasn't sure how long it would take me to get out there, especially with the security checkpoints. And I really didn't want to try my hand at four-wheeling through unknown territory in the dark. I called again, but still the voice mail. Shrugging (and swearing), I'd decided to head out, figuring she would call me on the cell any moment. Action felt better than inaction. And heading for the Point felt better than trying to go physically find Mrs. Augustine in a warren of county offices that I didn't know the location of anyhow.

Unfortunately, at that point, I did not yet know that cell phones wouldn't work out on the Navy end of the Point. As soon as Delgado told me that, sitting in his office, I borrowed his desk phone to call Mrs. Augustine once again, even though it was now well after five o'clock on a Friday. Good luck trying to reach a civil servant. Damn. Voice mail again. I left another message, this time including Delgado's office number and hung up with a little more force than was necessary. He grimaced in sympathy and assured me he would send someone down immediately if she called. He himself would be working late that night. Until nine or ten, he said. I wondered fleetingly what his job was.

But I didn't really care. And I'd given up on Mrs. Augustine for that day, mentally cursing the woman for being so hard to reach. And on a Friday! I didn't even have the address of the foster home where Katie was staying. Was I going to have to wait until Monday to pick the poor kid up?

But I should have had more faith in Mrs. Augustine's dedication to her job. Just as Delgado was letting us in James's cabin with a spare set of keys, the radio in the Navy truck squawked. The sailor, leaning against the hood, got back in the driver's side to answer it. Delgado called out to him from the doorway.

"What is it, Boyd?"

The sailor was nodding and still talking into the handset, but motioned to both of us with his free hand. I threw my purse on the couch and ran down to the truck. Mrs. A. had called Delgado's office and they were patching her through on the radio to talk to me. Boyd quickly showed me how to operate the controls, then he and Delgado removed themselves to the shade under the trees to give me a little privacy.

"Hello, Mrs. Augustine? Can you hear me?"

"Yes, dear, you're clear as a bell."

My relief at having finally caught up with her was soon erased by the next problem. It seemed I would have to meet her at a location near, but not at, the foster home so she could first establish my identity, then we could proceed to the house to pick up Katie. The problem was the foster home was out in the boonies past some place called Escondido, a good hour away. If I didn't get lost. By the time I got out there, identified myself and was finally allowed to spirit Katie away, it would be well after nine. Katie would be asleep in bed. If I jammed, I might— might—be able to get off the Point prior to sundown when the security gates closed for the night, but we wouldn't be able to return until the next morning. When the sun went down, the gates closed and no one was allowed on or off the Navy property. So, my choices were—go pull the kid out of bed and make her spend the night with another stranger (me) in a hotel, which I'd have to find in the dark…or make her spend another night in a foster home and go get her first thing in the morning to bring her back to the cabin, her home.

Fuck, I hadn't got to this chapter in Dr. Spock yet. Both choices seemed like bad choices for Katie. It was fucked either way.

"Miss McPeake, dear? What do you want to do?" Augustine was ragging me for an answer.

I quickly explained the situation, asking her what she thought was best for Katie.

"Oh, goodness…I really couldn't say. They're probably getting ready to put her to bed right now. It really would be best if you take her home. The poor little thing's been through so much, I don't know how she'd react to a hotel at this point… But, of course, you are her aunt, dear."

This was not helping. The sun was setting. I had to make a decision fast.

"Delgado," I called out, "what time do they close the gate?"

He didn't even have to glance at his watch. "Oh, they've already closed it down for the night, ma'am."

Shit. Well, there was my answer. Mrs. Augustine was agreeable to meeting at a coffee shop near Escondido at eight the next morning, telling me I would recognize her by her red eyeglasses. She gave me the off-ramp to take, telling me I'd see the coffee shop from the freeway. She also told me to bring at least two forms of photo identification and any other family-type documents I had. I said I'd see her then and thanked her.

A few minutes later, Delgado and Boyd set off back up the hill, leaving me behind with my groceries and the keys to the cabin.

Still no sign of the other marine biologist, Dr. Piper.

Apparently, my first night in San Diego was to be spent alone. I unloaded the Jeep, putting my suitcase in James's bedroom and the grocery bags in the kitchen. I shoved the Lean Cuisines in the small ice-clad freezer next to a tray of ice cubes and placed the wine, Coke and bottles of water in the fridge. I noticed there was hardly anything else in there. A plastic carton of milk on the top shelf, almost empty. (Milk! Damnit, that's what kids drink. I should have bought milk. Oh, well, I could pick some up in the morning. Katie could help me pick things out at the grocery store. How's that for a fun family activity.) Half a stick of margarine in its wrapper and an empty bologna package. A jar of pickle juice, devoid of pickles. Even though I'd conked out halfway through page two of Dr. Spock, I was pretty sure this barren larder would not meet with his approval. I checked the glass-fronted kitchen cabinets. More austerity. Surely, the only parent who'd be supportive of this would be Ole Mother Hubbard. I wondered why James was living this way. Was he broke?

In any event, it would be that much less stuff for me to throw out. At least there was a microwave to nuke my Lean Cuisines. And a little cooler in the corner too. That would be good for the beach.

I tried a couple of the drawers. One held a motley assortment of flatware, some steak knives, a butcher knife and a few other kitchen utensils. But no corkscrew—I'd correctly guessed James wouldn't have one of those in his house. Another was the usual kitchen junk drawer—pens and pencils, rubber bands, matchbooks, a pack of lightbulbs, a box of plastic sandwich bags, other oddments. No phone book, but I guess that made sense as there was no phone.

Putting the bourbon and the rest of my stuff on the countertop, I went to check out the rest of the cabin. There was no door between the kitchen and the living room, just a doorway, if that makes any sense. The screen door was latched but I'd left the living room door open, hoping to bring in some fresh air. It felt fuggy in there, dank, although I noticed the windows along the front were both open a few inches. Metal brackets screwed into the top of the window frame kept them from opening any wider. San Diego's climate was more desert than tropical—"semi-arid," they call it—so the humidity hanging in the air was a bit of a puzzle. The wind chimes were randomly clanging away on the porch. Why do people find that restful? It was bugging the shit out of me already. Or maybe it was just the absence of the constant sirens and car alarms I'd grown so used to in Boston. I knew that all the civilization a big city like San Diego had to offer was only a few miles away, but out here at the end of Shadow Point, it felt completely remote and isolated. Knowing that James had died down here just a few days ago was always in the back of my mind too, like the bug running along the baseboard you only see out of the corner of your eye.

The living room was maybe ten feet by twelve. The floor appeared to be plywood. The front door and two windows defined the front wall, looking out onto the porch, the cleared gravel parking area and what I assumed must be Dr. Piper's cabin. Semitransparent white drapes were limply gathered at the corners of the windows, barely moving in the nonexistent breeze. A box fan was plugged into the outlet in the corner.

A low bookcase ran underneath the front windows, with three framed photos and a tiny cactus in a three-inch pot on top of it. I went over to check out the books, which were all religious books or learned tomes on crustaceans. Except for a couple of Dick Francis mysteries. You see, that was the bitch—every time I was just about ready to give up on James entirely, he'd pull that on me and be marginally cool. Be like the brother he used to be.

I turned my attention to the photos. A formal wedding picture of James and Chloe, a more current snapshot of Katie at the beach and—my throat caught again. A picture James himself had taken of me when I was just about Katie's age, riding my red trike in our driveway. Our father was just behind me, ready to provide a push as needed, but cut off at the shoulders in the photograph, giving an odd perspective of a headless man reaching out. My face was serious, peering down, concentrating on my driving. I was wearing a dark blue sailor suit-looking dress with a red ribbon in my hair and white leather shoes.

I loved that picture. I had it on my own nightstand at home. I didn't even know James had a copy. I looked at it for a long time. Then I set it back down on top of the bookcase.

The cactus looked sickly. Somebody may have been watering it too much. I turned to face the sagging fabric couch. Scratchy, once white fabric, almost burlap in its coarseness, with multicolored stripes. Ugly as homemade sin, in my estimation. A crocheted throw, tossed over the back, did not conceal a large stain on the far cushion. Somebody had spilled their dinner (or worse) there. A small, grubby stuffed elephant sprawled across one arm, looking like Babar after a three-day binge.

A green metal footlocker that had seen better days separated the couch from the windows, sitting on a cheap beige dhuri rug. A Bible was open on the footlocker, yellow highlighting marking certain passages. The highlighter was in a little crudely made purple ceramic pot with some other pens, pencils, etc. next to the Bible. I picked up the pot, carefully, so as to not spill any of its contents and looked at the bottom of it—the initials "KM" were awkwardly etched in the clay. KM—Katie McPeake.

The front door of the cabin opened right into the living room. Beyond that small space, a hallway led back to the bedrooms, its position a twin to the front door like a shotgun shack. Standing in the living room, the kitchen was immediately off to the right. No TV in the living room, no stereo, no pictures on the walls, but in the corner along the back wall a small desk supported a laptop computer, a printer and stacks of papers. A rickety and mismatched wooden chair with a plum-colored cushion sat in front of it. An ancient upright piano and stool completed the living room, also hugging the back wall, next to the hallway entrance. Dusty and darkened with age, they looked a hundred years old. The ivory was coming off the tops of several keys. The curlicued little brass manufacturer's nameplate above middle C was dull and begrimed, but still legible—Nickerson, with both the Ns quite ornate. I didn't recognize the make. Music books were piled on top of the piano, so it looked like somebody had been playing it.

James and I had taken lessons as kids, but he was always the better player. I wondered if Katie was learning now. I reached out to hit a high E as I passed by into the hallway. Even that single note sounded seriously out of tune. The sea air and the humidity had to be hell on a piano, I thought. The decrepit old instrument fit right in with the cabin. Perhaps some previous tenant had left it behind. I couldn't see James hauling it all the way from Maine or wherever down to this place, but what did I know.

The little hallway was dark, with no light switch or fixture. Threadbare brown carpeting picked up at the edge of the hall and continued into the bedrooms. The larger of the two was on the right. James's room. The same limp, white see-through curtains hung in the window. A full-sized bed and a dresser, with a small lamp on top of it. An old-fashioned alarm clock also sat on three spindly legs on the dresser, ticking loudly in the oppressive silence. A two-drawer gray metal filing cabinet in the corner. Dust motes spiraled in a stray beam of sunlight by the window. A door in the wall common to the kitchen was presumably the closet.

I didn't go in, but continued my exploring to check out Katie's room across the hall. It was teeny, maybe eight by eight, but then I supposed she wasn't too big yet herself. A south-facing window. A low kid-sized bed made up with a flowered bedspread, a floor lamp in the corner beside it. A twin to the rickety wooden chair in the living room, this one cushion-less and draped with a very small pair of jeans. A pint-sized chest of drawers was painted a glossy white with a lumpy coating suggesting many previous applications. A collection of seashells, sand dollars and beach rocks adorned its top. A rather garishly colored paint-by-number headshot of Jesus was propped against a small, polished wooden box. Finger paintings on construction paper were haphazardly taped to all four walls as high as a very short person could reach. Tiny pairs of shoes and sandals were neatly lined up under the bed. A milk crate held a jumble of children's books and toys. No closet. Low-placed hooks on the back of the door held a bathrobe, a windbreaker, a rain slicker and a sweatshirt jacket. All in all, an impressively neat room for a little kid, I thought. Much neater than my own bedroom back in Boston. I was pretty sure I'd left the bed unmade. That would suck when I got home.

At the end of the hall, the bathroom appeared to have been tacked on as an afterthought. Maybe the original occupants of the cabin had an outhouse. Or just plenty of bushes. Like the rest of the dwelling, the bathroom was built on a petite scale. Just enough room for a tub with a shower, a toilet and pedestal sink. The murky mirror on the medicine cabinet reflected my dubious expression as I viewed this magnificence. A small window high in the wall above the tub was open just a crack but sufficient to admit the daddy longlegs perched up in the corner above the showerhead. A once white, opaque plastic shower curtain was pushed back to the far end. I shuddered to imagine it clammily adhering to my wet body. Yuck.

I went back down the hall to the living room. Like I said before, there were no pictures on the walls, but as I returned from this vantage point, I saw there was one piece of decoration above the front door. A small silver cross hung from a nail there. Was it decoration? Or protection? Or just a reminder James had set himself? Whatever it was to him, I let it be.

I plunked down on the couch. Thinking of the desk and the file cabinet, I knew I should get started on clearing out things, but I just couldn't bring myself to do it yet. I felt like an intruder, like a thief. I didn't feel James's presence there, probably because I'd grown so disconnected from him over the years. I was in a stranger's house.

I went back out onto the porch and lit a cigarette. The empty cabin was to my right. The one across from me showed signs of habitation—curtains in the window, stuff on the porch, picnic table, barbeque grill and even a garden gnome in the yard—but there was still no sign of James's only neighbor. I assumed the decrepit pickup belonged to Dr. Piper. I felt restless and displaced. Forty-eight hours ago, I'd been employed, flying home from a business trip with nary a thought for my brother or niece and not many for myself. Twenty-four hours ago, I'd been sitting in my apartment in Boston. Now here I was on another coast, without another living soul to talk to. Nobody except Delgado and Boyd, total strangers, even knew where I was. And James was dead at just thirty-three. I felt gooseflesh rise on my arms, but I wasn't cold.

Physically and mentally shaking myself, I decided to take a walk down to the beach to watch the sun set. No more of this melancholy lolling about. It was going to be a long enough night without that. Besides, the wine would be chilled by the time I got back. But, first things first—I took down those fucking annoying wind chimes and parked them on the railing. I thought about turning the porch light on so there'd be a light when I returned, but then noticed a couple of dusty wires dangling from the fixture and no bulb. Oh, well. The banging screen door on the empty cabin was driving me nuts. I marched over there, stubbing my cigarette out in the dirt on the way and wedged a metal porch chair up against the screen door to stop the racket. Big relief.

I peeked in the grimy windows of the empty cabin out of curiosity. There wasn't much to see. It appeared to be a twin to James's cabin: living room, kitchen, two bedrooms and a bath. Same plywood floors and white walls. Out of sheer nosiness, I wondered if the key I had would also fit this cabin's front door. I turned and surveyed the dell, but there was nobody around to witness my crime. I unwedged the metal chair and pulled back the screen, which made an awful screeching noise in the process.

"Shhh," I said to it. I have an unfortunate habit of speaking to inanimate objects from time to time. I really should get out more often. I positioned the chair so the half-open screen wouldn't revert to banging against the cabin door, then—just for kicks—

tried the knob. To my surprise, it opened readily. I guess there was no point locking the door when there was nothing to steal.

Unless you like dust. A thick coating of that covered the floor, the windowsills and every other flat surface. I sneezed as my shoes kicked up a cloud from the uncarpeted living room floor. I closed the door behind me. The latch clicked loudly in the silent, empty, dim space. The dirty windows let only a little light in, but at least there were no curtains to block its progress.

The cabin smelled of dust and abandonment. Like James's cabin, there was a light socket in the living room ceiling, but James's place included a glass shade. Here, there was only a bare bulb screwed into the fixture. I flipped the light switch by the front door, but nothing came on. It was quiet in there, except for the soft drip drip drip of a faucet in need of a new washer. Which was strange—surely they would have turned the water off when they turned the power off, right? Or maybe both the electricity and the water were still on and it was just that one fixture that was out. Nope. I flipped some other switches, all with the same negative result.

There was nothing in the living room except an empty cardboard box. The floorboards creaked loudly as I moved toward the kitchen. I hoped I wasn't going to put a foot through one of them. I then had to picture myself trapped, with my leg stuck through the floor, jagged ends of the floorboards impaling me, with no one to hear my cries for help. And blind white grubs from under the house crawling up my leg. Shut up! I told myself. Try, for once, to think of something positive. I tried. Nothing came. I went into the kitchen, careful where I trod.

Nothing there, including no leaking faucet. What was dripping? I didn't rummage too much in there, since I didn't want to open a drawer or a cabinet to be faced with something furry and eight-legged. I wasn't really looking for anything, anyhow. Just…looking.

There was nothing in the room corresponding to Katie's, either, except a dusty, unused, plastic trash bag lying on the floor and a little trash that had failed to hop inside it. A coat hanger, some balled up paper towels, a plastic cup… In the larger of the two bedrooms, however, things were different. First of all, it was quite dark in there because someone had taped black construction paper over the window panes. One piece in the top right corner had come undone, so a lonely beam of sunlight pierced the gloomy interior. In that minimal light, I could see a single piece of furniture. A rocking chair. Covered in dust like everything else. It was hard to tell in the dimness, but it looked old and made of wood so dark it was almost black. The only sound was the constant "plop" of the drip about every three seconds. The room felt cold, perhaps because the sun was kept from warming it during the day. In any event, I had no desire to sit in that ancient rocking chair. It seemed strange to have left it behind, in the darkened room. Creepy.

I backed out of the room slowly and told myself I was a chicken if I didn't check the bathroom, the last room in the cabin. Besides, some obsessive-compulsive part of me really wanted to turn that leaking faucet off.

As expected, the bath was a twin to the one in James's cabin. Oddly, neither the sink nor the tub was dripping. Maybe it was a pipe in the wall. That wouldn't bode well for a future resident, but the whole place was such a dump, maybe it didn't matter. I certainly was grateful I wouldn't be spending much time in James's cabin before heading back to Boston with Katie.

The aged mirror above the sink had black veins of disfigurement running through it. One big one on the left side looked like a six, or maybe a lower case b. I noticed I'd somehow managed to attract a vertical swath of dust down the front of my shirt—how did I do that? Maybe when I'd peered in the windows on the porch. I swatted at it, but that just made it worse. Grimacing in the mirror, I made the loser sign at myself. But I then recalled my vow to think positive and contritely gave myself a V for Victory instead. The V of my fingers on top of my upraised arm made more of a Y though, than a V…

A shadow passed by the living room windows, momentarily further darkening the cabin. I started and whirled about, then firmly told myself to buck up—it was only a cloud passing in front of the sun. There was no one out there. There was no one watching me. Although as soon as I thought that, I, of course, started to get that feeling like maybe there was someone watching me.

Paranoia aside, it was time to leave. There was nothing to see. I'd only been in there for a couple minutes, but that was more than enough. I probably wasn't supposed to be in there anyhow. I was ready for some fresh air and hurried back out to the porch. I again pinned the screen door closed with the metal chair. The screen made the horrible screeching noise for the last time, I hoped.

I still wanted to head down to the beach, but continued my self-guided tour by going over to peek in the windows of James's Explorer. Again, not much to see. But for the first time, I was on the passenger side of that vehicle and was shocked to see it was all banged up. It looked bad—lots of scratches in the paint and a minor dent toward the rear as if it had bumped into something solid and unyielding at a low velocity. Close up, the damage appeared to be recent. It must have been—the James I remembered, all neat and orderly, would never have driven such a blemished vehicle, except straight to the body shop. Katie's car seat was in the back, on the passenger side. I wondered if she had been in the car when it happened. I hoped she was okay. I fingered one of the long scratches, wondering what had happened. And knowing, like so many other questions I would have liked to ask James, I would probably never get the answer.

Delgado had pointed out the entrance to the path to the beach, between the McPeake and Piper cabins. I set out, figuring it was maybe ten minutes or so to sundown. Perfect timing. The walk down the path was like a replay of the drive down the dirt road. Instead of the tires sliding around, though, it was my sneakers finding little purchase on the sharp incline. Fifty feet in,

I found there were actually two paths, one to the left and one to the right. Decisions, decisions. I mentally flipped a coin and went left, hoping it would take me to the beach.

Wrong again. After maybe a hundred yards of fairly level path, I topped a slight rise to find the ruins of the old lighthouse below me. Waves crashed on rocks below it. The fire had clearly happened a long time ago, but the tower was still there, a blackened, decayed, lightless beacon for the unwary mariner. Most of the glass was broken out at the top, a few panes still bearing some jagged shards. A sparse crop of weeds encircled the base. A serious looking chain and padlock secured the door at the foot, although I couldn't imagine who would want to venture in there. Even from this safe distance, it looked bleak and foreboding. It must have been quite a sight from the sea, that long ago night when it burned. It almost seemed like I could still catch a whiff of the charred remains—something burnt, something rotten… Suppressing a shiver, I turned and hurried back up the path to the fork, where this time I headed down to the beach.

I slithered down the steep slope, bushes and sandstone outcroppings marking the boundaries of the path. Fortunately, it turned out it was only about another hundred feet down to the sand. The sky was gorgeous pink and lavender, gray clouds sitting out at the horizon. The sun was low in the sky. I thought about walking down to the water, but chickened out when I thought of all the sand in my shoes. Besides, I had a great view right here at the edge of the path. I sat down and frankly marveled at the perfect little beach. Sheer cliffs took over fifty yards down and fifty yards up, but in front of me was a beautiful stretch of sand right on the Pacific. The surf thundered onto the shoreline, where a line of sandpipers did a complicated dance with the advancing and receding waters as they found their dinner. Three pelicans in a V formation flew overhead, heading south. Somehow, that felt like a good sign. For the first time that day, I allowed myself to relax, deeply breathing in the pure ocean air. The sun continued its stately descent. That and the unending vista of the sea before me had me nearly mesmerized.

Finally, though, the sun set. The first star of the night was already twinkling above. While the air was still warm and with that peculiar humidity still cloying, I thought I'd better make it back to the cabin before it got too dim to see the path. Dusting my hands off on my pants, I started to rise, then paused. A shadowy figure was emerging from the waves. Was I seeing things? A solitary surfer, clad in a charcoal gray and black wetsuit. Toting an off-white surfboard with…some kind of hot pink floral design on it. Frangipani, maybe, or hibiscus. If I was seeing things, this was a really detailed hallucination.

Backing up a few feet, I sank back down on the path too intrigued to stop watching. How had he gotten all the way out there? We had to be miles down the coast from the regular surf spots. Had he come off a boat and surfed into shore? The beach seemed completely inaccessible, except from the way I had come. And this surfer didn't look like some brawny Navy guy. In fact, not like a guy at all. As the figure trudged up the sand, I could see now it was a chick. Slender, maybe five foot six. Somehow, the wetsuit didn't reveal as much as you might think, but it definitely looked good on her. Fair skin and dark hair were the only other features I could make out in the dwindling twilight. Dripping medium-length hair which she vigorously shook out as she reached her evident destination, a large rock about halfway up the beach. Stopping there, she parked her board upright in the sand and ran her hands through her hair to push it back up off her face. She reached down and came up with a backpack.

She hadn't noticed me. It was dusk. Both the waning light and a large bush hid me, but I could see her clearly. She couldn't have been more than thirty feet away. I knew I should go, but curiosity kept me rooted to the spot.

Facing the ocean, she opened the backpack and spread out the contents on the rock. She raised her arms above her head and lithely stretched her back, much as I had when I got out of the Jeep. She finished her stretching and reached back to find the toggle attached to the wetsuit's zipper. Pulling it down to the small of her back revealed smooth tanned skin uninterrupted by bikini lines. Oh my.

She was shrugging out of the suit now, twisting to pull the sleeves off. I could just make out the swell of a breast. The pounding of the surf could not mask a roaring in my ears. The wetsuit rode down low on her hips as she pulled a dark-colored tank top off the rock and donned it. Ah, now a tan line appeared as she worked the cumbersome suit down over her hips, her knees, finally stepping out of it entirely. The curve of her behind was truly lovely. The white of her buttocks a shock against the tan legs and dark shirt. Standing up straight, she gave the wetsuit a shake and laid it carefully over the rock. Her bare shoulders and arms looked graceful and strong, silhouetted against the now orange and lavender sky and the dark surf with its nearly phosphorescent foam.

My mouth was dry. I realized I was clutching handfuls of grit from the path. Part of my brain was urging me to get the hell out of there before she saw me, but the other part was urging her to Turn Around, Turn Around, Turn Around…

Instead, she was putting on board shorts. She slung the bag and the wetsuit over her shoulder. I realized she was getting ready to head up the path. As she reached for her surfboard, my brain finally released my body and I let out a breath I hadn't known I'd been holding. I scrambled backward and upward in the same movement, flipping over to gain my feet and haul ass back up the trail. It's one thing to be a pervert and quite another to be caught at it. The gathering darkness and the brush covered my quick retreat.

I flew up the path and hurtled myself into James's living room, collapsing on the sofa where my gasps for air soon degenerated into a fit of coughing. Patting myself on the chest, I reviled myself for not having quit smoking yet while I reached into my purse for a cigarette.

In that short interval, the surfer reached the head of the trail and emerged into the cleared area between the cabins. I had a great view out the front windows from James's couch. I realized this must be Dr. Piper. I hadn't turned on any lights. I hoped she couldn't see the lit end of my cigarette glowing red in the darkness. She paused when she saw my rental car and looked over toward James's cabin. I slunk down lower on my spine on the couch. Surely she couldn't see me sitting in the dark house at twilight? I needed to get a grip. Sheesh, it wasn't my fault she up and stripped in front of me. Why should I feel guilty? And she hadn't even seen me, so…

She turned away from her scrutiny of James's cabin and back toward hers, where she tended to rinsing off her surfboard and wetsuit with a garden hose, and, finally, her own feet and lower legs. She dried them with a beach towel hanging from her porch railing. With one more glance in my direction, she headed inside her own cabin. Lights came on. Then, music.

Country music. Ugh. I felt weird enough without Patsy Cline talking about being crazy.

I was in dire need of an ashtray. I went into the kitchen in search of something that would serve that purpose. The lid from the pickle jar sufficed. I poured myself a glass of wine, the fridge light reminding me I hadn't turned on any lights in the cabin yet. I went from room to room, flipping switches. It was time to get down to business. Start packing stuff up, going through James's papers.

I began in his bedroom. There was no washer and dryer in the cabin, but I found clean sheets in the bottom drawer of his dresser. I stripped the bed and made it up fresh, stuffing the dirty sheets in a plastic garbage bag. They were trash now. I certainly wasn't going to haul them back to Boston as part of Katie's inheritance. I figured I'd be throwing out ninety percent of his stuff. The sad truth is most of the things we're so attached to, that we can't live without, instantly turn into crap when we stop drawing breath. They're just a burden to be disposed of by the suckers left behind.

I wasn't going to touch Katie's room without her being present, but I figured I could pack up the rest of the small house pretty quickly. I decided to put the "good" stuff on his bed and bag up the rest as I went from room to room. First, his closet. Precious few garments were hanging in there, it turned out. I guessed James wasn't much of a clotheshorse. Would Katie want any of his clothes? Maybe a favorite shirt as a keepsake? I carefully folded all of the clothes and put them in a separate bag, just in case. Shoes went in the bag earmarked for the Goodwill. Miscellaneous items from the closet went in the trash. I made quick work of his dresser drawers. The trash bag was quickly filling up.

It was the file cabinet that brought me up short. Opening the top drawer, I saw that James had carefully labeled all the folders: insurance, bills, credit cards and important documents. That one contained the birth certificates for both himself and Katie. Her birthday was easy to remember—November 11th. 11/11. His marriage certificate was in there too, officially recording that James Matthew McPeake wed Chloe Juliet Lowe. Lowe—now I remembered her maiden name. Maybe that would help me track down her parents or other family members, who I frankly did not recall from the wedding beyond some vague sort of American Gothic grimness.

There was one more document in that folder—Last Will And Testament, it said. I mentally complimented James for being so responsible, at age thirty-three, to put his arrangements for Katie down in black and white. Then, I started to read.

The will, which appeared to be a simple form with blanks for him to fill in, stated he had left his entire estate to the Church of the Benevolent Fount and named one of their officials as the executor. It even gave directions for the disposal of his remains— cremation, ashes to be scattered at sea, a prepaid arrangement, agreement attached. No mention of Katie's name anywhere. It was dated a year prior. I couldn't believe it. I read it through three times, but it still said the exact same thing. I could not fucking believe it. How could he be so stupid? Not to mention mean. It wasn't like a million bucks were at stake, but it just seemed so cold to me to leave nothing to his only child. I couldn't understand it.

I checked the life insurance policy. It too, named Benevolent Fount as the sole beneficiary.

I'd assumed, as his only living relative, that I was executrix by default. I'd blithely jumped in, making preliminary arrangements with a funeral home for when the coroner released his body, talking with Delgado, calling CPS. Shocked, I stared at the Hefty bags littering the floor, the will in my hand, the sixty-watt bulb from the lamp on the dresser providing a weak glow of light.

If this will was legitimate—and why wouldn't it be?—I realized I had no need, no right, even, to be going through his stuff. It all belonged to someone else now, not me or Katie.

The loud ticking of the alarm clock caught my attention. Almost nine, which would be midnight in Boston. I started to go get my cell phone, then realized it wouldn't work. No signal. My thought was to call a pal from the firm's legal department, even if I rousted him out of bed and get the name of the attorneys we dealt with on the West Coast. Surely, they'd have a San Diego office. LA, for sure. I had to make sure the will was bona fide, for Katie's sake, at least. But that would have to wait until the morning, when I could get to a working phone.

While I was thinking about it, I set the alarm for five-thirty a.m. That should give me more than enough time to find Escondido, wherever the heck that was.

I added the insurance policy to the file with the birth certificates and the will. I took that and my wine back out to the living room, where I stashed the papers in my purse. If the estate truly belonged to James's church, then all I needed to do was put together some kind of memorial service and get Katie and myself back on the next plane to Boston. If nothing else, it would be a lot less work for me. A lot less paperwork, for sure.

I toasted that possibility with another glass of wine. And a huge yawn. Almost midnight in Boston…no wonder I felt so tired all of a sudden. Sitting down on the sofa, I took my shoes off, thinking I'd chill there for a bit before going to bed. Maybe read a few pages of Dick Francis. I must have closed my eyes for just a second.

Chapter 7

In the dream, I was back down on the beach. It was night and black as pitch, but a full moon directly overhead shone down on me as I sat on the big rock. Clouds flitted across the moon's face. I was all alone. A red glow emanated from beyond the cliffs down to my left and I calmly understood the lighthouse must be burning again. I knew I was down there for some reason and patiently waited for that to be revealed to me. The night was still hot and humid, sweat running down the small of my back, but I found myself shivering, wrapping my arms around myself. There was something out there, in the darkness, just beyond the limits of my vision. I could feel it, a nameless presence that filled me with dread. I wanted to run, but I knew I shouldn't leave the rock. I had to wait.

The roar of the surf was so loud it was hurting my ears. Even so, a slight noise behind me caused me to turn around, taking care not to let my feet touch the sand. A man was coming down the path. A stranger, tall and gaunt, dressed in a black suit and a white shirt buttoned all the way to the top, but no tie. Like a scarecrow. He even had the black hat clutched in his hand. The clouds must have obscured the moon, because the light trembled and failed. Toiling through the sand, he spoke as he approached.

"I'm from the church," he said. The Something out there in the dark edged a little closer. But I couldn't run from either. I felt paralyzed, speechless, hanging on to the rock like I was afraid it might lurch and tip me off at any moment.

"I'm from the church," he insisted, irritated at my lack of response. He loomed over me, angry now. I felt weak with terror.

Suddenly, the moonlight flooded back with full force. He threw his hands up to shield his face, but the light was too strong. He disappeared, freeing me to turn back to the ocean.

A figure was emerging from the waves, but not a surfer this time. Although as she came closer, I could see it was her. It seemed that the stars themselves twinkled more brightly as she advanced. The foam at her feet glowed like diamonds, then receded. She was clad not in a wetsuit, but in some sort of iridescent fish scale mermaid suit, leaving only her stomach, arms and shoulders bare. She smiled at me, making me ache. So beautiful. Closer and closer she came, until she was right in front of me, drawing me into an embrace. The shimmering scales, to my amazement, felt as soft to the touch as moleskin and as warm as the flesh beneath. Her face was in my hair, whispering words of comfort I couldn't quite catch. I tried to tell her I couldn't leave the rock, but she was pulling me in, tighter and tighter. I held on for dear life as the tide surged in to take us away. As my feet touched the sand, I heard it scream in rage. I knew it was coming for us...

Chapter 8

I awoke with a start, drenched in sweat, blinded by the light fixture glaring down at me from above the couch. Dead silence. Strange place. That nasty sulfur or methane or whatever smell back on the breeze. I struggled to an upright position, knocking over my wineglass on the floor in the process. Oh, well, piece of crap dhuri rug anyhow. Breathing deeply, I took stock. Stupid dream. Scared the shit out of me, though.

My watch said three thirty-three, so it was way too early to get up. The lights in the kitchen and the bedrooms were still ablaze too. I got up and took the wineglass into the kitchen, then turned out the light in there. Had I even locked the front door? Jesus, I must be losing it. I turned the deadbolt. The cabin across the way was dark. I turned out the living room light too.

Then went back to the bedroom and unpacked my suitcase to the extent of retrieving my toiletry items and the T-shirt I planned to sleep in. It was freaking hot in there. I thought about bringing the fan from the living room back into the bedroom, but it seemed like too much effort. The wind was shushing in the bushes outside. Grabbing the necessary accoutrements, I took a step toward the bathroom. But stopped in the dark hallway as I heard something. Probably just a branch from a bush scratching the outside of the cabin. I listened. The wind picked up, but I thought I could hear something more. Voices. Not whispering, but talking just low enough that I couldn't make out any words. Just the sibilance of soft speech in some language other than English.

The snap of a twig underfoot? I froze, petrified. Told myself I was just being foolish. There was nobody out here but me and the marine biologist sleeping across the way. But straining to hear what I was sure I had heard. People talking. I couldn't make out any words. But it didn't sound like a possum. I could feel and hear my heart beating. I was listening so hard I had my eyes squeezed shut.

A loud thump against the outside wall made my eyes fly open and further caused me to leap the short distance to the bathroom. I flung the light switch upward, hoping a courageous demonstration of my occupancy would frighten off whatever bogeys were out there, telling myself not to be an asshole, it must be a skunk or a possum or whatever and I was far too old and grown up to be scared of the dark.

But I *was* scared. I was keenly aware I didn't even have a phone. All alone.

God knows how I got back to sleep that night. I couldn't bring myself to lie down in James's bed for some reason. His room felt too hot and uninviting, but it was more than that—like the room itself didn't want me in there. Like I wouldn't be able to breathe in there. I finally left the lights on in both bedrooms and the bathroom, then went back to the semi-darkened couch. Every stray noise, every creak of the cabin was like a jolt of electricity in my veins. Although I didn't hear any more whispering. I tossed and turned on the itchy fabric, unable to find a comfortable position. God, if I had to live in that place, I thought, I would install every known burglar alarm, booby trap and motion sensor to man. And buy a big ole can of pepper spray. Only exhaustion and stress could explain the sleep that finally overtook me around four thirty.

I don't know if I dreamed that time, but I again woke with a horrible start, this time due to the lunatic clamor of the alarm clock in James's room. Loud enough to wake the—never mind, I thought, jamming back there to shut it off. It was still dark outside. Shutting my mind to everything but the need to get going and pick up Katie, I focused myself on my next goal: taking a shower in that bathroom.

It wasn't that bad, I told myself. Especially if I kept my eyes tightly shut. I got through teeth brushing and the other preparatory stuff, then reached in to turn on the hot water in the shower. With a couple of clanks and a groan, the plumbing reluctantly responded. I noted the daddy longlegs up in the corner had been joined by a friend overnight. Great. At least he had one.

I hadn't bothered to shut the door to the bathroom, since I was there by myself. Never did it at home, either. Besides, with no fan, I wanted the door open so the mirror wouldn't steam up too much. I waited for a while for the water to get up past mildly lukewarm, but it never did and I finally decided I couldn't wait anymore. I had places to go and people to see, so I braved the temperate water.

At least the tub was clean. The shower curtain, however, once expanded, revealed a wealth of mildew in its folds. Lovely. Good thing my favorite color is green.

Its remaining once white opaqueness enveloped me in a dreary, dreamy, milky light inside the shower. The rest of the bathroom could be seen only in vague, shadowy outlines through the curtain. I washed my hair as quickly as possible, being careful to not make eye contact with the spiders lest they viciously leap upon me. I was still plenty jumpy from the night before and felt ultra vulnerable in the shower. The less-than-hot water was not conducive to relaxation either. I kept thinking maybe I heard something. But, no, of course I didn't.

Head under the tepid flow as I rinsed, I then thought I *really* heard something. A thud or a bang or…something. I jerked my head out of the stream, frantically wiping suds out of my eyes so I could open them. Blinking away, I strained tensely to hear, but there was nothing but the rush of the water and the gurgle of the drain. What could I have possibly heard with my ears full of water anyhow? You dumb butt, I chastised myself. I took a breath. And realized with an agonizing spurt of adrenaline that a tall dark shape was visible through the curtain that hadn't been there before.

The worst and longest thirty seconds of my life followed as I stood, immobile with fear, with the now cold water cascading down upon me. And the shape unmoving outside.

After thirty seconds of chicken, however, I suddenly couldn't take it anymore. With a shriek, I threw open the curtain and threw up my fists, ready to take on my attacker.

Who, I realized with a gasp, was James's navy blue bathrobe, hanging on a hook on the back of the bathroom door, which had slowly swung shut while I showered. So, I'm standing there with the shower shooting water out on the floor, buck naked, fists up, ready to take on a terry cloth bathrobe and whup its ass. Ay yi yi. How humiliating. After all that, I was so shook up I couldn't even do conditioner.

I did put on the robe while I combed my wet hair, however, since I hadn't brought my own. Its warmth was welcome in the chill of the early morning hour. It was way too big for me, so I had to roll up the sleeves a few turns. As I leaned into the mirror to see just how bloodshot my eyeballs were, I could feel paper crackling in the robe pocket. I pulled out a much folded lavender sheet of stationery. A hint of lavender scent wafted up from the page as I smoothed it out to read it. Seconds later, I had to look in the mirror to see if I was blushing. (I wasn't.) The author of the note was someone named Patricia and hoo-wee, she had it bad for James. The note was addressed to him, but undated, so I wasn't sure how current it was. Patricia seemed to be a woman with few inhibitions and fewer limits to her imagination. Plus a background on her high school junior varsity gymnastics team. The letter mentioned a photo which had apparently been enclosed, but it wasn't in the robe. Believe me, I checked. I certainly hadn't come across it anywhere else in the cabin. Hmmm… I wondered if James had returned her interest. She didn't sound like the Bible-study type, but you never know.

Whew! I tucked the refolded note back in the robe pocket. What with one thing and another, this was about the most exciting shower I'd ever taken. (Well, by myself.) My priority, though, was still to get out of there and pick up Katie as soon as possible.

I dressed quickly and in multiple layers, thinking ahead to the drive. Why in the world had I put the top down on the Jeep? I seriously doubted my ability to correctly put it back up—it wasn't one of those easy push-a-button deals. There were snaps and straps and heaven knows what else. And I'm mechanically challenged on a good day. What a moron I am, I thought. I must have been thinking of San Diego's vaunted year-round perfect weather, not about driving through fogbanks or hitting the freeway in the predawn darkness. I added a hooded sweatshirt and Levi's jacket to my jeans and polo shirt, topping off that finery with my prized black 49ers baseball cap. Great—raggedy hat on top of damp hair should make for a fabulous first impression on Mrs. Augustine, but I figured my two forms of photo ID were more important to her than my fashion sense. I was too nervous to bother with any makeup, either—I just wanted to hit the road and substitute activity for thought, at least for a little while. Some previously unused part of my brain cycled on with a click just before I went out the door, telling me to grab a jacket for Katie too. And the animal crackers! Oh, yeah. I stuffed them and her little windbreaker in the side pocket of my capacious bag.

Since I wasn't a coffee drinker or a breakfast eater, a cold can of Coke was all I needed for the road. I turned out the lights and locked the door behind me. I paused on the porch to get my bearings. There was light in the sky now. The top of the Point above was outlined in blush tones. Good—I could use the light for the drive up. I had been feeling more than a little nervous about getting up the dirt road in the dark. As I glanced across to the other occupied cabin, a light came on inside. Maybe I'd get to finally meet the neighbor later today. And maybe up close she'd have a face like a bullfrog so I could stop dreaming about her and focus on business. The first chance I got after picking up Katie, I'd be calling my pal Ben from Legal, so I could find out about the merits of the will.

I fired up the Jeep and cautiously made my way uphill, with no problems except for a few jackrabbits startling me as they darted across the road in front of my high beams. It was actually a little easier going up than it had been coming down, or maybe I was just getting more comfortable with the vehicle. The light was growing stronger with each passing minute and that helped too. In any event, I made it up to the main road in maybe ten minutes time, very glad for the additional layers of clothing.

Delgado had given me a placard for the dashboard which identified me (or the vehicle, at least) as having some legitimate reason to be on Navy property, but would not exempt me from the watchful eyes at the guard shacks. Even so, the armed sailors at the first kiosk waved me through without comment. Maybe it was easier to get out than in.

There was no traffic on my side of the road, but a few cars were coming past me on their way to the labs. Must be the day shift—but on a Saturday? Coming up on the kiosk marking the exit from Navy property, I slowed, but the guard again waved me through with only a cursory glance. His partner on the other side was checking each southbound vehicle before permitting entry.

Free at last! My spirits picked up a little as I cruised down the city street leading off the Point. My rental car map guided me toward an on-ramp to the right freeway. It was a nice enough morning, although not particularly sunny. June Gloom, they call it in Southern California. I was tired, no doubt, but feeling energized and shaking off the effects of the creepy night before. I even found a semi-decent radio station and cranked up the tunes, hoping they would offset the anxiety I felt growing inside the closer I got to Escondido.

Mrs. Augustine's directions were as good as gold and I pulled up outside the Koffee Kup at seven thirty-five after only one wrong turn. Which gave me time to peel off my jacket and sweatshirt and do some much-needed damage control on the hat hair in the rearview mirror. And smoke a cigarette. It was probably about sixty-five degrees, but that felt wonderful to my Boston-attuned senses. I shoved the sweatshirt and jacket under the driver's seat, leaving the hat on the passenger seat. As far as I was concerned, this was bikini weather. Maybe Katie and I could hang out on the beach later. I'd seen a plastic pail and shovel in her milk crate of toys…

If she didn't hate me. If she wasn't a perfect little replica of James, with a cross clutched in one hand and the Old Testament in the other. To tell the truth, I was very close to completely freaked out. I was keenly aware that this morning was a turning point in my life. Prior to today, I was single, carefree (sort of) and at liberty to be as stupid and reckless as I cared to be. After today, I was A Parent. A Responsible Adult.

Yikes. For a second, I really thought I was going to throw up, but the last slug of Coke in the can calmed my stomach. Get a grip, Madison! Whatever's happening, it's happening, so let's just get on with it. Steeling myself, I grabbed my purse and headed for the door of the Koffee Kup. It was one of those strange purple and orange "space age" monstrosities from the sixties. "Futuristic" design, banal food. It was still not quite eight o'clock, but I thought I spotted an Augustine possible drinking coffee in a booth by the window. Stiff Blonde beehive in a markedly unnatural tone, oversized red glasses on a round face and a bright blue and white muumuu. She fit right in.

The place was half empty. I bypassed the vacant hostess station and went directly to Beehive's booth. She was working on a cinnamon roll as big as a dinner plate.

"Mrs. Augustine?"

It was. Muumuu and enormous pastry aside, she was very professional. She got right down to business, showing me her county badge and closely examining my IDs and the other documentation I'd brought. She explained again, as she had over the phone, that this was temporary custody only and that the court would notify me of a hearing date, etc. I was too nervous to eat, but was grateful for the Coke the waitress brought me. My mouth was dry as a bone.

"Well, dear, this is all in order," she said, pushing the documents back to my side of the table. "If I can just get you to sign here...and here..."

More promises on paper for me to keep. I sucked down the last of my drink, rattling the ice for no reason other than to be doing something with my hands.

"Now don't be nervous, dear. I'm sure little Katie will be just thrilled to meet you."

I wasn't so sure.

"How much does she understand?" I asked. "Do you know what they've told her? About James and...me?"

"Not really, but the Jennings can tell you much more. They live just around the corner. Are you ready?"

No, but I didn't really see any other choice, so I followed her Plymouth in the Jeep. We drove a few blocks to a tree-lined street of modest stucco tract homes in pastel and earth shades. Lots of dads already out mowing the lawn or changing the oil. Kids on bikes. We stopped in front of a small beige house with a straggly looking yard, littered with toys and sports equipment. I guess they were watching for us, because as I climbed out of the Jeep with my purse slung over my shoulder, a bunch of people came out the front door. A man, a woman carrying a baby and about twenty-seven kids. Okay, it was only four, but three of them were whirling dervishes, creating the illusion of many more. The fourth lagged a little behind the rest of the group.

My heart stopped. It was Katie. It had to be. The other kids were bellowing and running around the yard like maniacs, but it was like time slowed for this moment to allow me to take in the sight of her. She looked so small, dwarfed by the kid-sized backpack on her back. She looked…perfect. A perfect little girl. Ten fingers, ten toes (I assumed), two eyes, two ears… Still with the wispy Blonde hair and big blue eyes. She wore jeans and a pink T-shirt with a little denim jacket, twin to the one under my seat. White sneakers with pink stripes that made her feet look clumsy and big, like a puppy whose body hasn't caught up yet to his paws. Her face wasn't sad, exactly—more like expressionless, although I caught a brief moue of distaste when one of the dervishes bumped into her. She grabbed the straps of the backpack and jacked it up a little higher, screwing her face up as she glanced toward the sun. She hadn't seen me yet.

My feet, without me realizing it, had carried me from the Jeep to the edge of the property. Mrs. Augustine joined me there, hailing the foster parents in tones calculated to carry over the banshee wails of the other kids. She introduced me to them, Mr. and Mrs. Jennings, but I could barely put two words together as I stared past them at my niece, who was closely examining a mosquito bite on her left wrist, ignoring everyone else.

Mrs. Jennings hefted the baby to her other hip, telling me the family resemblance was just amazing, wasn't it?

The kid really did kind of look like a little me. Boy, that must have pissed James off. Mrs. Jennings was now plying Mrs. Augustine with her genetic theories. Augustine seemed unimpressed. Probably ready to clock out—enough with the Saturday overtime already.

I eased past the Jennings and crouched down on one knee in front of Katie. I took my sunglasses off. She gave me the full beam of those blue eyes.

"Hi, Katie," I said. "I'm your Aunt Madison."

Her look was skeptical at best. She went back to the mosquito bite.

I tried again. "Your daddy was my big brother. We used to play together all the time when we were little kids."

She gave me another quick glance, biting her lower lip meditatively.

Augustine was going into the house with Mr. Jennings to do the paperwork. Mrs. Jennings was saying something to me. I stood up.

"I beg your pardon?"

She explained that Katie had all her stuff in her backpack and was ready to go. She didn't look ready to me, but I again realized neither one of us had much choice in this deal.

"She's been a real good girl too, haven't you, Katie?"

I was happy to see I wasn't the only one getting the silent/skeptical treatment. I stuck out my hand.

"Do you want to come with me, Katie? Let's go back to the cabin, okay?"

Much to my relief, she took my hand and we walked to the curb. I found myself making more or less idiotic small talk to fill the silence.

"I brought your windbreaker," I said, pulling it out of my purse and holding it up for her inspection. "But I guess you don't need it since you got your denim jacket, huh?"

She spoke her first words to me. Accusingly.

"It's wrinkled."

I looked at the windbreaker. It was pretty damn wrinkled.

"Oh. Well, we can fix that." I stuffed it back in the side pocket, then stashed the purse on the floor in front of the passenger seat.

"Okay, well, let's get you in the back here." I opened the passenger door and looked down at her. She climbed right in like a little monkey, pausing to put her backpack on the floor before settling in the car seat. Between the two of us, we figured out how to strap her in.

After assuring myself she was secure, I went around to the driver's side. The day had warmed up a bit and was probably at San Diego's traditional seventy degrees. I thought she'd be okay in the open car in her little jacket. I left my sweatshirt under the seat, but pulled out my Levi's jacket.

"Hey, look, I've got a jean jacket just like yours," I tried.

She took in this pearl of wisdom without comment.

I shrugged into the jacket. Mrs. Augustine had resurfaced, leaving the foster family thankfully behind. We shook hands and parted, her duty done. We both got in our cars. I watched as she sped off in her Plymouth, then followed her at a sedate speed down the residential street. I glanced back at Katie to see how she was doing. The wind was whipping her hair in her face, but she bore it all stolidly. I'd never thought of five-year-old girls being stolid before.

I raised my voice a little to ask her, "Have you had breakfast yet? Are you hungry?" She shook her head to indicate no and no. Which was when I remembered I'd forgotten to give her the animal crackers. Oh, well. They'd keep. She was saying something.

"What?" I glanced back again.

"Are we going to the Point?" Her eyes glittered for a moment. Maybe it was just the sun.

"Do you want to go back?"

She considered that for a moment. "I have to…be there."

I noted the pause, but assumed it was a reference to her father. On the road in an open vehicle was not the place for this conversation. We'd have plenty of time later to talk once we got back to the cabin.

"Yeah, we're going back to the Point. We'll stop at the store first and get some groceries, okay? You doing okay back there, kiddo?"

She nodded. Saturday morning traffic was light, so we flew down the freeway. In no time at all, I had taken the off-ramp onto the main drag that bisected the Point and led all the way out to the labs. Now that I'd gotten through the picking-up-the-kid part of the process, I suddenly realized I was hungry. Really hungry. Breakfast is the most important meal of the day. Yeah, right. But the kid had said she hadn't had breakfast either... I definitely did want to stop by the store and pick up some more groceries, but the thought of buying and cooking a breakfast was way too much for me. Between you and me, I'm not much of a cook. I could just see the kid looking at me disgustedly when I served her burnt scrambled eggs and some twisted little black sticks that used to be bacon. I didn't want that to be our first culinary experience together. Plus, I was starving. I wanted real food, for myself and hopefully her too.

Since I already knew there were no restaurants on the Point, I made a right turn when a sign pointed us toward Ocho Beach. Once again, my Internet research from two days before came in handy. Ocho Beach was the neighborhood hugging the westward, Pacific Ocean side of Shadow Point, at least the non-Navy part of it. The original land grant for the area had been four miles of coastline, extending roughly two miles inland. Four by two equaled eight, thus Ocho. Most of the coastline section, however, was nothing but craggy rocks and crumbling sandstone cliffs. And a lot of the two miles inland now belonged to the United States Navy. Modern day Ocho Beach (or "OB" as the locals called it) was roughly a mile square—a quaint, if shabby, little beach town, with one main street devoted to businesses and the rest residential. Lots of the original little stucco or board and batten bungalows, with the occasional, newer, big, fancy house on the larger lots.

As I turned onto Ocho Beach Boulevard, Katie called out from the backseat.

"Where are we going?"

"Let's get some breakfast, okay and then we'll go to the store? All right?"

She seemed ready to argue, but then subsided without answering and merely looked off to the side as we climbed a steep hill lined with houses topped by red-tiled roofs. At its peak, a breathtaking view of the Pacific was unveiled. I drew in my breath as we started down the other side of the hill, an equally steep decline into the heart of Ocho Beach. Houses gave way to a school—Newport Elementary—and a library, across the street from each other. Then came the business district, a scant three blocks long. The street ended at the beach—coming down the hill, I could see the waves tumbling onto the sand and a fishing pier extending out into the surf. We stopped at a red light in front of the school. A young guy wearing swim trunks and flip-flops crossed in front of us with a black Lab and a shepherd mix on leashes. Both dogs wore red bandanas. The ocean air was clean and invigorating, this close to the water.

"Do you know a good place to get something to eat?" I turned around to ask Katie, but she merely shrugged, seemingly uninterested. I was a little disheartened by her lack of enthusiasm thus far, but took a deep breath and persevered. What else could I do?

"We'll just cruise the street and see if we find something good then."

I gave her a bright smile in the rearview mirror. Nothing. Oh, well.

What traffic there was slowed to about twenty miles per hour as we entered the business strip. It was kind of funny to see Small Town USA plunked down here in the midst of the San Diego metropolis. Cars pulled in diagonally to park at the curb, their rear bumpers protruding into the broad, palm tree-lined street. No fast food, no major brand stores. Not even a grocery store. Most of the buildings looked like they'd been built no later than 1950. Only a few were two story. None were higher. At this relatively early hour, a few tourists roamed the sidewalks, along with a scruffy assortment of locals. Surfers on their bikes, their boards clutched under one arm, kept pace with the leisurely traffic.

I looked for a kid-friendly restaurant with an "A" sign from the health department in their window. I saw a dime store, a liquor store, a beauty parlor, a couple of surf shops, a bar, a crappy tourist souvenir store, a youth hostel... And a gorgeous art deco movie theater. The huge and colorful neon sign identified it as The Grand. I slowed as we passed. A Hitchcock retrospective was playing, plus Rocky Horror at midnight on the weekends. I couldn't be sure, but I thought I saw the Goth cashier from the day before smoking a cigarette in the shadows with some other kids near the box office.

We were running out of road. The beach loomed just ahead. Since there was so little traffic and no cops in sight, I made an illegal U-turn at the light and tried another pass down the boulevard. A clothing boutique...a bicycle shop with a poodle asleep on a pillow in the window... Aha! I spotted a restaurant and pulled into the first available parking space, which was in front of the bright blue building next door. An oddly vibrant shade of bright blue, one usually found on retail businesses south of the border, not north. I glanced at the rainbow-colored sign as I helped Katie out of her car seat. "The Blue Moon," it was called, with a rascally looking man-in-the-moon winking down at us and smoking a corncob pipe. I grabbed all our possessions from the Jeep and grabbed Katie's hand too, as we made our way onto the sidewalk. We both were drawn to the window display— silly T-shirts, the OB seagull bumper stickers I'd seen on Dr. Piper's truck and an assortment of smoking paraphernalia.

Oops! I belatedly realized "The Blue Moon" was a head shop and quickly drew my five-year-old niece with me into the restaurant next door. Man! There was a ton of stuff in this world I'd need to conceal from her, for a while, at least. This was going to be a lot of work, I thought, with a sigh.

Mi Amiga was a bright and cheerful little one-room Mexican restaurant. The floor was scuffed linoleum, the tables and chairs were mismatched and tippy, but the line of patrons waiting to be seated, the happy faces on the outgoing customers and, above all, the pleasing aroma told me we'd found a winner. Saturday morning and the place was packed. Turnover was brisk, though, so we found ourselves seated at a tiny table for two in less than ten minutes. Whoever had been sitting there before had left behind a copy of the local beach newspaper, *The Grunion*, folded up with the laminated menus in the little metal rack placed on each table for that purpose. I pushed aside the salt-and-pepper shakers and a bottle of Mexi-Pep to glance at the paper's folded front page for a second before I grabbed the menus. Ocho Beach was getting ready for the annual Fourth of July holiday fireworks extravaganza at the pier. Whoopee.

Holidays. Oh my God. I would now be required to do holidays, something I hadn't had to bother with for at least five years, except to cadge the occasional free meal at other people's houses. Thanksgiving. Christmas. The horror of it all. I felt like I might start to hyperventilate, so I grabbed a menu and started fanning myself with it. Where was the water? I looked around for the waitress.

I felt flushed. Katie was looking at me kind of oddly. I fanned a little harder. Her head barely cleared the table. Probably needed one of those—what do you call them?

A smiling waitress brought a booster seat (that's it!) for her and got her situated, then returned with glasses of ice water. I downed half of mine in one gulp. I handed Katie one of the menus, just to give her something to look at even though I assumed she couldn't read it. There was no children's menu in the little metal holder. Now more or less at eye level with me, she glanced down at the large menu crammed with size ten font and no pictures, then back up at me with doubt and a furrowed brow. She seemed a little abashed and uncertain of her surroundings. I suddenly wondered if she had ever eaten in a restaurant before. I tried a smile on her, but couldn't raise one in return.

I scanned the menu for the children's section, but there was none. Oh, crap. Well, we'd have to improvise. The busy cafe buzzed with conversation and activity around us as I quizzed Katie on her breakfast likes and dislikes. She didn't like eggs, she didn't like oatmeal and she seemed downright suspicious of all pork products. She didn't know what a bagel was. Well, frankly, I was a little worried about ordering a bagel in a Mexican restaurant anyway. We settled on pancakes for her, huevos rancheros for me and two orange juices. We both barely made a dent in the huge portions that were quickly brought to us, but I, at least, felt a little more ready to face the rest of the day. Although I could have used a couple of the mimosas the other customers were so joyfully sucking down. I dutifully drank my orange juice. Straight. For the most part, we ate in silence as the noisy chitchat and clatter of plates around us precluded any meaningful conversation. My chair faced the street, so, in between bites of my food and glances at Katie's impassive face, I watched the traffic drive by. I thought I saw Dr. Piper's aged white truck pass by at one point, but it was gone before I could be sure or catch a glimpse of the driver.

After our meal, we headed back to the main drag. Shortly thereafter, I pulled into the Shadow Point General Store parking lot. Things were looking much busier this time. Several big trucks were coming and going from the freight depot. In the rearview mirror, I noticed Katie eyeing them with some unreadable emotion. I freed her from the car seat much more easily this time and she again took my hand with no complaint as we walked the few yards through the busy parking lot into the store. Kids loitered beside a bike rack to the right of the store entrance. Some were teenagers, some were only a few years older than Katie. I figured the general store must be the major hangout spot on Shadow Point, with so little else going on.

She jammed off ahead of me as I grabbed a cart just inside the entrance despite my call to her to wait. I followed after her as quickly as I could, challenged by a wayward wheel on the shopping cart which seemed determined to head nor'northeast. Katie was skipping down the aisle devoted to salad dressings and condiments. She was obviously very familiar with the layout of the store and I decided to let her lead the way. What did we need anyhow? Milk. Juice. Cereal, maybe? Rounding the corner at the back of the store, we were into the dairy section. I grabbed some milk. Catching up with Katie, I told her to pick out some cereal. She scampered off to that aisle and I followed in her wake, keeping her in sight. We rounded another corner, this one with a display devoted to juice boxes. I grabbed an assorted twelver, then pulled my cell phone out of the depths of my purse. Plenty of signal—hallelujah. I found Ben's number and pressed send.

"Hello?" I could hear his nine-year-old twin boys yelling in the background and the dog barking.

"Hey, Ben—it's Madison."

He was less than thrilled to hear from me, partly because of my black cloud status, partly because it was a Saturday, but he owed me and he knew it. We'd worked together for almost three years. Although our jobs were quite different—me being a trainer and him an attorney—we'd become buddies, sharing wiseass remarks in the backs of staff meetings and more than a few after-work margaritas. More to the point, we'd been at a corporate retreat in Tahoe a couple years back and…well, the less said the better. But he owed me a favor, big time.

I brought him up to speed in about thirty seconds. Katie was capering about in front of the Lucky Charms and Cocoa Puffs about twenty feet ahead of me, but hadn't yet made a selection. As if I didn't know there was no way James would have let her eat that crap. Well, we could figure out the all granola diet plan later. Right now, I wanted her distracted while I had this conversation with my favorite attorney.

"I don't know, Mad," he was saying. "It sounds legit. If he wanted to leave all his money to the church, I mean, he could, you know. His call. Damnit, Rusty!"

I think that last bit was for the dog, a spastic hound who'd peed on my shoe when I'd last visited their household at Thanksgiving.

"Okay, I hear you. I think I need to run these papers past somebody out here, though. Who's our West Coast counsel, again?"

He gave me the name of the firm. Then, telling me to hang on, found the name of a particular attorney and his phone number. I punched it into my phone's memory.

"You're a prince, Benjie. Thanks a bunch!"

"Yeah, well, you take care of yourself out there, Madison. People are worried about you, you know."

"Yeah, right," I scoffed.

"Okay, well, I'm worried about you. I didn't even know you were gone until the meeting yesterday. Rumor is the boss wanted to fire your ass, but HR held him back at the last minute on some technicality."

Hmmm. I knew I hadn't exactly been Employee of the Month lately, but I didn't think I was on the brink of being fired. Close, maybe, but really, truly, *actually* fired?

Ben was still talking. "Seriously, Mad—are you doing okay?"

This conversation was not going the way I had anticipated.

"I'm fine, Ben. Thanks. Look, I'll be back at work in a few weeks and we can talk more then, all right?"

There was a pause on the other end.

"Ben?"

"I'm here, Mad, but…I don't know if you should plan on coming back anytime soon. Or at all. You might want to think of looking for another job. They're pretty pissed at you."

"Come on," I said, trying to be positive. "It's not that bad."

"Mad, buddy—look, I didn't want to say this before and you know I love you, but those people…they, uh…they hate you, Mad."

Wow. That hurt. I hadn't thought they actually hated me.

"Madison?" Ben said in my ear.

I was clogging the aisle. A woman with a full cart passed me on the left with a sniff. Maybe she hated me too.

"Look, I gotta go, Ben. Thanks for your help. I'll catch you later, okay?"

We hung up. Great, now I could add career uncertainty to my list of woes. I'd thought I could just serve my three-week sentence and they'd get over it, but Ben had made it sound a lot more serious than that.

Katie was approaching the cart with a large box of Captain Crunch, carefully not making eye contact as she deposited it within. I yanked her chain a wee bit.

"Is that what you usually get?"

"Yes." In a small voice, still with the eyes looking everywhere but my face. She hooked her fingers through the front of the cart, leading me on.

I let that pass with no comment since I love Captain Crunch too. Although I rarely eat it these days since it's about ten thousand calories a bowl. I figured we both deserved some comfort food, though. We could always walk back to Boston.

"What else do we need?"

Silence. We were passing the deli section now, though, so I grabbed some prefab sandwiches, chips and potato salad. There. Done.

The cashier this time was a man in his sixties. No sign of the Goth. As we waited in line behind another customer, I tried the attorney's number just to see. Nope. Voice mail. I decided to not leave a message since Katie was standing right there. I'd catch the guy on Monday.

The store was very busy, especially for a Saturday morning, it seemed to me. Although I usually spent Saturday mornings in bed, so for all I knew this was what the normal people did. The assistant manager hustled over to help the cashier bag up our stuff. Craig B., his nametag said. He looked to be about my age. He sported a natty red vest, an obsequious manner and a prominent Adam's apple.

"And how are you two pretty ladies doing this morning?" he said to me and Katie with an oily smile. She looked back at him with a complete lack of expression. His smile dimmed a bit. He looked at me.

"Fine," I responded, although with a similar lack of gusto. He showed us, though—didn't offer to help us out to the car. Which was fine by me.

As we pulled out of the parking lot, another big truck was pulling into Conrad Bly Freight.

"C—B—F," Katie sang out from the backseat, reading the letters off the trailer. I thought that was pretty good for five years old. I felt a flush of familial pride—the kid was smart! Could I read anything at that age? I couldn't remember.

It was getting close to noon by the time we made it back to the cabin. The clouds were starting to clear to reveal patches of cornflower blue sky. Perfect timing for a lunchtime picnic on the beach, I thought. The sailors had still closely examined my ID and vehicle, but we got past both checkpoints with no problem. One of them—the sturdy Latina from the night before—even greeted Katie by name, to which she responded with a regal nod. Not exactly a chatterbox, that kid.

I told her to hang on tight as we edged our way over the lip of the dirt road leading to the bottom. We slowly bumped and slid down the track. I was even more careful with Katie in the back, but she seemed unconcerned, bored even, when I checked on her in the mirror. I parked the Jeep this time under the trees next to the other cars, on the far side of James's Explorer. Dr. Piper was just coming out of her front door as I got Katie unhooked from the car seat.

"Pipe!" the kid yelled joyfully, making a beeline for the doctor at a dead run. The first real show of emotion I'd seen from her. I picked up the backpack she'd left behind, wondering if this was the first of about a million times I'd be doing that. Slinging the pack over my shoulder, I then took off my Niners cap and stuffed that in my purse. I ran my hands hastily through my hair, trying to reassert some semblance of order. This was not destined to be a good hair day. Oh, well. I collected my purse, my sweatshirt and the groceries and trailed along behind her.

Dr. Piper had gone down on one knee to receive Katie's hug. Regaining her feet, she picked her up and swung her around in a circle, setting her down at the foot of the porch steps. Katie grabbed her hand and looked up at her adoringly, excitedly telling her where she'd been and what she'd been doing in a tumble of words, ending with "…and I got to ride in her car that has no top!" as I walked up. I laid down my assorted parcels as they both looked at me. Dr. Piper's small smile was more in the eyes than on her lips and more in response to Katie's recitation than for me.

"Hi," I said to her. "Madison McPeake." I held out my hand.

"Alice Piper," she replied, shaking my hand briefly.

Her easy drawl marked her as a southerner. Texas, maybe. Her grip was cool and firm. She was maybe half an inch shorter than my five foot seven and slender, like I'd thought the night before. Late twenties. Fine featured. She was wearing faded olive green cargo shorts and an ice blue tank top that set off her coloring nicely. She was too fair to tan much, but I knew from the night before that her natural skin color was a few shades even lighter. Soft-looking, dark brown, medium-length hair in no particular style. Mirrored sunglasses hung from a rainbow cord around her neck. Her eyes were a clear blue gray. Beautiful skin too and eyebrows that… I realized I was staring. She didn't look like any Alice I'd ever seen. Nothing like my dream either, not that I could really remember what she looked like in that.

"You don't look like an Alice somehow," I blurted out like a fool, since I couldn't think of anything else to say.

Her smile widened. "Well, I guess that's why everybody calls me Pipe."

She looked down at Katie, who was tugging at her hand. "Maybe you could say hello to Norm, huh? He missed you," she said to her. Katie's face lighted in a smile and she ran off to the corner of the yard to embrace the plaster garden gnome, scarcely shorter than herself. She busied herself with patting the tip of his triangular red hat and making sure he was arranged just so amongst some potted succulents. She was talking to him too, but I couldn't catch any of her words.

Pipe gave me a shrug. "She loves Norm."

I couldn't help but smile at her.

"I'm sorry for your loss."

That wiped the smile off my face.

"Oh. Thanks." I glanced over at Katie, but she was still occupied with the gnome. "Did you know James well?"

"Not that well, actually, although we've been living across from each other for almost a year. But Katie and I get along real good. She's just a pistol," she said, gazing with obvious affection at my niece who was now locked in a full body embrace with Norm, struggling to move him to a better spot.

"Don't worry," she said to me, "she can't break him." We watched her for a moment.

I said, "I just met her for the first time this morning." I wondered why I was sharing personal info with this total stranger.

She turned to me and looked into my eyes for a long moment, then briefly touched my arm, saying, "You must be completely freaked out, right?"

I had to laugh. "Yeah, that sounds about right."

Katie heard us laughing and came galloping over. This time, she grabbed both my hand and Pipe's. Which shot my heart right into my throat and brought tears to my eyes, which I furiously blinked away.

Pipe looked at me like I couldn't fool her.

"Well, I got some work to do, but I think y'all should join me for dinner tonight. What do you think about that, Miss Katie Lou McPeake-a-boo? Madison?"

Somehow I'd never heard my name pronounced like that before. I can't even describe it to this day. Madison. Sent a shiver down my spine.

I looked down at Katie. Her little face was upturned to me, reminding me of James, reminding me of me, telling me we were in agreement.

"Sure. Pipe." I tried out her name. Pipe. "That sounds good."

Chapter 9

The plan was to reconvene at six. She pooh-poohed my offer to contribute anything, saying she had everything we could possibly need. Which saved me a trip back into town, thankfully. She was headed topside to do some work in one of the labs, she said. As she pulled away in her truck, Katie and I hauled the groceries and other stuff into our cabin. She paused impatiently while I unlocked the front door, then surged through into the living room. And then abruptly stopped.

"What?" I said. "What's wrong?" I stepped in behind her, shutting the screen door behind me.

"Yuck!" she said, looking up at me. "It stinks in here." She threw her backpack, then herself onto the couch, grabbing the elephant with the exclamation, "Babs!"

"What?" I said again. Didn't smell *that* bad, at least not to my nicotine-dulled senses. Oh. Maybe it was the smell of cigarettes she was reacting to. For the record, some small part of my consciousness had already noted I would have to quit smoking now that I had Katie. I was trying to put it off. But I knew the time was now. Damn it. I should have been happy to have the excuse to finally quit and be healthy. Damn it. The very small amount of fun I had left in my life seemed to be whirling down the drain.

I took the groceries into the kitchen. Eww, it did kind of stink in there. Then I saw it. The fruit I'd bought just yesterday was still there on the counter, but brown and rotting. Liquid seeping from some putrid grapes had pooled on the countertop and was slowly dripping onto the floor. As I watched, a fly landed on a nasty looking banana and walked its length. Gross. The two apples were shrunken like little decomposed heads. What the hell? Must be the crazy humidity or something. Man, this place was weird. The sickening sweetness of decay filled the air in there. I opened the kitchen window over the sink, then hurriedly emptied one of the plastic grocery sacks, so I could use it to scoop up the fetid mess. I wasn't sure what the garbage arrangements were down here. I had a sneaking suspicion they would involve me packing out the trash like an expedition to Everest. I took the bag outside, back around the rear of the cabin. Nothing but bushes out there as far as I could see. I chucked the bag as far as I could into the brush. So long, putridity. Merry Christmas, possums, fruit bats, whatever the fuck was out there.

Wiping my hands on the seat of my jeans, I went back inside. Having decided I must quit smoking, I was, of course, now dying for a cigarette. Will power. It's all about will power, I told myself.

I broached the subject of a picnic on the beach to Katie. She ran to go change into her swimsuit. Returning to the kitchen, I put the milk and some of the juice boxes in the refrigerator. I organized our lunch components and a baggie of ice cubes in the little cooler, then went to change into my own suit in James's bedroom. I peeked into Katie's open doorway on the way to see how she was doing.

I had to bite my lip to keep from laughing. She was pivoting around and around in a circle, wearing a little red one-piece tank suit with a froo-froo and frilly white skirt and struggling to pull a much twisted strap over her shoulder.

"Here," I said, coming into the room. "Let me give you a hand with that."

She stopped twirling and let me fix it. Part of what was making me laugh inside was the fact that my own suit was also red. Great minds think alike.

Suit squared away, she hunkered down beside her bed deciding which pair of sandals to wear. I left her to that important fashion decision while I quickly changed into my bikini. I added some truly trashed cutoffs, black rubber flip-flops and my always useful Niners hat. I found beach towels in a closet and sunscreen in the medicine cabinet. Not having dealt with a five-year-old before, I actually thought we were ready at that point.

The Kate-ster had gone with the yellow sandals (bold choice), but was now engrossed with the dilemma of which beach toys to take. We sorted out a plastic pail and assorted digging implements, then located a denim bucket hat for her to wear.

A battle then ensued over the sunscreen. Meltdown on her part, unswayed firmness on mine. Tears, wailing, you get the pic. I found myself down on my knees trying to get some eye contact. She finally caved. It basically boiled down to she didn't want me to put any on her face. Okay. Further negotiations revealed her concern that it would get in her eyes and hurt like a son of a bitch. (My interpretation, not her words.) We compromised to the extent that I was permitted to apply the sunscreen to her back, while she handled the extremities. I then applied a small amount to her upturned palms, which she vigorously but randomly applied to her face, careful to avoid the sensitive eyeball area. I stuck the bottle of sunscreen in the back pocket of my shorts. I gently placed two fingers under her chin, to lift her face for my inspection. I was careful, again, not to laugh. Broad streaks of white marked her visage like war paint, with whorls of lesser whiteness where she'd applied more pressure. Got the job done, though. I ran a fingertip down her nose and gave her a grin. She looked at me with no expression.

"Good job, kiddo. Let's hit the beach."

It had taken longer—much longer—than I'd anticipated, but we were finally ready. I schnagged the cooler on the way out and grabbed a low aluminum folding chair from the porch. Katie charged ahead of me to the path, carrying the towels. I called to her to slow down. I didn't want her out of my sight, even down there where I knew there was nobody else around. Overly protective, no doubt.

I can't properly explain the mix of emotions flooding my brain at that point. But just imagine a single twenty-eight year-old woman who had never expected to have a baby of her own, suddenly blessed with a beautiful child who looked just like her. Not that there wasn't going to be a lot of shit involved too, but shazam—now you are a Mother. Some (probably ovarian) part of my anatomy was absolutely singing. Later on, when we got into the serious tantrums and the boyfriends and the rebellion, it would suck, but for now—in this moment—I was having a picnic on a perfect beach with my niece for the very first time ever. And she seemed pretty cool so far. And we were both McPeakes. That settled it. That fluttering pain in my chest might even be...love. Now that I had somebody to love.

We found a spot on the sand not far from that big rock. I eyed it uncertainly, feeling some kind of vibe left over from my dream, but Katie had no reaction to it whatsoever. By now, it was an absolutely gorgeous San Diego beach day. Maybe seventy-five degrees, perfect sea breeze, blue skies. Katie ranged up and down the small beach, always staying within my view as she dug holes, collected shells and ran, ran, ran, always staying just out of reach of the incoming tide. Apparently, she didn't like to get wet.

I laid one towel out in the sand and draped the second one

over the chair. Shedding my shorts and flip-flops, I applied copious amounts of sunscreen to my pale East Coast bod. Bad habits aside, at least I was in decent shape thanks to regular visits to the gym and a really nasty spinning instructor. I called Katie to come get some lunch as I set up the victuals.

I was starving, but she turned her nose up after just a few bites of her turkey sandwich and a hit from a juicebox. I didn't make a big deal out of it. I figured she could wear herself out running the beach and would eventually get hungry. And maybe we could talk a little bit then.

Seemed like I was letting a lot of stuff pass until we got back to Boston. I knew I would have my work cut out for me once we got back there, but what could I do? We had to get through this hardest part first.

I wasn't through it myself yet. James was dead. My brother was dead. It just didn't seem real. I didn't know how to make it real, especially on a Saturday afternoon at the beach. No doubt reality would hit with a sickening crunch on Monday morning. I'd have to call the attorney then. Who would no doubt tell me it was my duty to advise the church—unless they already knew? Maybe some friend of James from the lab had gotten word to them already. I hoped they were in the phone book. Maybe I wasn't the executrix (such a cool title, huh?), but I was still next of kin, so I figured I might still be involved in the decisions regarding a memorial service.

I'd have to call the coroner's office and the funeral home too, to let them know I wouldn't be making funeral arrangements after all. Monday was shaping up to be no fun at all.

I'd have to try and track down Chloe's side of the family as well. I knew they were from somewhere in the greater San Francisco area, or at least had been. Maybe the local branch of the church could contact the Bay Area folks and help with that... Heaven forbid any of them would have any designs on custody of Katie. My stomach knotted up just to think of it. Not that I was such a stellar choice, but she deserved a better life than those

73

crazies would give her. Besides, James had put *me* down as next of kin—that had to count for something, right? And I was pretty sure I knew better lawyers than they did... I shook it off. No point worrying about something that might not even happen.

I'd been keeping an eye on Katie throughout these musings. I watched as she scampered back up to my chair and the spread out beach towel next to it. She eschewed the potato salad with a look of five-year-old horror, but sucked down some more juice and allowed herself to be talked into another bite from her sandwich and a couple of chips.

She jammed back down to the waterline with her bucket, shovel and other accessories to get some "good" wet sand. She didn't seem to have mastered the full concept of sandcastle building to my limited architectural eye, but hey—who cared? She was busy and I was almost prone in my chair, leaning back as far as I could. Wondering what the going rate was for a nanny in Boston these days. Hmmm...

Warmed by the sun and lulled by the surf, I managed to daydream the rest of the afternoon away with one eye on Katie while eating my lunch and envisioning a twenty-year-old French au pair named Claudette...

Chapter 10

I ventured down to the water line as the afternoon waned. I knew how to swim, but that was at the Y, in the pool. Not in the open ocean. I had no desire to test my skills against the waves, but I thought sticking a toe in the receding tidal surge might be pleasant. The water was cool. And the current was strong, surprisingly so to me. It sucked at my feet and the sand underneath, eating it right out underneath me. I was glad Katie hadn't wanted to get in the water—it felt like it would take her little body directly out to sea with its power. Pipe must have been some kind of swimmer to feel confident enough to take her board out there.

Katie shrieked from the safety of her spot ten feet up the beach as the waves came back in, lapping at my calves. The cool water did feel great after baking in the sun all afternoon. And it was beautifully clear as this section of the coast was untrampled by tourists or other pollutants. I leaned down and cupped a few handfuls, pouring them over my face and body. I glanced back at Katie. Her back was to me, her attention fixed on the east side of the beach where the path lay. I looked that way and saw Pipe heading down to us, backpack slung over her shoulder.

I was suddenly keenly aware I was wearing nothing but a red bikini, a baseball hat and shades. Oh, well. I tucked a wayward strand of hair behind my ear and walked up to meet her. Katie had already run up. They split the distance at my beach chair. Pipe sat on the towel and Katie dropped down in the sand next to her. They watched as I slogged up to join them. I fervently hoped nothing was sticking out where it shouldn't.

As nonchalantly as I could manage, I sank down into the beach chair, saying "How's it going?" I passed out drinks from the cooler to all of us. Juice box, water, water.

Inscrutable in her mirrored shades, Pipe was saying, "I'm just on the way to get my twenty-four-hour samples. From the tide pools." She eyed both me and Katie, gauging our reactions.

Katie jumped to her knees. "Can I come?"

They both looked at me. "Can I?" Katie pleaded eagerly to me.

Me? Oh, yeah, I was supposedly in charge here.

I looked back at them. Pipe gave me a subliminal nod, like it was okay for Katie to visit the place where her father had died. I had to admit, I was curious to see it myself. Whether that was morbid or just closure, I don't know.

"Is it safe?" I asked Pipe. She nodded again. Did I trust her? I don't know why, but I found that I did.

"We'll all go then," I said.

Katie and I donned our sandals and followed Pipe as she led the way to the cliffs. It looked to me like there was nowhere to go.

"The path's right over here," Pipe said.

Sure enough, there was a narrow path along the foot of the cliff. Fortunately, the tide was out. It looked like the path would be underwater once it came back in. Katie followed Pipe and

I followed Katie as we traipsed around the corner of the cliff. With the tide out, a whole area of small tide pools was exposed in a small inlet, invisible from the beach. Looking up, I could see scrub brush lining the top of the sheer cliff rising up from the back of the little cove. The sandstone was slippery footing and I was glad Katie had her sandals on. Pipe led the way to the largest pool, right in the middle. She knelt down beside it and pulled some stuff out of her backpack. Katie crouched down beside her, her little butt in its frilly skirt almost—but not quite—touching the ground. I envied her flexibility. I was still picking my way toward them in my flip-flops, careful not to step on some washed up kelp or any other flora or fauna. Katie seemed completely unperturbed to be down here, but it did not escape my notice that James had died here just a few days ago. At least, I guessed it was here. Belatedly, I wondered whether Katie and I shared the same allergy that led to James's death. What the hell was I thinking, letting Pipe bring us back here?

As I reached the two of them, Pipe was gathering a sample of the water from the tide pool into a test tube. She stoppered it and put it carefully into a side pocket of her pack. Katie was pointing at something in the pool. I walked to her side. Katie stood up, putting a hand on Pipe's shoulder to steady herself.

"Look, Madison," she said to me. My heart leapt into my throat—did she just call me by name for the very first time?

We were apparently skipping the aunt appellation, but that was okay with me. "Aunt Madison" sounded like some old broad about a hundred years old anyway.

I followed her pointing finger and saw a cluster of three beautiful golden brown starfish attached to the side of the tide pool. They looked so perfect they almost seemed fake, like some guy from the aquarium store had just stopped by and stuck them in there.

"Wow," I said to Katie. "Those are cool." Clearly, she'd been here before. "What else is in there?"

"Fishes." Sure enough, there were a few minnows darting in

the corner of the pool. And something else...

"What IS that?" I asked Pipe. A long spindly whitish stick thing was moving around from under a rock.

"Crab," she answered shortly, absorbed in getting another water sample. As I watched, the white stick thing moved some more and I realized it was the leg of the crab. Had to be a good eight inches long. The whole crab slowly came into view, looking like some nightmarish water spider. Yuck. Hideous. I hoped we weren't having crab for dinner after seeing that thing.

Putting that test tube away, Pipe returned her attention to the two of us, both watching the crab.

"Want to know the Latin name?"

"No," Katie said as I simultaneously said, "Not really." We all three laughed.

Katie let go of Pipe's shoulder and bopped over to the adjacent pool, peering into its depths from a safe distance.

Pipe stood and hiked her bag over her shoulder. "We better get going. You don't want to be caught back in here when the tide starts coming in."

She didn't have to tell me twice, as I'd been thinking the same thing. We headed back toward the beach, but Katie was lagging behind.

"Katie!" I called. "Katie!"

Something was wrong. The whole scene seemed to shift, like a movie skipping a frame. Katie suddenly looked far away, not just a few yards.

"Madison!" She was calling now too. Yelling. "MADISON!"

Chapter 11

"Madison!" I awoke with a start. Damn, I must have drifted off just for a second. Katie was right next to me, though, her hand on my shoulder, ready to yell in my ear again as needed. I twisted around to put my hands on her waist.

"What?! Are you okay?"

"You fell asleep," she said reproachfully.

Uh…busted.

"You're not 'posed to sleep at the beach," she continued. Serious, now, lecturing me.

"I'm sorry, baby, you're right. It won't happen again. And it was only for a second, right? And you're okay, right?"

"I'm okay," she agreed. She gave my shoulder a little pat, like the general letting the new recruit know his screwup had not gone unnoticed, but would nevertheless be excused this one time. I let go of her.

"Come on," I said, "let's go down to the water."

Just like my dream, the water was cool and the current was strong. And just like my dream, Katie wanted none of it, preferring to continue her sand castle building just out of reach of the tide. I found myself visually checking on her every thirty seconds or so, overly vigilant now in my guilt and not a little dismayed by my lapse.

Way to go, Madison, falling asleep on the job in your first six hours, I chided myself. Although the logical and detached part of me noted I'd had very little sleep in the last couple of days and was exhausted, as anyone would be. God, how did people do this solo parenting thing? I glanced at Katie, who was busily digging. I knelt down to splash some water on my face, then looked back at Katie's sand castle spot. She was gone.

Shit! I scanned the beach for a single heartstopping second, then calmed down when I realized she was back up at the chair. Whew! Katie was waving, but not at me. I followed her gaze and saw Pipe emerging from the path. Too weird—just like my dream. I splashed some more water on myself to make sure I was really awake and went to join them.

By the time I reached them, Katie had plunked herself down in the chair and was giving me a big grin because she'd "stolen" my seat. Pipe was gracefully seated Indian-style in the sand, a plastic tackle box beside her.

Feeling rather underdressed, I took the opportunity to pull on my cutoffs, catching a glance from Dr. Piper that I couldn't quite decipher. Approval, perhaps, that my pearly white Boston ass was finally covered. I sat down on the towel and asked her what was up.

Gesturing toward her box, she explained that her research project involved taking daily samples of water to test certain bacteria levels over the course of a twelve-month period. She and James had worked independently of each other, each focused on a different project. She went on to say that her year was almost up.

"So, you're done here?" I asked, obscurely disappointed.

"Just about. I've got all my findings on a CD up at the lab that I'm due to turn in to Delgado next week," she replied in that easy Texas drawl. "I'm really just gathering these samples out of habit, more than anything else."

"So, you just wade into the surf and fill up a test tube?" I asked.

She gave me a small smile for my ignorance, but addressed her next remark to Katie.

"Hey, Katie Lou, you see that big pile of kelp down the beach?"

It was all the way down to the southern cliff face. Katie peered down there, then nodded to Pipe, who said, "Bet you can't run down there and back in less than two minutes." She tapped the diver's watch on her left wrist, adding "I'll time you, okay?"

Katie leapt from her chair and ran off toward the pile of kelp. I'd have to learn that trick.

Pipe turned back to me, having bought us at least two minutes of adults only time.

"I get the water samples from the tide pools, Madison," she said.

Oh.

"Are they far?" I asked.

"Right behind the cliff," she responded, gesturing to the north, the opposite direction of Katie's kelp. The kid had almost reached the pile.

Pipe continued, "There's a path along the cliff face when the tide is out, so this is the best time of the afternoon for me to go in there."

Weird. Just like my dream.

Katie was headed back toward us, laboring in the deep sand.

I asked Pipe, "So, is that where it happened?" I was trying really hard to keep my tone matter-of-fact—not sure I pulled it off.

She nodded, "Yeah. It really was a one in a million kind of thing. I mean, sure, some of these creatures can sting or bite you.

Or pinch."

I thought of that nasty ass crab. Oh wait—that was a dream crab…

"But," she went on, "even though the sting would hurt, the chances that you'd be allergic to it are slim. And the chances that it would kill you are, well, one in a million. It was just a hell of a thing. I still can't believe it."

"Me neither, to tell you the truth," I said.

"Has Katie said anything about him?" Pipe asked me.

Katie had slowed to a walk now, maybe thirty feet away from us. The white noise of the surf and the wind completely masked our quiet conversation.

"Not yet. I think she needs some time to get used to me first. I'm not sure how much she really understands. But we'll talk about it later today, for sure, at least a little bit."

She nodded sympathetically. "It's got to be tough for you. I don't envy you that conversation. She likes you, though—I can tell."

I gave her a grateful look. And hoped it was true.

Katie collapsed back into the chair like she'd run a marathon. And looked at Pipe, who announced her time was one minute and forty-seven seconds. Without checking her watch.

"Excellent time under these conditions, wouldn't you say?" she asked, cocking an eyebrow at me which made it very difficult to keep a straight face.

"Oh, absolutely," I agreed. Katie smirked triumphantly.

I then ruined the moment by suggesting we get ready to leave the beach. Yikes! That innocent proposal triggered serious opposition from the five-year-old. She was loath to leave, but the possibility of ice cream after dinner finally motivated her compliance. We compromised on ten more minutes at the beach to finish her sand castle, then we would leave. God, this negotiation stuff was exhausting! She was worse than an attorney.

Which somehow made me think to ask Pipe if she knew the names of any of James's church friends, as we watched Katie furiously dig and shape.

"No, I've never known James to have any visitors down here at all. And we really weren't, uh, friends, you know."

Something in her tone clued me in.

I gave her a smile. "It's okay if you didn't like him. I hadn't spoken to him myself in several years. We didn't get along either."

"Well, I wouldn't say I didn't like him," she answered, obviously reluctant to speak ill of the dead. At least to his sister's face. She propped her sunglasses up on her forehead before she answered me.

"I guess I thought we'd get along better since we were both marine biologists, but he just never seemed to take to me. He certainly didn't approve of *my* visitors. I think he thought I was a terrible sinner. Probably right about that too." She flashed me a wicked grin, one that made my stomach give a little jump.

"So what visitors did you have down here? Your family? Boyfriend?"

She laughed as though I'd said something funny, then shot me a quick sideways look. "Heck, no, my family's all back in Texas."

No comment regarding "boyfriend," I noticed. No rings on any of her fingers either.

"Dallas?" I guessed, trying to place the twang.

"Austin, actually."

A sudden and dire thought struck me.

"You're not a Cowboys fan, are you?" I asked with ill-concealed dread.

"I don't really follow football," she said, looking at me half-quizzically, half-laughing. My obvious sigh of relief was also amusing to her. Her eyes sparkled when she laughed. I didn't even care that she was laughing at me.

Luckily, before I could embarrass myself any further, Katie called out that she was done and we were to inspect the finished project immediately. We obeyed and pronounced the edifice to be a true work of art. We admired it for a few more moments, then I enlisted Katie's help in gathering up our things. Pipe bid us adieu then, saying she'd see us at six for dinner, adding she still had some work to do. Katie nodded, unconcerned and took my hand. It had amazed me all day how perfectly willing she was to be alone with me. But I guess children are supposed to be all trusting and innocent, right? That part of my past seemed a thousand years ago. Too many broken promises and disappointments ago.

I watched Pipe's back view head toward the tide pools. Not a bad view at all.

"Madison?"

I turned my gaze back to Katie, still holding my hand. We were standing on the beach towel, having tossed all the food-related items into the cooler.

"Yep?"

"Is my daddy in heaven?"

Good Lord, here we went.

"Yes, he is, Katie. Do you know what that means?"

She considered me for a moment. "What?"

"Well…your daddy's in heaven now, with God and all the angels. And your mom."

She was squinting at me. I forged ahead.

"So, it's okay for us to be sad for a while and miss him. But you'll always love him and he'll always be watching over you from above."

I thought that last part might be laying it on a bit too thick, but she didn't flinch. She looked up at me, then down at the sand.

She said something in a low voice I couldn't hear. I got down on my knees in front of her and touched her arm.

"What?"

"So he's not coming back? Not ever?"

"No, baby, he's not. I'm sorry."

More sand gazing. Finally, she looked back at me. She looked sad, but didn't say anything. Seeing those big puppy dog eyes, I couldn't help myself, I had to pull her into a hug. She wrapped her little arms tightly around my neck for a few seconds. I teared up, but told myself severely that I was the grownup and I should be strong for Katie. Nonetheless, I had to wipe my nose and eyes on the corner of the beach towel when she unclenched a few moments later. Classy, but who takes a box of Kleenex to the beach? Katie sat back down in the chair and accepted a dollop of sunscreen from me without comment, smearing it on her arms and legs. She seemed to be mulling something over. I gave her one more half dollop, which she applied to her face.

Wow! Could I be up for Mother of the Year on my first afternoon already?

Probably not.

I thought I should probably say something warm and sensitive at this juncture, but I couldn't think of anything, so I tried staring out to sea for a while. She had wrapped herself up like a sausage in the beach towel I'd draped over the chair. She finally broke the silence with another "Madison?"

"Yep?"

"Is there enough room at your house for Babs too?"

I couldn't help it—I burst out laughing. She laughed too, then, a charming sound to my admittedly biased and sunburned ears. I grabbed her off the chair, towel and all and swung her around in a circle, exclaiming in an astonished tone, "An elephant?! You want to move an ELEPHANT into my apartment?!" She knew I was only kidding. Her delighted giggles and shrieks mingled with the sounds of the surf and the wind.

Chapter 12

We got back to the cabin a little before five. Based on how long it had taken us (well, her) to get ready for the beach, I wanted a full hour to prepare for our dinner with Pipe.

Before we got inside, however, she had to arrange the new additions to her seashell collection on the porch railings. She paused when she saw the wind chimes lying there, but didn't comment. Maybe they'd been driving her batty too. Having regrouped her treasures to her satisfaction, she was then ready to go inside.

I was dying to take a shower after spending the afternoon at the beach, but I couldn't figure out how to do that without leaving Katie unobserved. I guess I could have made her sit on the closed lid of the toilet while I showered, but that seemed kind of creepy. How did people do these things?

Maybe I could foist her off on Pipe at six for a few minutes while I grabbed a shower. Which didn't seem like a good idea for our first date, so to speak.

All right, I knew it wasn't really a date. But I can dream, right?

In any event, I did think Katie needed a bath in a bad way, after rolling around on the beach all afternoon. Thanks to her liberal coatings of sunscreen, she was looking a little gritty around the edges, like cookie dough rolled in granulated sugar. Just looking at her made me itchy, so I thought she'd welcome the idea of a bath.

Wrong. So wrong. Man, that kid did NOT want a bath! But even in the midst of my insufferable, Dr. Spock-less ignorance, I was fairly certain children required water and soap at least at semi-regular intervals. And I wanted her to look good for dinner. Well, okay, I wanted me to look good in Pipe's eyes. Which required both of us McPeakes to be clean, sweet-smelling and properly attired.

Properly attired for Katie turned out to be overalls, the yellow sandals and the same pink T-shirt she'd been wearing earlier. This after three other outfits were tried on and discarded. What a diva. But whatever, she was clothed and bathed.

Yes, bathed as well. A mere thirty-five minutes of coercion, arguing and intimidation finally resulted in a bath being drawn and her deigning to get in it. I stuck to my guns, so it was both a moral and an actual victory, but she was wearing me out. And this was only the first day. Fucking A. I hoped Claudette had the patience of a saint to go along with the smokin' bod.

I wasn't sure if she was old enough to be trusted to take a bath alone, but I didn't think so, so I hung out and supervised while she splashed most of the contents of the tub on me and the floor. Refreshing, really. Almost solved my need for a shower, but I still felt a pathological need to wash my hair in a more conventional manner. Once she was in the tub, she entered into the spirit of things and didn't give me any more grief. Talk about your mood swings. By this time, I was dying for both a drink and a cigarette, but there was neither time nor opportunity. By the time we got Miss Katie hosed down and redressed in her fourth and final ensemble, it was 6:05 and we were late for Pipe's.

I left her in the bathroom for a sec, slowly combing her wet hair with a look of great concentration. I hadn't noticed a little green stool underneath the sink before, but she pulled it out and stepped on it so she could see herself in the mirror. (Note to self: buy little green stool in Boston.)

There was no point in changing out of my now drenched swimsuit and cutoffs, since I was hoping Pipe could watch the Kate-ster for a few minutes while I jumped in the shower. I threw on the black polo shirt I'd been wearing earlier and reinserted my feet in my flip-flops. It was still plenty warm out, so I wasn't concerned about either of us having wet hair. Maybe I'd have time to blow-dry mine...

Pipe had said I shouldn't bring anything, but that just didn't seem right. Although, come to think of it, I didn't have much to offer. I went out to the kitchen. Half a bottle of wine? Yeah, right, why not just take the jar of pickle juice? The full bottle of bourbon? That might not send the right message. Probably shouldn't be drinking at this meal anyhow. Probably should just stop drinking altogether. Right. Where had I heard that before?

Damn it. All right, what did I have? Dessert? One freaking box of animal crackers. Flowers? Again, probably not the right message and all I had was one ailing cactus anyhow. All right, fuck it. Nothing.

I stepped into the living room. "Katie? You ready, kiddo?"

She was still on the stool, leaning over the sink to get a better look in the mirror while she grappled with a blue scrunchie behind her head. I helped her make a pigtail and get that through the scrunchie. She looked a hell of a lot cuter than I did. Oh, well.

She again grabbed my hand to pull me the short walk across the gravel to Pipe's. Our hostess was in her yard, presiding over a smoking barbeque grill. She put the top back on it as we walked up. A battered wooden picnic table stood nearby.

"Good evening, ladies," she said. "You're just in time to help set the table, Katie Pie."

Amazingly, Katie skipped right on over to the picnic table and started sorting out paper plates and napkins from a bag Pipe had put on the bench. Was this how it was going to be? She'd give me total grief over a freaking bath, then be a perfect angel for non family members? Probably.

I watched as Pipe hung the barbeque tongs on the side of her grill. I liked her hands. I thought about how they'd feel on me, then silently told myself to (a) shut up and (b) get a grip. Again. I then worked it out with Pipe that she would watch Katie for the next ten minutes while I jumped in the shower. Thank God.

I returned to the soiree much revived and a little more fashionably dressed in a pair of close-fitting white jeans, white leather sandals and a lavender tank top. Just for your information, my ass looked awesome in those jeans.

I had hesitated for a moment over the dual questions of drying my hair and putting makeup on. I bagged the blow-drying as it would take too long—pulled my hair back into a ponytail, tied it with a ribbon and told myself it would do. Same deal for the makeup. She'd already seen me without, so no big deal, right? Plus, I didn't want to be the overdressed "Easterner" for the casual SoCal barbeque. I usually wore makeup at work, but not so much anywhere else unless it was a formal occasion. Hadn't really made a difference in my social standing or overall success level as far as I could tell. I'd only brought some on this trip because of the funeral. Would there even be a funeral now? I shrugged the thought away for the moment, stuck my tongue out at my reflection in the bathroom mirror, decided this was as good as it was going to get (looks-wise) and headed across the way.

The party was in full swing. Pipe was back at the grill, overseeing burgers and one all-beef hot dog for you know who. Katie was standing on one of the benches next to the picnic table, carefully pouring chips from the bag into a bowl. Sheryl Crow was coming from a boom box perched on the porch railing. I hadn't noticed before that Pipe had strung little white lights over and around her porch railing. Maybe she'd turn those on once it got dark. Might make the crappy little cabin look almost festive. I wondered what it looked like inside…

Katie jumped down and ran over to Pipe as I walked up.

"Chips are done," she pronounced, handing me the empty chip bag. Why? What did I want with an empty chip bag? I looked around for the trash.

"Okay, what else do we need?" Pipe replied, noting my return and my predicament with a grin, pointing out a trashcan at the corner of the house with her barbeque tongs.

"Uh…" Katie clearly had no idea.

"Starts with a C," Pipe hinted, sounding out "Kuh…" to get her started.

"Cake?" Katie guessed hopefully.

Pipe shook her head no.

"Cookies?" I said, joining in the game.

"Yeah, cookies!" Katie did a little jig of excitement.

Pipe laughed. "No one would ever guess you two are related! We haven't even had dinner yet and you're already thinking about dessert. But, actually, I was thinking of cups. They're on the kitchen counter if you want to get them, Katie."

The kid immediately shot off toward the door. All that energy and she hadn't even had a nap that day. Oops! Forgot to give her a nap. I was going to have to start writing this stuff down. I was feeling a little like a nap myself, but then I was old and feeble.

"I'll help," I said belatedly, curious to get a peek in her cabin. I deposited the chip bag in the garbage can, then followed Katie inside. Pipe's cabin, of course, looked an awful lot like James's, although this one was even smaller with apparently just one bedroom. The front door opened right into the living room, just like James's, though and there was the same small kitchen off the living room.

Her surfboard and wetsuit were both on the porch, which was good as there was precious little space in the miniscule living room for them. No TV, of course, since there was no signal and no cable down here. A small, square wooden table was in one corner, supporting a laptop and papers. The printer sat underneath, on a milk crate. There was a bookcase filled with books and CDs. A huge surfing poster covered most of the wall behind it, some guy on a forty-foot wave in Tahiti. There was nothing else on the walls. No plants, unless you counted the baggie of pot I spotted on the top shelf of the bookcase, next to some rolling papers, a lighter and a Pez dispenser with Sylvester's head. A comfortable-looking dark brown velvet loveseat took up most of the rest of the small room. A chenille throw was tossed over the back of the faded loveseat. An equally faded Oriental rug covered the floor in front of it.

Pipe's bedroom was just down the brief hallway. Two steps away from me. Katie was futzing around in the kitchen, getting plastic cups out of the bag. I checked out the window—Pipe was doing something at the picnic table, her back to us. Curiosity got the better of me. I ducked down the hall for a quick peek at the bedroom. A full-size futon looked hastily made, but I could see cream-colored flannel sheets in a tasteful pine tree and moose design. Flannel sheets in June? Hey, why not. A lightweight dark green cotton blanket was pushed all the way to the foot. Nothing on the walls in here. Some clothes had been tossed on a dilapidated wicker chair, with a few more on the floor nearby as if she'd aimed but missed. No dresser, but maybe that was in the closet with the rest of her clothes. A bag of golf clubs reposed in the corner. A milk crate sat beside the head of the futon, with one of those alarm clock/CD player combos on top.

I rejoined Katie in the kitchen, who, for some reason, was lining up all the plastic cups from the package along the countertop.

"Whoa, there!" I said. "How many more people are you expecting?"

We decided three cups would be sufficient and I helped her put ice in all three. In the fridge, we found a pitcher of iced tea and a quart of pink lemonade. Some cans of Coke too, which gladdened my heart. I couldn't help but also notice some wine coolers and a couple of bottles of Stella Artois, but told myself to be cool and just drink tea. It's important to pretend to be normal when meeting someone for the first time.

I sent Katie back outside to see if Pipe wanted tea or lemonade. Which gave me a chance to check out the kitchen. It was so small, I could basically take it in at a glance. The only items of interest were several photographs on the refrigerator door. One was clearly a posed family studio portrait with a fake autumny background behind them. Mom, Dad, four boys and a girl. Looked like a recent shot. So, Pipe was the baby with four older brothers. Big, good-looking guys, all of them. They looked like lumberjacks or farmers or something—something rugged and active that would provide them with lots of stories for family get-togethers about trips to the ER when Billy Joe cut his toe off with the axe, or how Bubba broke three ribs when he crashed the tractor. Pipe favored her mother, a slender, serene-looking woman standing with her husband behind their seated brood.

The other photos were of Pipe. Pipe skiing. Pipe in Europe somewhere with a Blonde woman (hmmm, now who was that?), arms thrown around each other, mugging for the camera. Pipe and a seriously hot brunette on a beach somewhere, both in bikinis. I studied that one closely.

Katie banged the door open and ran back in, Pipe following just behind. I busied myself with the drinks, pouring some lemonade in Katie's cup.

"Tea."

I cocked an eyebrow and looked a question at Katie's rather terse declamatory statement, hoping to generate a "please."

She looked right back, finally deciding additional explanation was needed for the dullard aunt.

"Pipe wants tea," she stated, slowly spacing each word.

I noticed the tea drinker was attempting to discreetly move her pot, etc. into the bedroom.

Catching her eye, I said, "You can leave the Pez."

She smiled sheepishly and went on into the bedroom,

returning a moment later to collect her glass of iced tea. We all went outside to eat a dinner that turned out to be remarkably good. There's just something about eating outside on a beautiful summer evening. And not having to cook anything yourself. I nibbled on a perfect slice of watermelon and idly wondered why Pipe's fruit hadn't rotted, like mine. Probably because she put hers in the fridge, the voice in my head said. Duh.

As we talked during dinner, I occasionally glanced over at James's cabin. I'd forgotten to leave any lights on, not that it mattered. The third cabin was, of course, dark as well. It looked just the same as James's cabin, but the thought of that black rocking chair alone in the blacked out room made it seem creepier by far to me. But still, I wondered why Pipe had chosen the smallest of the three cabins instead of the other two-bedroom model. Had there been a third marine biologist living down there?

"No," she said when I asked her. "James and Katie were down here first."

She paused. We both looked at Katie, but she was happily struggling with a large slice of watermelon and making a glorious mess in the process. She spat a seed onto the ground with obvious delight and gave us a big grin before diving back in. We both chuckled at the sight. Suppressing an urge to wipe Katie's sticky little face, I decided to wait until she finished. And seeing that the kid wasn't bothered by the reference to her father, Pipe went on.

"The Navy signs us up to twelve-month contracts. He was on his second and I'm almost done with my first, like I told you. So, when I moved in last June, they were already here. They were originally living in the third cabin there, but they'd moved into the other one before I got here. Delgado told me I had my pick of either one, but it turned out James had been storing some stuff in his old cabin and, well, let's just say he wasn't too happy about the idea of having to move it the one time the subject was broached. And since it was just me and I don't have that much stuff, it was just easier all around for me to take the small cabin. No big deal. I didn't really care—and when you live out here on the back end of nowhere, it's a good idea to try to get along with your neighbors, you know what I mean?"

I nodded. I told her I'd taken a peek in there on Friday night and there was nothing in there now except some trash and an old rocking chair. She shrugged and said, "I guess he must have moved his stuff out then."

"Why do you think they moved from one cabin to the other?" I asked her. I loathed moving. I couldn't imagine what had motivated James to pack up all his shit and move fifty feet west to an identical abode.

"I don't know," she said. "I wondered about that myself, but James had his own way of doing things."

I'll say. She flashed me a smile and said she'd go get the ice cream if I wanted to run Katie under the garden hose for awhile. She was joking, but not by much. As she went inside, I did wet some napkins with water from the hose and tried to clean up the watermelon aftermath as best I could. The girl had seeds in her hair! She giggled and squirmed under my ministrations and I finally gave it up. And I had just given her a bath before dinner. Criminy.

I took advantage of our moment alone, however, to ask Katie if she knew why they had moved from one cabin to the other.

She said, "It wasn't the right one."

Since they appeared identical to me, I wasn't sure what that meant, but Katie couldn't explain it any better to me. She just kept saying "Because it wasn't the right one" like We Hold These Truths To Be Self Evident. I then asked her if she'd been back in the empty cabin, but she told me her daddy wouldn't let her.

"Not ever, since you moved?" I said.

"Not ever."

Further discussion was shelved due to the arrival of the Neapolitan ice cream, which we all enjoyed, although I noticed Katie gravitated toward the chocolate, Pipe toward the strawberry and I scarfed down all three flavors without prejudice.

After dessert, Pipe was telling me that Shadow Point was named for the gloom cast by its many trees and cliffs.

"That's really just a name cooked up by the real estate developers, though. It used to be called Bly Point."

"Bly? Like...Conrad Bly Freight?"

"Yeah," she responded. "You noticed the trucks, huh?" She had turned on the little white lights as the sun went down and they twinkled now fairy-like as the moon rose above us. Katie had lasted just long enough to collect on the ice cream, then crashed in the canvas butterfly chair on the porch. Pipe's eyes gleamed across the table at me as the darkness gathered. I felt like I could listen to her for hours.

"Conrad Bly," Pipe went on, "lived out here for years with his family and his workers, tending the old lighthouse back in the twenties and thirties. And, some say, doing much more besides that."

"Like what?"

"Smuggling, maybe. Bootlegging, probably. That was big business back in Prohibition days. There's a little cove at the tip of the Point where they used to anchor their boats. Anyway, legend has it that back in those days, anything you needed—legal or illegal—Conrad Bly could get it for you. For a price. Some say he and his gang are still running around out here, haunting the Point."

I could tell she loved the story. Rumrunners and pirates and ghosts. I wasn't that into it, but I sure liked hearing her talk. That Texas drawl and those eyes were mesmerizing.

"So is there a map with an X and a buried treasure in this tale?" I asked her.

"Nope," she said. "Conrad poured every penny right back into his various business concerns, which flourished. To this day, Bly family descendants own lots of property on the Point, plus the freight company, of course and the general store. One of Conrad's far-flung nephews is the assistant manager there right now, as a matter of fact."

A vision of the oily Craig B. in his red vest rose before me. That old buccaneering blood must have thinned considerably, I thought. I told Pipe that Delgado had mentioned something about a curse and the old lighthouse.

"Oh…yeah." Her enthusiasm dimmed suddenly. I wasn't sure why.

"If you're really interested in that stuff," she went on, a little reluctantly, "you should talk to Mr. Bohannon."

"Who is?" I prompted.

"He's this old guy, head of the local historical committee. They've been trying to turn the old lighthouse into a museum. He's always poking around down there."

Since I was probably headed back to Boston in a couple of days, the likelihood of me seeking out the historical committee chairman seemed low. If anyone, actually, I was hoping to spend more time with Pipe before Katie and I had to leave. Maybe we could hang out a few extra days…and nights…

That reminded me. "Say, Pipe, did you hear anything weird last night?"

Even in the semi-darkness, I caught a glimpse of the dimples and the white flash of her teeth. "Like what?" she said teasingly.

"Well…I know it sounds crazy, but I thought I heard someone moving around outside the cabin last night. Voices."

It did sound crazy, now that I'd said it aloud. But I had been afraid at the time. With all the events of the day, I hadn't had a lot of time to dwell on it but I knew I wasn't looking forward to spending another night out here.

Pipe said, "What did they say?" She was still smiling, indulging me.

"Oh. I don't know." I shrugged, trying to act like it was just a joke since she obviously hadn't heard anything. "Maybe it was just a possum or something in the bushes."

"Or Conrad Bly," Pipe supplied. We both laughed then.

"Do you want to see a picture of him?" she asked. "I've got a book in the cabin about the history of the Point."

I readily agreed and we got up to go inside. At the foot of the steps, though, Pipe stopped and put a hand on my arm, then a finger to her lips, motioning toward the butterfly chair. Katie was out like a light, all curled up in the chair.

"I guess it's past her bedtime," I said quietly, close to Pipe's ear. A nearly perfect ear, I noticed. Good—nothing worse than funky ears. Maybe it's just me, but the sexiest woman in the world gets downgraded from a ten to a one instantly if she's got weird ears. Her fingers were warm on my forearm. My heart was thumping in my chest.

Pipe turned toward me. Our faces were about three inches apart. She seemed to study me for a moment, then spoke in a low tone. "I can help you put her to bed, if you want."

I nodded dumbly, went to the chair and picked Katie up. She didn't wake as I carried her back to our cabin. Pipe went ahead to open the screen and front doors. She preceded us into the house, turning on the living room light as she entered. She led the way back to Katie's bedroom where she turned on the lamp and turned down the bedspread. I laid the little girl down. Pipe got one sandal off and I got the other, both of us kneeling down by the bedside. The overalls were a bitch, but I wrestled them off finally. Katie never stirred.

"Kid's a sound sleeper," Pipe whispered, her breath warm on my ear which caused a flip-flop in my stomach.

We stood, surveying our handiwork. I didn't want to hassle with pajamas and figured she was fine in her little T-shirt and panties anyhow. It was too hot to tuck her in, so I left her on top of the sheets, her head on the pillow. I turned off the lamp and we retreated to the doorway. I turned back to take one more look at Katie. Pipe stood close beside me in the doorway. Very close.

"Looks like an angel, doesn't she?"

That hot breath in my ear again. That tingle of excitement running up my spine. I turned my head slowly and met her eyes. She didn't move. I put my hand lightly on her forearm. We both took a breath, her gaze still locked on mine. I leaned in. If I was wrong—again—this was going to be really bad…

But her lips found mine as if they had been looking for a long time. And the search was finally over.

We stepped out of the doorway. She pressed me up against the side of the hallway. Her hands moved down to my butt, pulling me even closer. Her mouth was hot on mine, tongue seeking. Marshalling my forces, I pushed her back against the opposing wall, my hands underneath her T-shirt now, running up her spine. She kissed me there in the dark hallway until I thought I might melt, then walked me backward the few steps into the living room until my rear hit the back of the couch. We went over it backward, her body entangled with mine. I heard her give a little moan as my fingers went down the back of her shorts to find the crack in her ass. Her lips were soft and urgent, then momentarily withdrawn as she moved down to kiss the side of my neck, then to lick the hollow at the base of my throat. Oh, God. It felt so right. And it had been so long.

"Pipe…wait…" I gasped in a whisper. It felt like every nerve ending I had was on fire, but I had to stop this before it went any further. If I could.

She sighed and sat up, running her hands through her hair and tucking it behind her ears. She gave me a smile as I sat up too. Opposite ends of the couch.

"Bad timing, huh?" she said. We spoke in hushed tones to avoid waking up Katie.

"I'm sorry. I just can't do this right now—with the kid, in his house? Do you understand?"

"Yeah," she said. Awkward silence. She gave me another, smaller smile and said, "Well, I guess I should be going."

We stood. I walked her the five feet to the front door. We stepped out on the porch. The illumination from her fairy lights was nearly swallowed by the darkness.

"Good night, Madison," Pipe said calmly.

I grabbed her arm again. "Wait…" I couldn't quite let her go. Not like that.

She paused, clearly waiting for me to make the move. My hand found hers. Her fingertips slid slowly over mine, traced a line down the center of my palm. The night was warm, but the heat between us had nothing to do with the weather. Putting my hands on her hips, I steadied her against the cabin wall. I couldn't have told you afterward how long we stood there and kissed. Kissing her was new, familiar, strange, fast, slow, delicious, thrilling...and tasted like strawberry ice cream. Like no other first kisses I'd ever had. I couldn't believe I'd just met this woman less than twelve hours ago.

When we finally pulled apart, she gave another of her little sighs, but this one sounded like a satisfied exhalation to me. She gave a little tug to a strand of my hair, running her fingers down the length of it. Fingers which continued ever so gently down my tank top to just barely graze the side of my breast.

"I'll see you tomorrow," she told me.

"Oh, yeah," I replied with certainty, taking a deep and much-needed breath. Her smile was luminous in the moonlight. A multitude of stars shone high above the dell in the deep velvet sky.

She headed home. I watched her door close behind her, then heard the music start up. Dwight Yoakam. Smiling and shaking my head, I closed my own door and locked it. I felt so good I didn't even want a cigarette. I went in the kitchen and looked at the bottle of bourbon. A long moment passed, but I finally got a bottle of cold water out of the fridge and went to check on Katie. Still asleep. I turned the light on in James's bedroom, but it still felt prickly and unwelcoming in there. I returned to the living room to settle down with Dick Francis for the evening. The memory of Pipe's kisses was a recurring glow amongst my worries for the future and my grief for the past, like a winking ember in the cold dead ashes.

Chapter 13

I woke up on the couch again in the dead of the night. The darkness was almost absolute in the living room, but a thin glow of ambient light illuminated the front window perimeters. And the smell was back—the foul odor I'd experienced the day before hung on the air like a pall of smoke.

I had read until twelve thirty, then called it a night, turning out all the lights and drawing the living room curtains. I had no idea what time it was now, but it was dead quiet. Unsettling to my city-fied nervous system, but better than ghostly voices. I regretted kicking Pipe out for more than one reason. It would have been nice to have another adult there in that strange and unfamiliar place. But I knew that had been the right decision. Sigh.

Since I was now wide awake, I decided to go check on Katie. And pee. And get a drink of water. I thought about smoking a cigarette on the porch…but I really didn't feel that comfortable with hanging out on the porch in the pitch black with the rabid possum or the ghost of Conrad Bly or whatever. And I'd promised myself I wouldn't smoke in the cabin anymore. Man, this place was better than the patch.

Shrugging off the throw, I stood up from the couch and turned toward the hallway. My heart nearly leaped out of my chest when I saw a pale figure standing there, looking at me. Then I caught myself, realizing it was Katie.

"Holy sh…moke, Katie, you scared the—"

Her unnatural stillness stopped the words in my throat. I realized she wasn't looking at me, she was staring at the front door with an absorption so complete she wasn't even listening to me. I crossed the few feet of floor between us and dropped to my knees at her feet.

"Katie? Sweetie? What's wrong?" I grabbed her hands. They were ice cold. I wondered if she were sleepwalking, or if this was some kind of delayed reaction to her father's death.

"Katie? Can you hear me?"

She turned her head slowly, finally meeting my gaze as if she were returning from many miles away.

"He says it's time," she said. Her lack of affect was chilling.

My heart was hammering in my chest.

"Who says?" I asked.

"The man," she said, pulling her hands out of my grasp and taking a step backward.

She took another step backward into the dimness of the hallway. Her face was a pallid blob.

"Who?" I persisted, my voice a little higher and louder than I wanted it to be.

"The man on the porch."

If I didn't drop dead at that very second, maybe I never will. I whirled to stare at the windows, but saw only the drawn blinds and locked door. I ran to the door to confirm it was locked and it was. Steeling myself, I pulled back the curtain to check out the porch, but there was nobody out there.

Get a grip, Madison, I told myself. You're way overreacting to a five-year-old's dream. Still, I was getting a little tired of these middle-of-the-night panic attacks.

When I turned around, Katie was gone. The bathroom door was closed and I could see a strip of light under the door. The toilet flushed. I heard her dragging the little step stool in place so she could wash her hands. She emerged a moment later, calmly regarding me in the light from the bathroom, then went into her room. I followed, turning on the lamp beside her bed. I checked my watch—almost four a.m.

I busied myself with putting Katie back to bed. She was drowsy and unresponsive to my tentative inquiries. Like I really knew what to ask her. Did you have a bad dream, dear? Or is one of us losing her mind?

At any rate, she went back to sleep. I went through the cabin one more time, making sure all the windows were latched and the door still locked. I sat on the floor by her bed, listening to her even breathing, the lights on, the butcher knife in my hand.

It wasn't the foul smell that kept me up.

It was the fact that I could hear the wind chimes clanging again out on the porch.

Katie woke up about six thirty. Dawn had come right on schedule and full sunlight was now cheerfully flooding in through the windows, although the morning was cool and still. She seemed unsurprised to find me by her bed. Instead, yawning, she wanted to know what was for breakfast. Climbing out of bed, she grabbed my free hand. The other one had slid the knife under the bed to conceal it from her view.

"Come on, Madison! Come *on*!"

She was rarin' to go. It was surreal to me that the care and feeding of this small person was taking precedence over everything else in my life, including strange visitations in the night. In any event, I certainly felt both saner and safer with the sunrise. The wind chimes had died away with the dawn. Groaning, I let her pull me to my feet whereupon she spontaneously hugged my thighs. Startled, I patted the top of her head. She looked up at me, smiled happily and scampered off to the bathroom. I made another quick circuit of the cabin, glancing out the windows as I went. All looked secure and normal in the burgeoning daylight, both inside and out. I exchanged the tank top and flannel boxers I'd slept in for blue jeans and a long-sleeved, dark blue, ribbed Henley shirt. I needed the warmth psychologically as much as physically.

Katie joined me in the kitchen, having donned jeans, socks, sneakers, T-shirt and sweatshirt jacket all on her own. I congratulated her on this, then got her squared away with a bowl of Captain Crunch. Juice box for her, Coke for me.

I was exhausted, but she was fired up, keeping up a running stream of commentary concerning proposed activities for our Sunday, a recap of last night's dinner, the pros and cons of Neapolitan ice cream as opposed to "regular" ice cream, a long story about a friend of hers from day care named Kipper (who was either a small boy or a hamster—I wasn't quite sure,) and on and on.

But nothing about bad dreams or a man on the porch.

I opened another can of Coke and positively yearned for a cigarette. And a shot of bourbon in the Coke. A headache was raggedly gathering at the back of my brain.

I was also feeling withdrawal symptoms from not having had access to e-mail for…how long now? I couldn't remember. No e-mail, no cell phone, no voice mail…hell, I hadn't even seen a piece of real mail from the U.S. Postal Service in days. I felt weird, remote from my usual reality and hung over. Which I didn't deserve, since I hadn't had anything to drink.

Katie gestured with her spoon, emphasizing some point in her story and giggled when that caused a piece of Captain Crunch to fly through the air. It landed on the table, next to my elbow, since my arm was propping up my head. I was too tired and too much in the throes of a nicotine fit to care about this minor breach in decorum. The cigarettes were in my purse, on the couch, just in the next room… Katie was asking me something.

"Sorry, what?"

"Are we going to church?" she asked me again.

Oh, wow. Church. Yeah, I guess it was Sunday. My lawyer friend Ben had taught me to answer a question with a question when I was caught off guard or simply had no good answer.

"Did you and your daddy always go to church on Sundays?"

Mouth full of cereal, she nodded. Those big blue eyes pinning me down with guilt.

"Do you like going to church, Katie?"

She looked at me quizzically as if "like" didn't enter into it, but nodded again, after a moment.

"It's church," she said, as if that settled it.

"What do you do there?" I asked.

A somewhat convoluted tale emerged in which she described Sunday school activities like occasional coloring (which she liked), required memorization of Bible stories (which she didn't), plus sitting on really hard wooden pews (ditto), some singing, long sermons she didn't really understand with a lot of shouting in them, giving witness (we were both a little fuzzy on what that entailed), more miscellaneous praising the Lord, and in general, spending pretty much the whole day at church on Sundays.

"The Church of the Benevolent Fount, right?" I clarified.

She nodded.

"So, are we going? We're supposed to go," she said, somewhat severely.

Come to think of it, I did want to have a word with those folks. Although not with Katie present… And I had no idea where the church was.

"Do you know where the church is, Katie?"

Working on another mouthful, she shook her head, giving me a look that said, plain as day: "Hello! I'm only five years old—

how am I supposed to know where things are?"

Katie said through her cereal, "It's pretty far."

"Okay," I replied. "But don't talk with your mouth full, please."

She gave me a radiant, close-lipped smile, swallowed and pronounced herself done. We proceeded to work out that we wouldn't go to church that Sunday, that we wouldn't get in trouble for that, that God would indeed be okay with this since it was a one-time deal (oops, little white lie there, but no lightning came through the ceiling to take me out) and the next order of business would be tooth brushing, to be immediately followed by trike riding on the short sidewalk in front of the cabin. She seemed pretty enthused to be let off the ecclesiastical hook, I thought. As was I.

She ran off to the bathroom. I engaged in another staring contest with the bourbon bottle. Finally, with a sigh, I got up and stuck it in the back of a cabinet. Out of sight, out of mind. Sure. I found some aspirin in my purse and got another Coke to help wash it down.

Katie raced back through the living room and out the front door to her tricycle. I followed, more slowly, onto the porch. Where my eye was caught by two things. The wind chimes lying on the railing right where I'd put them. And two sets of muddy footprints on the steps to our front door, drying in the morning sun. One pair belonged to someone with a shoe size much larger than mine, the other much smaller.

Chapter 14

I had no idea what the fuck was going on, but the one thing I did know was that I was not spending another night in that place. The sun was brightly shining down on us, a gentle sea breeze playing in the trees, my niece riding her trike up and down the sidewalk in front of the cabin, but something was seriously wrong here. I had my issues, sure, but I was used to having a tight grasp on reality. This slippery slope was foreign and frightening territory. I had to get me and Katie out of there.

I had another sudden shot of desire for a drink, but that was ridiculous. It was not even eight o'clock in the morning and I had stuff to do. Keeping one eye on Katie out the windows, I marched back into the kitchen, yanked that bottle of bourbon out of the cabinet and poured it all down the sink. For good measure, I dumped the rest of the wine as well. I didn't even want to have to think about that shit until we were well out of there.

I dropped the empty bottles in the trashcan under the sink.

Ran the water in the sink to wash away the smell of booze. And checked on Katie again out the kitchen window while I was doing that.

Pipe emerged onto her porch with an oversized mug of coffee in her hand. She had her mirrored shades on to guard against the morning sun. Well-worn, faded and raggedy blue jeans and one of those Mexican hoodie deals the surfers wear. Even from across the way and in my disturbed state, I couldn't help but notice how well those jeans fit her.

It had certainly crossed my mind that she was the only one out there besides us, but besides the obvious shoe size mismatch, I couldn't believe she was behind any of this.

I washed my hands at the kitchen sink and splashed some cold water on my face. Katie had dismounted and run over to say good morning to Pipe, who was seated on her steps. Katie sat down next to her, just a couple of gals catching up on the morning gossip. As I watched, both stood and looked up the road toward topside. A pickup truck was gingerly making its way down. Not one of the little white ones the Navy favored, this was a full-size, glossy black, late model with big off-road tires, brush guards, mud flaps, spotlights, big shiny toolbox in the bed—all the bells and whistles. And, in case you were still in any doubt, the foot high characters "4X4" emblazoned in bright red across one side. I went out on the porch as Pipe shooed Katie back toward our cabin. She ran across and zipped past me into the house, in search of something. I belatedly noticed her passing had all but obliterated the footprints—just looked like we had a dirty porch now and some crumbled dirt on the steps. Even as I looked at it, the wind blew some of it into the yard.

The truck had reached the foot of the hill. The driver parked it next to Pipe's International Harvester. An old guy got out. Khakis, work boots, white T-shirt and red, white and blue suspenders. Probably late sixties. Looked like he was about five foot ten and despite the serious gut which necessitated the suspenders, he was solidly built, like he'd done heavy work all his life. Pipe walked over to greet him.

Katie came bursting back onto the porch with her hat on and took my hand. I looked down at her.

"Are we going somewhere?"

"That's Mr. B.," she said, as if that explained anything.

When I didn't immediately respond, she pulled on my hand and said, "Come on!" Her intent was clearly to go join him and Pipe. I let her lead me over there. Somehow, I could tell from their body language that Pipe was updating the man on James's death and my arrival. He flicked me a shrewd glance as we walked up, then spoke directly to Katie, who had let go of my hand to hoist herself up on the truck's back bumper in a familiar fashion.

"Well, hello there, young lady."

"Hi, Mr. B.!" she replied happily. "Are you going down to the lighthouse? Can we come? Did you bring Henry the Eighth?"

"Whoa, now," he responded. "That's a lot of questions so early in the morning."

During this exchange, Pipe and I had exchanged a long look that was making me feel a bit lightheaded. She gave me one of her slow smiles like she knew exactly what I was thinking.

"Madison," she said and touched my hand briefly. I could only hope the jolt I felt was not visible to the rest of the party.

She went on—"I'd like to introduce you to Mr. Bohannon, president of the Shadow Point historical committee. This is Madison McPeake, Mr. B.—James's sister."

Bohannon extended a hand that was rather small in comparison to the rest of his bulk. I took it, glancing down at his feet as I did so. They too, were small for a man his size.

He was one of those bonecrusher handshakers, though, so I was glad when he finally relinquished my digits. I resisted the urge to massage them.

"Walter Bohannon, Miss McPeake. I'm sorry to hear about your brother's passing. He was a fine Christian man."

I glanced over at Katie, who was swinging her feet back and forth from her perch on the bumper. She gave me an anxious look, then stared off toward the lighthouse.

"Thank you, Mr. Bohannon," I said. "Nice to meet you."

We were thankfully saved from further stilted conversation by an eruption of snuffling and grunts from the front seat of his truck.

"Henry the Eighth!" Katie yelled and jumped to the ground.

"Guess I better let him out before he starts chewing on the steering wheel again," Bohannon said. He opened the driver's side door and lifted out an English bulldog that was as old and fat as him. He set him down on the ground with a grunt from the exertion of bending over. The bulldog shook his head and snorted, then sat down and sneezed three times in rapid succession. He was more or less tan in color all over, a sandy shade they call fawn, I think. He waddled over to Katie and accepted her gleeful pats with what I can only describe as a smirk.

Bohannon grabbed a camouflage-style canvas backpack out of the truck and shut the door. "Well, ladies, I'm off to work now. You take care." He whistled to the dog, who was ecstatically unaware of this call to duty as Katie was now scratching the area just above his stumpy little tail.

Katie heard the old man, however and stood up, repeating her plea to accompany him to the lighthouse. The dog barked at the sudden withdrawal of her attentions, then sat down again with a sound that sounded suspiciously like a whoopee cushion. I wondered what it was that Katie found so interesting about a burned-out old lighthouse. Looked pretty creepy to me in the one brief glimpse I'd had of it.

"Actually," I started to say, but Pipe jumped in just ahead of me so I didn't get to finish my sentence, which was: Actually, my only goal today is to get me and my niece the hell out of here before sundown.

"Maybe we could all go down there after lunch," Pipe said, flashing another one of those perfect smiles, this one encompassing both me and Katie. Who was giggling because the bulldog now had the laces of one her sneakers between his teeth and was energetically tugging at her shoe.

"Yeah, please, please, please, Madison?!" she entreated me, toppling over in the process whereupon Henry the Eighth immediately began licking her face, to peals of laughter from the little girl.

Well… I realized I probably should formulate a plan and a destination before I just threw the kid in the Jeep and started driving. And we needed to pack, although that wouldn't take long… As long as we were gone before sundown.

Bohannon reached into his pack and came up with a leash which he attached to the mutt's collar. Dragging him off in the direction of the path, he called back over his shoulder, "Okay, thirteen hundred hours then, ladies!"

It appeared the decision had been made. The sounds of both man and beast wheezing diminished as Bohannon disappeared down the path. Katie picked herself up and ran to wash the dog slobber off her face with Pipe's garden hose. Pipe and I strolled at a more sedate pace. She slowed me even further when her index finger gripped the back belt loop of my jeans and pulled me in, her hip touching mine.

"Sleep well?" she asked.

That stopped me in my tracks.

"Actually, no. Did you hear the wind chimes?"

She looked over at my porch. We could both see the wind chimes on the railing.

"You took them down Friday night, didn't you? I noticed I couldn't hear them when I came back from surfing that night. It's weird—I never really noticed them when James had them up, but I noticed right away when the sound was gone."

"But last night," I insisted. "Didn't you hear them last night?"

I could tell I had spoken too intensely. She took her hand off my belt loop and moved a step away, glancing again at the porch railing, then back at me. She shook her head and said, "I don't understand, Madison. You took the chimes down, right?"

I nodded.

Pipe went on, "Well, I didn't hear anything last night except the surf and the wind. Did something happen?"

She gave me a look. A look that said "And will you be needing a ride back to the sanitarium?"

We were at the foot of the sidewalk in front of the McPeake cabin. Katie finished her ablutions and ran past us to resume her trike riding.

Pipe took a step closer to me. Better.

"Is everything okay?" she asked, her face showing concern. Not better.

"I'm fine," I said. "It was nothing. No big deal, really." I smiled at her. See? Not crazy after all. No point showing her muddy footsteps that were no longer there.

"Okay," she said and smiled back, although not with the full wattage.

Katie rode up to us at maximum velocity, then sailed past us off the edge of the sidewalk and into the gravel, where her trike ground to an abrupt halt, which cracked her up. Pipe and I had to laugh too. We helped Katie get the trike turned around and back up on the sidewalk. She cruised back toward the house, making engine noises with her mouth.

The engine noise of another vehicle, however, caught my attention. One of the Navy's little white pickup trucks was slowly coming down the hill.

"Who's that?" I asked Pipe. She shrugged and said she didn't know, watching with interest to see who it could be. The truck maneuvered its way down into the gravel parking area. With four vehicles under the trees, there was no space there, so the driver pulled up right in front of us. Delgado was behind the wheel, but someone else was getting out of the passenger side.

"Oh, Lord have mercy," Pipe said under her breath. Emphatically.

"Who is it?" I said again. Katie rode back up to us and peered at the visitors over her handlebars.

"It's the teacher!" she exclaimed with some alarm, looking up at me perplexedly. Pipe was still muttering.

"Who?" I said with exasperation.

Delgado got out, a package under his arm. He and his passenger walked up to us.

"Good morning, Ms. McPeake, Katie," he said to us. We said hello. Pipe got a "hey" to which she responded with a head jerk, although I could detect a gleam of affection in her attitude toward him which was clearly missing in regard to the other visitor.

Delgado, blushing for no good reason I could see, was introducing the newcomer to me. She turned out to be Miss Klein, Katie's preschool teacher from the topside day care facility. Did everybody work on Sunday except me, I wondered? Maybe I was a slacker and didn't know it.

"How do you do?" I said, while shaking the limp fingertips she extended me. Miss Klein was a size eight body in a size six blouse and skirt. She looked young, like twenty-two and despite the physical endowments she was obviously determined to display to their best effect, somewhat homely of face. Dry, fried-looking ringlets of strawberry Blonde hair were pulled back in a French twist, but two long stiff tendrils had escaped to frame her narrow face. A fine dusting of freckles covered her face, her hands and the considerable amount of chest I could see thanks to the top three buttons of her lavender blouse being undone. Her perfume was rich and cloying. Her heels were ill-chosen for the gravel parking area, but she made her way self-confidently onto the sidewalk where we stood. Thin gold bracelets and big hoop earrings jangled as she walked. Lots of other jewelry, makeup and a sharp little manicure colluded to dazzle and attract (if not blind) the unsuspecting male of the species. Fiercely plucked brows outlined small hazel eyes. She had "high maintenance" written all over her. Ewwwww, I thought and resisted the urge to wipe my right hand down the side of my jeans. Delgado appeared to be in heat, however. She was working every asset she had and a couple she didn't. E for Effort, Miss Klein.

She said hello to me and Katie, who mumbled a glum greeting

and proceeded to tell me what a wonderful student my niece was and offer me her condolences on the loss of my brother. I thought she was wildly overdressed for a Sunday.

Somewhat icily, I thought, Miss Klein then greeted Pipe with the single word "Alice."

In her driest drawl, Pipe came back with, "Patsy." Clearly, they knew each other.

"It's Patricia," Klein said furiously. "Pa-tri-cia."

Pipe smiled disarmingly, that twinkle in her eye shining brightly. Say—hold the phone—Patricia? Writer-of-the-naughty-letter-to-my-brother Patricia? I eyed her with a sudden surge of interest.

"You must be very dedicated to your pupils to come in on a Sunday, Miss Klein," I said to her. Pipe made the tiniest of snorting noises at my shoulder.

Miss Klein primly informed me that she often came by on Sundays after church to prep for the week ahead. If those were her church clothes, I thought, she clearly was not a member of the Benevolent Fount congregation. Her prim and proper manner was a strange contrast to the rest of her presentation, which was busily shouting S-E-X to the world. I wondered what James could have thought of her. I also wondered just how much prep she could possibly need for a week with people five years old and under. But that was probably just my corporate snobbery.

"What's in the box, Gato?" Pipe said to Delgado.

Katie, who had dismounted, perked up and grabbed my sleeve. I looked down at her.

"That means cat," she informed me. The kid just kept impressing me—was she speaking Spanish now? Wow. I gently patted her on the back with approval. She beamed up at me.

Miss Klein said, "We're teaching the children Spanish this year as a way to bridge the cultural divide and celebrate diversity."

We three females digested that gem in silence, while Delgado gazed at her in whatever the horny equivalent of awe is. Pipe impatiently gestured at the box under his arm.

"Oh! I almost forgot," Delgado said. "This came in the mail for you yesterday and I thought you might like it today, so I brought it down. And when I ran into Miss Klein here, she said she'd love to come along and see how Katie was doing."

He handed Pipe the box, which was about the size a pair of boots would come in. Since the return address was boldly marked "Mrs. Donovan Piper" with an Austin, Texas address, I guessed it was from her mother.

"How come you always hand deliver the boxes with cookies in them?" she teased him with a grin.

He started to stutter through some excuse, but Klein interrupted him.

"Byron, why don't you and Katie and Dr. Piper"—she gave Pipe the gimlet eye here—"check out her package while I speak with Miss McPeake?"

I caught Pipe's eye and somehow semaphored that I wished to speak with the teacher alone. Although obviously loath to comply with La Klein, Pipe gave me a nod as she gathered up Katie and Delgado and took them over to her picnic table to investigate the contents of the box. Muttering a not so sotto voce "good luck" as she passed me and rolling her eyeballs.

Delgado called over his shoulder, "And I have something for you too, Ms. McPeake."

Whatever it was had to wait as Miss Klein firmly took my elbow and guided me up the steps and indoors, making me feel like she was the hostess and I the guest. Was this a parent/teacher conference? If so, I was so not ready.

Once inside, though, her demeanor made another abrupt shift. All business.

"Miss McPeake," she said, then paused. "May I call you Madison?"

"Sure," I said. "And it's…Patsy?"

"Patricia," she said shortly.

We passed a few moments in uncomfortable silence, while she looked about her, taking in the room and its meager furnishings.

It finally dawned on me that she was probably there to get her letter and who knew what else, back. I devoted five seconds to a silent and intense prayer that her dominatrix outfit wasn't hidden under a loose floorboard in his bedroom.

"Well, Madison," she finally said. "I'm not sure what Katie's told you about me."

"She hasn't actually mentioned you at all."

She seemed aggrieved by this, but rallied quickly.

"This is a little embarrassing. Ummm…I sent James a letter. A very…personal letter. I'd like to get it back."

Her small eyes gazed ferociously at me from under those over-plucked brows.

I went to the bathroom and pulled the letter from his bathrobe. Returning to the living room, I put it in her hand.

"And the photograph?" she said, her voice shaking a bit.

"I'm sorry, Miss Klein. I haven't come across any photographs."

She cocked her head, trying to decide if she believed me. I gave her my best poker face. I didn't have it, whether she believed me or not. Two spots of color appeared, high on her cheeks.

"Mind if I look?" she finally asked.

"Be my guest."

She didn't just look. It was a systematic search from room to room, with cold, calculating resolve. Miss Klein was clearly a force to be reckoned with. I couldn't imagine James being interested in her, but stranger things have been known to happen, I guess. She started in his bedroom, but found nothing there. I followed her from room to room (except Katie's—she seemed to sense I would draw the line there) as she checked in, under, behind and on top of every fixture and piece of furniture. She looked askance at me when she saw the empty booze bottles in the kitchen trash, but whatever. Glass houses, Patsy. I wasn't the one with the naughty boo boo picture. Finally, the only room left was the living room. She went through every book in the bookcase and the Bible on the footlocker too, shaking them by their spines. Hoping to speed up the process, I did the same to the music books on top of the piano, setting them on the stool as each passed muster. Nothing in Bach, nothing in Haydn, but something fell fluttering from the pages of Chopin's nocturnes. Patsy looked up from where she was rifling through a hefty volume devoted to the mollusks of North America.

"What is that?" she demanded.

I picked it up off the piano keys. It was an item well known to me, but I felt surprised nonetheless. It was one of those little navy blue paper folders for airline tickets. There was another one still partially stuck in the book. I opened first one, then the other. One-way plane tickets from San Diego to Boston—one for James, one for Katie. The departure date was the very next day, Monday.

I was absolutely floored. Why would James be coming to Boston? On a one-way ticket, no less. To see me? Why would he be going anywhere, one way? I couldn't fathom it.

Miss Klein was yammering at me. I dragged my attention back to her.

"What?"

"Is the picture in there?" she asked.

"No," I said, showing her one of the tickets before replacing it and folding both folders shut. "It's just plane tickets."

My purse was still on the couch, so I stashed the tickets in there, in the important documents folder. Maybe I could at least change the date on Katie's ticket and use it later, saving a few bucks in the process. Lucky for me, it was on the same airline I always use for both business and pleasure. (Since frequent flyer perks are the only things that make business travel even faintly pleasant.) My own return ticket was open-ended since I hadn't known how long I'd need to stay. We certainly wouldn't be leaving for Boston on Monday since the whole memorial service issue was still up in the air.

Klein looked disappointed. The search had clearly taken a toll on her. She was sweating and had gone quite pink in the face and the bosom. More tendrils of combustibly dry hair had escaped her 'do. She impatiently pushed them behind her ears, but they immediately popped out again. She looked around the cabin with frustration. But there was no place left to search. With a last burst of inspiration, she went to the piano and wrenched open the top with some difficulty. She sneezed at the dust that stirred up, but the picture wasn't in there either.

"Do you know why James would have been taking Katie to Boston tomorrow?" I asked her.

"What?" she said, still distracted and dejected by her lack of success. "No. He hadn't spoken to me since...well, since I sent the letter."

She seemed very young and on the verge of tears, suddenly. A smudge of dust marred her too-snug, eggplant-colored skirt.

"Maybe he kept the letter and tore up the picture," she said to me, hopelessly.

"Maybe." Unexpectedly, I felt a little sorry for her. "Look," I told her, "if it's any consolation, I don't think he would have kept the letter if he didn't like you at least a little bit."

Especially in his bathrobe pocket (ewwwww again), but I kept that to myself. Another, less kindly thought struck me—maybe he was keeping it as evidence in case she turned out to be more of a stalker than an admirer, but I kept that to myself too. I didn't really think she was dangerous—just not in possession of the best decision-making skills. And who among us hasn't been guilty of that from time to time? I handed her a tissue from my purse.

"I'm sorry," she said, sniffling and dabbing at a tear with that don't-mess-up-the-mascara move high maintenance women master in their early teens. "I just really thought your brother was great." She could have stopped right there, but went on to say, "You don't really seem much like him."

Then she caught herself. "Oh. No offense."

"Hardly any taken," I said, with a small smile.

Still dabbing, she flicked me a glance in which I read a lack of comprehension and a growing dislike. Gee and we'd just met.

Oh, well. I got the sense witty repartee was not Miss Klein's strong suit. I gave her a couple more tissues and she pulled herself together enough for the walk back outside. I promised I would give her the photo if I came across it.

Pipe, Delgado and Katie were seated at the picnic table, laughing it up and sharing the contents of the care package. I trusted Pipe (more than myself, maybe) had doled out only a small and sensible amount of cookies to the five-year-old. Klein and I crunched across the gravel. She quickly regained her pissy composure at the sight of them as she carefully picked her way in her three-inch heels.

Katie came running across to me with a brownie nestled in a bit of pink tissue paper. "Pipe says this brownie is specially for you, Mad," she said as she handed it over like an ambassador giving me a medal. I looked over her head at Pipe, who was smiling at me so devilishly I actually had to put my hand on Katie's head to steady myself. Ducking out from underneath, she went off to saddle up her trike again and work off some of her sugar high. I took a bite of the homemade brownie—oh my gosh, sheer heaven! So good I had to consider dumping Pipe for a second and moving to Austin to pursue her mother instead.

Klein was telling Delgado she was ready to go, but I paused him by asking him and Pipe about James's plane ticket. Both seemed as startled as I was.

Delgado said, "His contract with the Navy was through the end of the calendar year, so I can't imagine why he'd be leaving now. He certainly hadn't said anything to me about it."

Pipe shook her head in bafflement. I sat down next to her. With an irritated look, Klein sat down by Delgado.

He went on, "Although…" He stopped, looked at Pipe, then looked at me, cast a glance at Klein, then hurriedly looked down at the peanut butter cookie in his hands. The kind with the Hershey's kiss on top. Mmmmm.

"What?" I said, refocusing. Finding himself the center of attention from three highly interested females, he blushed again and adjusted his spectacles before he could speak.

"It's just that…he'd been a little…off lately. You know?"

"Like how?" I asked.

Delgado squirmed, plainly uncomfortable with the conversation. He manfully continued, though. "Well, James, I mean Dr. McPeake, was always very professional, very attentive to the quality of his work. But lately, he'd been a little erratic. Missing deadlines. Skipping over details. A little hostile sometimes. Especially since his car accident last week. You know?"

Erratic. Hostile. Two of the very adjectives my boss had so recently and warmly applied to me. Great. I felt my muscles clenching and tried to relax.

Delgado went on, "Even his workspace up at the lab was a mess when I checked on it this morning. Papers and stuff everywhere. He usually kept it as neat as a pin."

For some reason, I glanced over at Klein when he said that. Her post-search pinkness had been fading into lesser splotches on her neck and chest, but those two bright spots of color on her cheeks returned when I caught her eye. She hastily looked away. I wondered if she had talked her way into the lab and looked for the photo there too. Or conned some poor schlub of a sailor to do it for her. I wouldn't put it past her. I didn't say anything, though. I was much more concerned with trying to figure out why James had been headed to Boston.

Delgado had mentioned a car accident. What with everything else going on, I'd forgotten about the dinged up side of the Explorer. I asked him what had happened.

"I'm not really sure," he answered. "He came into work one day last week with a bruise on his forehead and said he'd run off the road when a tire blew. Up near the cemetery, I think it was."

I looked at Pipe and Miss Klein, but both shook their heads like they didn't know anything more about it.

"Cookie?" Pipe said to Klein, offering her the box. That southern hospitality runs deep, I tell you. Patsy shook her head again, looking like she'd been offered a bug on a stick. Delgado reached down and came up with a large envelope he'd evidently had on the bench beside him.

"This is for you, Ms. McPeake," he said to me, handing it over, his manner apologetic. "It's not much—just the personal items James had in his lab space. I cleaned out the area this morning."

The envelope was quite light, like he said. I thought about opening it later, but they were all looking at me expectantly and I was pretty darn curious to see what was in there too. I undid the clasp and dumped the contents out on the picnic table. A wallet-size picture of Katie that looked like her "school picture" from the day care. A finger painting she must have done for Valentine's day that featured a lopsided heart, clumps of glitter and the message "i lov u dady." Pipe put her hand on the small of my back for a moment when I had to blink back tears over that one. I set it aside.

Klein was looking at us with sudden speculation, but so what? I could care less what she thought. My date was way hotter than hers, anyhow.

What else? A roll of antacid tablets, a white envelope and a small wooden cross on a leather thong were the next three items. The fourth and final item was a bit curious. Tarnished metal, about five inches long, it was roughly the size of a pencil, but flat and with a hook at one end. Not sharp like a fish hook, but like the rounded hook you use to fasten the screen door. The top four inches of the non-hook end were beaten flat and grimy with age, but I could tell it had a fancy design etched into it. Like a piece of silverware, but this was no fork, knife or spoon.

"What is this?" I held it up for everyone to see.

"You know, I asked him about that once," Delgado said. "He had it in a cup with pens and pencils on his desk. He said his kid had dug it up in the yard down here, but he took it away from her so she wouldn't hurt herself with it. It's a...what do you call it? A..." He snapped his fingers, trying to remember the word.

"Buttonhook," Miss Klein said unexpectedly. We all stared at her.

"Well, it is," she said, somewhat crossly. "My grandmother collects them. People used to use them a hundred years ago to do up the buttons on their shoes."

Delgado was nodding enthusiastically, happy to agree with her. "Right, a buttonhook! There's a lot of history out here on the Point, you know. People find all kinds of things, from Native American artifacts to relics from the Portuguese explorers to more recent stuff, from when the Blys lived here."

I jumped a bit when he said the name. I don't know why, but it just caught me like an icy breath on the back of my neck. This time, Pipe's hand came down on mine on the bench seat, warm and reassuring. Delgado and Klein couldn't see that from where they were sitting. I looked at Pipe and felt the connection between us. Or maybe I felt it and she didn't. I wanted to think it was something you could only feel if the other person felt it too.

"There's one thing left," she said gently, bringing me back to the current situation. Oh, yeah. The envelope. Sealed, I could see, as the flap side was up on the table.

"Uh, you probably want to open that in private," Delgado said, squirming again.

I turned it over and saw why. The time-honored words "To Be Opened In The Event Of My Death" were neatly typed across the back of the envelope.

Chapter 15

I had to stop for a second and wait for the heart and lungs to reboot. The world was whirling a bit about me and I couldn't seem to take in any air. Pipe looked at me with concern.

"Are you all right, Mad?" she asked.

I must have looked a little weird, based on the way she was looking at me. I nodded, since I couldn't get any words to come out yet. I still had that funny feeling in the pit of my stomach you get when the roller coaster has just crested the summit and is headed down. A long way down.

"Do you want us to leave you alone?" she said.

Speech returned. "No, stay," I told her. Told all of them. "You guys stay. I want you to see what's in here too."

I'd been alone too much, I thought. The last thing I wanted was to open that envelope and have to deal with whatever was inside all by myself. I took a deep breath and opened it. They all three watched with avid interest. I was glad Katie was still into her trike riding across the way and out of earshot. I withdrew the single sheet of plain white paper and read the single sentence typed on it: "In the event I die on Shadow Point, I direct that my ashes be scattered on Shadow Point."

He had signed and dated it. One week earlier.

I didn't know what to make of that. I passed it to Pipe, who read it and passed it to Delgado, who did the same and passed it to Klein.

Delgado cleared his throat and said diffidently, "Uh, that's actually going to be a problem. I'm pretty sure the Navy's not going to allow that."

I agreed, but told him it wasn't going to be my problem since James had named a member of his church as the executor, not me. Delgado blinked, but didn't seem that surprised. Neither did Pipe or Klein. It seemed James's devotion to his church was well known amongst his colleagues.

But the burial instructions…or rather the ash-dispersing instructions… That was strange. None of us seemed to have any clue as to why James would want that. I certainly didn't. Klein handed the letter back to me. I held it in my hand and thought: My brother touched this paper one week ago, planning for his own death. The sun was shining, but I was cold again.

Klein finally broke the silence by asking me a question.

"Do you want that?" she said, gesturing toward the buttonhook, reminding us It Was Really All About Her. Inappropriate! But I absolutely did not want it, knowing it might have some connection to the Blys or at least this creepy-ass place.

"It's all yours," I said, handing it to her, then surreptitiously wiping my hand on my jeans under the table.

"Thank you," she responded. "I'll clean it up and give it to my grandmother for her collection."

I suddenly hoped it was indeed going to grandma and not being added to some candlelit voodoo shrine for James, but it was too late to worry about that now. She stood up, more than ready to depart.

"Can we go now, Byron? I have work to do." Like she was the only one who had things to do. She flounced off to the pickup truck after a cursory farewell to me, a wave to Katie and a curled lip for Pipe.

Delgado and Pipe stood as well, but my legs felt a little weak from too much information in too short a timeframe. I asked them one last question.

"You guys can't think of any reason he might have been planning a trip or heading off to Boston tomorrow?"

No, they couldn't.

Nobody said it, but they were probably thinking the same thing I was. If James's ticket had been for Wednesday instead of Monday, he might be alive right now.

All I could think was—what had he been trying to escape?

We said our goodbyes. Delgado was dusting powdered sugar and jimmies off his shirt and filching one last cookie from the box for the road. Patsy was already back in the truck, impatiently waiting for him to join her.

Pipe walked with Delgado over to the driver's side and leaned in the open window as he fired up the engine. "'Bye, Byron," she said sweetly.

I could see him blushing as he drove away.

Chapter 16

Pipe came back to the table and (embarrassingly) caught me rummaging through her care package in search of one of those peanut butter cookies with the chocolate kiss on top. Because those are only the best ever. Damn it. Delgado must have gotten the last one. Katie had her back to us, crouched by the rear wheels of her trike, making some needed adjustment to the power train. Pipe sat down next to me and planted a real kiss on my cheek instead, which I did not disdain.

"Are you okay?" she said.

When you are perceived to be a Tough As Nails Girl, no one ever asks if you are okay. The world, instead, neatly divides itself into two groups: Those who assume you must be okay because you are Tough As Nails and those who don't give a crap how you are. The latter group usually outnumbers the former. So, to have her ask me if I was okay, under such circumstances and with such a warmth of empathy in her voice, meant a lot to me and brought me instantly to the verge of tears. Where I didn't want to be, because I am Tough As Nails.

"Hey," she exclaimed, then drew me in for a hug. "It's all right."

I snuffled for a moment, hugging her back, then regrouped.

"I'm okay, I'm okay," I told her, letting her go. "I'm just…" My voice trailed off. I didn't know what I was, to tell the truth.

"Well, here, have a cookie," she said pragmatically, offering me the box. I took one of those ones you make with condensed milk—you know, the recipe's on the can? Layers of graham cracker crumbs, chocolate chips, coconut… So good.

Pipe smiled at my expression.

"I know I'm way too old to still be getting care packages from home," she said, "but every time I tell my mom that, she says I'm still her baby. She'll probably still be sending me these when I'm sixty-two."

We laughed a little about that, then wrapped it up. She told me she had some stuff to do in town, but she'd meet us at twelve forty-five for our lighthouse trip. She took off a few minutes later.

Okay, fine, twelve forty-five lighthouse trip and then we're out of here, I told myself firmly. With Pipe and the rest of the visitors gone, I keenly felt the eerie isolation of the dell. Yes, the sun was shining and big puffy clouds were now scudding through the sky at a pretty good clip, but the surface friendliness of the place didn't fool me. I needed to get us out of there. The more I thought about it, the more I wanted to bail on the lighthouse visit, but I didn't want to upset Katie more than I was already going to that day or stand up Pipe. Just a quick visit, I kept telling myself and then we're gone, long gone before another sunset would overtake Shadow Point.

Alone again with Katie, I wanted to ask her about the plane tickets, but again, not in a way that would upset her. I sat on the porch in one of the aluminum chairs and watched her ride her trike for a bit while I pondered the best way to casually bring it up. She finally took a break and joined me in another one of the chairs.

"So…" I said. "Are you excited about going to Boston and seeing my apartment?"

She shrugged. From all the excitement, no doubt. I tried again.

"We get to fly on a big plane. That'll be fun, right?"

Another shrug. Ehhhh.

"Have you ever flown on a plane before?"

She said no, but she probably had since James had moved all over the country since she'd been born. She probably just didn't remember. In any event, the mention of the plane ride elicited no other reaction from her. I tried a few other routes, but it was obvious she didn't know a thing about the plane tickets James had bought for her and himself. Another mystery.

While I was at it, though, I asked her about the car accident as well. I didn't know if she'd been in the car with James at the time, but it turned out she had. She verified she hadn't been hurt at all, having ridden it out in her car seat.

"So, you were driving by the cemetery and you got a flat tire?" I coached her.

"No," she looked at me oddly. "We didn't get a flat tire."

"But you guys ran off the road, right?"

"My daddy had to turn the wheel, 'cause that girl was in the road," she told me.

Girl? It must have been my turn to look at her oddly, because she insisted.

"That girl was right in front of us, so we had to drive off the road real fast. And we hit the fence and the car got all scratched." She nodded several times for emphasis.

"A girl from your school?" I tried.

"No," she said, a little exasperated by my denseness, "that other little girl. She just shows up sometimes."

As if that explained anything.

"She's mean," Katie confided.

"The little girl is mean?" I asked.

127

"Yeah. But her dress is pretty," she added, just to be fair about it.

I still had no idea what she was talking about, but gave it up. Seeing I had no more questions, Katie lost interest in further discourse and wandered back to her trike. I seriously doubted a little girl had been in the road by the cemetery, miles from anywhere. Maybe a squirrel or something had dashed in front of them and James had had to swerve... If, God forbid, James had struck a child with his vehicle, wouldn't I have heard all about that from Delgado or somebody else by now? As much as I already adored Katie, she was five years old. I didn't always understand the things she said to me. No doubt she would have said the same of me.

I spent the rest of the morning packing up our stuff and loading the Jeep. There were several big hotels near the airport and I was sure one of them would have a room for us, but I'd have to wait until we were off the Point to make some calls on my cell phone and confirm. In the meantime, I sat down on the living room couch where I could keep one eye on Katie, who was now puttering about on the porch. The front door was open and I could hear her talking to Babs through the screen. I found an empty page at the back of my day planner and drew up our plan of action.

Packing. Check.

Hotel. Soon to be check.

Talk to attorney, church people, coroner's office, mortuary and Chloe's family on Monday.

Fly back to Boston—when? It depended on what the Monday conversations brought, I guessed. Boston...did I even have a job to go back to? I couldn't just quit the bastards now, as much as I would have liked to. Now that I had Katie, I had to be all responsible and grown up.

Crap. But I couldn't help it—when I really thought about it, I hated that fucking job. I couldn't even remember how I'd fallen into it. Surely, there was something better for me out there somewhere. But where? Being in California always reminded me of how much I loved my home state. Boston was great, but California was home. I felt homesick suddenly, certainly not for my apartment or my solitary life on the road, or even for a specific place, but for a time when I'd had a home and a family and the comfort of knowing that somebody cared…

Snap out of it, Madison, I told myself with disgust. You've got work to do. I shook off my glum thoughts and brought myself back to the unsatisfactory present. I added Delgado to my list of Monday people to talk to. I felt I owed him the closure of letting him know I'd decamped and giving him any relevant updates I had at that point.

So, great, there was my plan, all neatly annotated on paper. And where did Pipe fit in with all this? Probably nowhere, I had to admit to myself. I'd seen that look she'd given me about the wind chimes before on other people's faces—most recently and notably, my boss. It was not a look my interpersonal relationships tended to recover from. But I wasn't crazy! I knew that. I heard what I heard and I saw what I saw.

Great. Now I was sounding like Dr. Seuss.

"Katie!" I called out.

She appeared on the other side of the screen, Babs under her arm.

"Want some lunch?" I said.

She nodded vigorously.

We split a Lean Cuisine. Two peas in a pod, us McPeake girls.

Pipe met us as promised at twelve forty-five and the three of us struck out for the lighthouse. We left Babs on guard in a porch chair. The path seemed less treacherous in the light of day. Plus, I knew where I was going this time. But the sight of the burned out structure was still alarming, even though I knew what to expect.

"Why are we doing this again?" I asked my two companions.

The short one didn't answer.

Pipe said, "I thought you wanted to see it. And Katie loves the lighthouse. James used to bring her down here all the time."

Seemed like a strange place to take a kid, but James was a strange guy, no doubt about it. Katie was skipping along at my side like we were going to Disneyland. We were all three still in long sleeves as the day hadn't really warmed up, although the mid-sixties temperature with the cool, clean air off the ocean still felt wonderful to me.

Katie picked up the pace and zipped a few yards ahead of us. I took the opportunity to quietly ask Pipe what the hell Miss Klein's deal was. She laughed and shook her head.

"How do you even know her?" I asked. Surely, the childless scientist types didn't have much reason to mix with the preschool teacher?

"Oh, it's a pretty small community out here. And Delgado likes to make it one big happy family, you know, with potlucks and stuff like that from time to time. He always includes the civilian contractors like her and me. There's nothing really wrong with her, she just bugs me, you know?"

I knew.

"For a teacher who's supposed to be so worried about Katie, she barely said two words to her—did you notice?" I said.

"Yeah, well, she's got poor Gato under her spell now, so I think most of her energy is focused on that," Pipe said ruefully. "So what were you guys talking about inside there for so long anyway?"

Before I could answer, Katie had heard me say her name and bopped back to us, wanting to know what we were talking about. I told her the topic was Miss Klein.

"She liked my daddy," Katie volunteered.

"I'll bet she did," Pipe muttered under her breath.

"Did your daddy like her?" I asked Katie.

Her face wrinkled as she considered this. "I don't think so," she said.

"And how about you—do you like her?" I asked.

"She's okay," was her tempered judgment. She went back to concentrating on her skipping, opening up a twenty foot lead on us. We trudged along behind her.

"I guess I can't really blame Patsy," Pipe said. "She's stuck out here with all these horndog Navy guys—I think she's worked her way through almost every one of them by now."

I'd thought about not telling Pipe about the letter and photo, but in the end it was too juicy a tidbit to keep to myself. Besides, I trusted her discretion.

"Whoa." Pipe whistled. "I guess she's moving on to the civilians now." She shook her head disparagingly. "It's such a soap opera out here, between the labs and the day care and the Navy. Sheesh. Is your work like that?"

I thought about it. Thought about the backstabbing, the whispering and gossip, the cliques, the constant jockeying for position, the sycophants and haters pouring their lies and venom into the boss's ear…

"More like a slasher movie," I told her. I couldn't believe I had once actually liked that job.

"Hmmph. Anyhow, I guess it's not Patsy's fault she's such a—" Pipe hesitated as Katie came back into earshot. "Well, such a dang ot-pants-hay, if you know what I mean."

I successfully decoded it, but had to laugh at the Ph.D. resorting to pig latin. Katie heard us laughing and wanted to know what "opp-ass-ay" was. Pipe told her it was French for Super Good Teacher, which Katie accepted. With her boundless energy, she again skipped down the sunny path ahead of us. Pipe grimaced at me. I laughed some more and grabbed her so we could stroll arm-in-arm, which she seemed pleased to do.

We passed the point where I had turned back on Friday night. A few more feet and a path opened up which would take us down to the lighthouse. Wooden steps had been built into the side of the hill. Henry the Eighth appeared at the foot of the stairs, woofed once, then trotted back through the open

131

door at the foot of the lighthouse. What had been chained and padlocked the other night was now wide open. We made our way down the steps and to the door. I kept a grip on Katie's shoulder as we entered the dim interior and resisted the urge to take Pipe's hand as well.

It was cool inside and not so dim after all as my eyes adjusted to the light streaming in through a tall, dirty, multi-paned window. The heavy wooden door was propped open with a wedge. We were in the base of the tower, in a round room perhaps twenty feet in diameter. The center was dominated by a narrow, wrought iron, spiral staircase with wooden steps that wove sinuously up to and through an opening into the tower some thirty feet above our heads. Bohannon was nowhere in sight, but I could hear hammering somewhere upstairs. His dog, panting heavily, lay under a long wooden workbench with all kinds of tools, a radio/walkie-talkie setup, cardboard boxes, fast-food wrappers, plastic cups and other crap piled on top. Sawdust and wood scraps littered the hardwood floor.

Either there hadn't been any fire damage in this interior level before, or they'd already fixed it up. Framed black-and-white photographs lined the white-painted wall at eye level. A low table covered with green felt sat under the far window. A scale model of the lighthouse rested on top of it. It was almost like a dollhouse, in that it opened up so you could see the cutaway view of the interior, complete with some small figures representing the lighthouse keeper, his wife and child. So far, it looked like the photos and the scale model were the only steps toward converting the place into a museum. Even though it looked pretty bad from the outside, I guessed the renovation efforts meant the building must still be structurally sound. Still standing after all these years, at least.

"Walter!" Pipe called out.

The hammering abruptly stopped and we could hear the old man's footsteps creak across the floor above our heads. Katie giggled as he gingerly eased his considerable bulk down the well-worn steps, which looked original. I kept a hold of her—this was not a kid-friendly environment. And the last thing we needed was a trip to the emergency room for a tetanus shot.

"Well, ladies," Bohannon boomed as he finally made it back down to sea level. "What do you think, eh?"

His remarks seemed mostly aimed at Pipe, perhaps fishing for a compliment on whatever progress he'd made since her last visit. Before she could respond, though, Katie had a question.

"Can we go up to the tower, Mr. B.?" she asked, bouncing up and down at my side with excitement.

"Sorry, little lady," was his reply. "It's not safe for visitors up there yet."

Katie looked philosophical, apparently not having expected a positive response anyhow. Bohannon turned his glance back to Pipe.

"Looking good, sir," she said. "Have you got some new photos up?"

He did and proceeded to give us the tour. The pictures were of the Point and the lighthouse back in the twenties and thirties. I remembered Pipe telling me that was when Conrad Bly and his family had tended the place. A blurry photo of a white Victorian-style house caught my attention. Two stories, with a wide porch in the front. The next picture showed a stoic young woman in a high-collared dress standing next to an upright piano. Nickerson, said the shiny metal nameplate on the instrument. Wow, just like the one in James's cabin, I thought.

I went back to the photo of the white house. Something there looked familiar too…

"Noticed the house, did you?" Bohannon said, right behind me. I tried not to jump. He gave me another one of his shrewd looks.

"Recognize anything?" he said with a sly grin. I didn't, but there was something about the picture—not the house, I'd never seen that before. There weren't any people in the picture. Just the house and a couple of scraggly trees off to the side that looked like they'd just been planted… It finally clicked.

I looked at Bohannon, who was waiting for my response.

"It's where the cabins are, right?"

"Got it in one, young lady. The Bly family house stood right there in the dell where you've been staying."

"Did it burn too?" I asked him.

"No, that was just the lighthouse. But no one ever lived in that house again after that night. Some say the ghost of Conrad Bly still walks the dell on moonless nights, looking for all he lost and working his mischief. But, look at me, I'm telling the story all backwards! Let's start from the beginning, shall we?"

I didn't really give a shit, but it seemed rude to demur when it was clearly his only purpose in life. Katie was now engrossed in the model lighthouse, with Pipe overseeing. Bohannon drew me over to his workbench, where he unerringly found the book he wanted in one of the cardboard boxes. He opened it to a well-thumbed page, then pointed.

"There," he said.

Another black-and-white photo. Probably sepia-toned, originally. This one was one of those stiff studio portraits from early in the twentieth century. A man standing behind a seated woman with a little child on her lap. The man's look was bleak and jaded, his big mustachios drooping but not defeated. He was a big guy, with deep-set eyes and fierce brows. Not a man you'd want to cross, in my opinion. The woman was similarly unsmiling. I recognized her sad stoic stare from the piano picture. She looked much younger than her husband. The child's gaze was diverted off-camera. She was a girl, perhaps three years old. Her tiny hand rested on top of her mother's. She was dressed up, no doubt for the picture, in a velvet dress and bow in her hair and wearing leather shoes that would require a buttonhook. The picture was black and white, but I imagined the velvet for the dress and bow had been a deep red, or maybe a deep ocean blue.

I looked up at Bohannon.

"Conrad Bly and family, circa nineteen twenty-eight," he

said. "That's his wife, Rachel and their only child, Lily."

Lily…that was Katie's middle name. Katherine Lily McPeake.

Bohannon was on a roll now. "That's the only known picture of the three of them together," he told me. "It was shortly after this that the troubles began." He looked at me expectantly.

"What troubles?" I asked, as he clearly wouldn't go on until I fed him the line.

"Well, it's a sad tale. A tragedy, really. First, the little girl took sick. By all accounts, Conrad doted on that child, but he was also infamous for being a terrible skinflint. Nobody was tighter with a nickel than old man Bly, which is probably why he ended up so rich. He figured the kid would get better, but she didn't. Rachel begged him to have a doctor come out to the Point, but Conrad didn't like having strangers on his land and didn't want to pay for a doctor anyway. He told his wife it was her job to take care of the child. By the time he finally gave in and took her into town to see a doctor, it was too late. She was dead by the time they got there. There was apparently an awful scene at the doctor's office. The doctor rebuked Conrad for not bringing his daughter in sooner and Conrad horsewhipped him within an inch of his life. I've got the reprint of the newspaper article around here somewhere…"

"That's okay," I murmured.

Bohannon hitched up his trousers and continued the story. "Anyhow, Conrad got back in his wagon and drove right back to the Point, with his dead child in his arms. They say he went a little crazy that night."

"You said *first*," I reminded Bohannon. "So what happened second?"

"Might have been the strain of losing her only child or living out here all alone, or the strain of being married to a man like Conrad Bly. No one knows for sure, but in nineteen twenty-nine, Rachel Bly killed herself. Hung herself right there on the porch of their house."

Involuntarily, I shuddered. I had a quick vision of a woman's body, clothed in a long dress, dangling and twisting in the wind, hanging from a porch beam. Right outside where my current front door stood.

Bohannon was watching me with a gleam in his eye, clearly delighted by my reaction to the tale. Creepy old bastard, I thought.

He went on. "After Rachel's suicide, no one saw much of Conrad. The men who worked for him—smugglers and scoundrels all—were a pretty tight-lipped bunch. They came and went off the Point, but Conrad was never again seen in town. Rumors circulated that he'd gone completely mad, locking himself up in the lighthouse for days on end and screaming at God for the fate he'd been dealt." He paused to hitch up his trousers again.

"So, was it true?" I prompted. "Had he gone mad?"

"Probably not," he sighed. He seemed disappointed. "Probably too mean to go crazy. His various business concerns continued to flourish, that's a known fact. His smuggling enterprise eventually turned into a legitimate shipping business that still exists—maybe you've seen the trucks?"

I nodded, hoping we were near the end of the story. The dog had waddled over at some point to join Katie by the scale model. She was sitting on the floor with him now, Pipe crouched nearby to join in petting him. Katie and the pooch seemed quite devoted, really. Maybe I could get her a puppy in Boston...and a bicycle. Although God knows where she would ride it—up and down the halls of my apartment building? No. Clearly not. I foresaw a lot of trips to the park and down by the river...

Pipe turned and met my gaze, the jolt still taking me by surprise. Maybe I could get *her* a puppy in Boston... She stood and walked over to join us. Bohannon, perhaps sensing he was losing my attention, cleared his throat to regain it.

"So, with both wife and child dead and buried, things went on the same way for several years. No one saw or heard anything of Conrad Bly, except the men who worked for him. Many people had almost forgotten about him until the night of November

11th, 1933, which was known as Armistice Day back then. That was the night when the lighthouse caught fire and almost burned down, trapping and killing Conrad in the tower. Some said it was a bolt of lightning that struck the lighthouse and set it aflame, although that's unlikely given the climate around here. Others said it was the final blow of a vengeful God to strike down an unrighteous man. A more likely theory is just plain accident, or perhaps a takeover bid by one of Bly's own men. There were some real cutthroats in that gang of his. Or maybe Bly finally did go 'round the bend and set the fire himself. I guess we'll never know."

Pipe had joined us during this recitation. "Okay, Mr. B.," she said. "That's enough ghost stories for today, don't you think?"

Bohannon responded, "Oh, but there's one thing left to tell, you know."

"Mr. B.," Pipe said in a warning tone.

"What?" he said in an aggrieved tone. "Isn't it better she hear it from me than read it in the newspaper or hear it from some stranger?"

Pipe looked troubled, but said nothing. I couldn't begin to guess what they were talking about. I gave Pipe a puzzled look, but she was walking over to Katie, announcing it was time for them to take Henry the Eighth for a walk. Both Katie and the dog scrambled to their feet and all three were out the door before I could voice any opposition.

I looked at Bohannon. "All right. What is it? What's the big secret, Walter?"

"It's no secret, young lady. It's the legend of Shadow Point. The curse, actually."

"The curse of Conrad Bly, you mean?" I said.

"Oh, no, this started long before Bly ever came here. He just became a part of it. The Portuguese sailors who discovered the Point were the first to write of the curse. And they learned of it from the Native Americans who lived across the bay. I've got the documentation in one of these boxes here…"

"Let's just cut to the chase. What's the curse?"

"That anyone who dies on the Point can never leave and is doomed to haunt us here for all eternity."

Chapter 17

Pipe and Katie were waiting for me at the bottom step of the hillside staircase, the dog panting at their feet. Pipe's sunglasses were perched on top of her head, so I could clearly see the concerned look on her face—worried, perhaps, that I was upset.

I had parted abruptly from Bohannon, having had enough of him. How dare that old bastard say such a thing to me, when my only brother had just died on the Point a few days ago? What an asshole. I wasn't upset. I was fucking pissed. I swear to God, people say the stupidest things. All the time.

A piercing whistle behind me split the air and galvanized the dog, who shot off to the lighthouse, moving far more quickly than I would ever have suspected he was capable of.

Pipe touched my arm. "Are you okay?"

I nodded, rather shortly.

"I'm sorry," she said. "I tried to shut him up."

"It's fine," I said. "Not a problem."

Katie was looking from one to the other of us, obviously wondering what the heck the grownups were babbling about now.

Pipe's hand tightened on my arm. She took a step toward me.

"No, really, Madison," she said with some emphasis. "It's just a stupid story. It doesn't mean anything." She looked me in the eye.

"It's fine," I said to her again. She looked skeptical, but released my arm. I glanced down at Katie, who was looking up at me open-mouthed. "We're all fine," I said to her, in a more moderate tone. I put my hand out and she took it. "Ready to go, Kate-ster?"

She nodded and set off up the stairs, dragging me in her wake. Pipe followed. We made our way back to the cabins with little conversation. Katie was chattering away, remarking on this rock, that leaf, a small lizard that darted across the path in front of us…in any event, filling any and all conversational voids between Pipe and myself.

I wasn't sure if Katie realized we were minutes away from leaving the Point, probably forever. The Jeep was all packed. There was really nothing left to do but put me and the kid in it and drive away. No reason to stay a moment longer…

"Madison." Pipe's voice brought me out of my reverie.

She and Katie were now just ahead of me, emerging from the path back into the cleared area between her cabin and ours. Both stopped short as they reached the gravel. As I came up beside them, I saw why. A fifth car had now appeared and was parked right in front of my cabin—an extra large American car, late model, maroon—a car like somebody's grandma would drive. Its driver was sitting on my porch steps. He didn't look like anybody's grandma.

"Friend of yours?" Pipe said to me.

"I was just about to ask you the same thing," I said, then turned in dismay as Katie burst into tears.

"What's wrong?" Pipe and I said in unison as she dropped

to her knees beside the now wailing child. Katie threw herself into Pipe's arms. I felt completely useless and taken aback by this unexpected turn of events. Pipe looked up at me in bafflement, gently patting Katie's back as she finally wound down into a few last hiccupping sobs, then accepted a tattered Kleenex from the pocket of Pipe's jeans.

"Blow," Pipe told her. Katie complied, then wiped her face on the sleeve of Pipe's hoodie. Five points for Pipe—she didn't flinch.

"What was that all about?" Pipe asked Katie conversationally, the child now standing in the protective circle of her arms. Katie turned to face me, but made sure I was between her and the man on the porch.

Oh my god. The Man On The Porch. The hair on the back of my neck rose as I remembered Katie saying those very words to me the night before…

"I told you," Katie was saying to me now, somewhat accusingly. "I told you we were going to get in trouble."

"What?" Now I was baffled. "In trouble for what?"

The waterworks were starting again. "'Cause it's S-s-sunday and we're 'posed to go to church and we didn't g-go and now we're in t-t-t-trouble…" She wrapped her arms around Pipe's neck again, who rose, with some difficulty, the kid clinging to her like a limpet.

"Busted," Pipe said to me with a small grin, shaking her head.

I reached out for Katie and she handed her to me. Katie transferred without complaint, burying her face in my shoulder.

"Katie," I said in her ear. "We're not in trouble, I promise."

She lifted a tear-stained face to me.

"Promise?" she said, dubious.

"Promise," I said solemnly. I used the sleeve of my shirt to wipe her face, then got a laugh out of her with a witty remark about boogers. I gave her a quick hug and a kiss and set her back down on her feet. Whereupon she immediately claimed a hug from Pipe as well.

That little drama having been resolved, I was finally able to ask the question.

"Katie, do you know that guy? Is he from the church?"

She nodded. The man on the porch was on his feet now, having seen us. He took a few steps into the yard, then stood there, waiting for us.

"What's his name?"

She shrugged. "I don't know. He's a Church Man." Her inflection capitalized it.

Pipe asked her, "Did your daddy know him?"

"Yes," Katie answered.

Pipe and I exchanged a look.

"Well," I said. "I guess I better go talk to him."

The three of us walked to James's cabin. The man eyed me and Pipe as we approached and seemed to reach a decision.

"Miss McPeake?" he said directly to me. I guess the family resemblance was there.

"Yes?"

"My name is Daniel. I'm from the Church of the Benevolent Fount."

"How do you do?" I responded and shook his hand, which was cold, dry and bony.

He clasped my palm in both of his, his dark eyes pinning me with a mournful look. He looked to be in his forties, tall and ectomorphic. A long nose, droopy earlobes and five o'clock shadow somehow contrived to give him a basset hound look. He was wearing a dark suit, white shirt and surprisingly tasteful dark red tie with a subdued paisley pattern. A class ring with a big red stone adorned one of his fingers.

"My sincere condolences on the loss of your brother, Miss McPeake. James will be much missed by our congregation."

My hand felt lost between his big paws. I retrieved it with some difficulty.

"Thank you, Daniel. And please call me Madison. Are you the pastor?" I wasn't sure if that was the right term, but whatever.

His face moved as if I had offended him, but he answered civilly enough.

"No, we don't believe only one soul should lead us. All men who are righteous shall take their turns."

I glanced over at Pipe to see how she was taking this in. Her face reflected nothing but mild and benign interest. She returned my gaze blandly, but I could still feel that palpable force between us. Something at the back of the eyes, that something that was just for me. How could I know her so well when I'd only just met her?

She took that moment to take her leave, telling me she'd be in her cabin for a while before heading up to the lab to do some work. I told her we'd be leaving soon, but would say goodbye before we left. She nodded at me, then at Daniel, then held out her hand for a low five from Katie, who promptly swatted it. Obviously a double act of long-standing. Pipe went over to her place. Katie was standing to the side of and slightly behind me. She had a hold of my pants leg with one hand.

I turned my attention back to the visitor.

"So, what brings you down here today, Daniel?" I asked him. Although I had a pretty good idea. The will. I was tempted to add "on Sunday" to the end of my question, but restrained myself. Church people make me snappish. It's probably not their fault.

"We wanted to pay our respects," he said. The words were all right, but there was something in the delivery that left me in no doubt that I had been judged and found lacking. Again.

"Katie," I said to my niece, "why don't you ride your trike some more while I talk with Daniel here?"

"I don't wanna," she said, tightening her grip on my pants leg, her gaze fixed on the middle distance.

I went down to her level, turning my back on Daniel. The hair on the back of my neck rose again.

"It's okay, sweetie," I said, making eye contact. "Don't you want to ride your trike?" I used my very best Director-of-Training-with-a-reluctant-trainee tone, but she was having none

143

of it.

"No." She said it under her breath, flicking her eyes amongst me, the ground and the man behind me.

I took a breath. "How about you play on the porch then?"

"Can I play in the house?"

"No," I said, more sharply than I intended to. I did not want her alone in that place. Her face started to crumple—tears were imminent.

I picked her up. "Come on," I said softly in her ear. "It's okay."

She looked back at me, lower lip quivering, tears magnifying the big blue eyes.

I said to Daniel, "Give me a minute" and took Katie up to the porch, depositing her in the chair with Babs. It took more than a minute, but I got her going on a tea party with Babs, with rocks and shells predominant on the menu. While we haggled over the details—and trust me, there were many—I peripherally noticed Bohannon and his dog reappear, get in his truck and drive away. Thankfully, he did not intrude on us further. God knows what I would have said to the old SOB by that point. Katie was too absorbed in filling her teapot—a green plastic watering can unearthed from beside the steps—from the faucet on the side of the cabin to notice him or the dog before he was roaring up the hill in a cloud of exhaust.

Finally, she was set and pouring "tea" for her pachyderm pal into an abalone cup while daintily proffering a scrumptious selection of petit fours. Also known as dirt clods. (I sincerely hope they were dirt clods.) The hostess thus occupied, I was free to return to Daniel at the foot of the walk, which was sufficiently out of earshot given the ever present background noise of the ocean, the wind and the gulls. Big feet, I noted disjointedly as I walked up to him.

"So what's up?" I said to him curtly.

He again looked like he tasted earwax, but I didn't feel like wasting a lot of perfunctory etiquette on him. I wanted him to say his piece and be gone, so I could load up the kid and head to a hotel. ASAP.

The foul smell—what the hell was that anyway? sewage? rotting seaweed?—was faintly back on the breeze. Just a hint at the back of the throat, really. Nasty.

I squinted up at Daniel, towering over me in his suit and disdain.

"I hate to bring this up at such a time…" he started.

"Just spit it out," I encouraged him.

He considered me for a moment, then got on with it.

"The will."

"The will," I agreed.

"As a God-fearing member of our congregation, Brother James left everything to the Church of the Benevolent Fount."

"Yes, he did," I agreed. Daniel tilted his head and looked at me quizzically—he evidently wasn't expecting such an easy victory. But there was no point arguing—not at that moment, with that man. I'd talk to the attorney the next day and then we'd see.

"So, I'll be taking the girl," he said. The sun was slanting down sideways, obstructing my view of him. Time stopped for a moment while I tried to process what he'd said. So I'll be taking the girl… Some kind of gut-level rage scorched through my veins, energizing me. Did this preposterous skeleton think I'd hand over my family to him? My voice came out hoarse and low.

"What did you say to me?"

For all his lugubrious height, he took a step back at my tone and words. My feet took a step forward of their own accord as my voice rose.

"Miss McPeake, please…" he said.

"You get the hell out of here." All of my hovering anger/depression/headache/need for a drink/stress/anxiety just launched itself out of my chest at his face. He took another step back, trying to say something. He was backed up against his own car now, holding out his hands to calm me down. Some small part of me noticed that Katie was on her feet on the porch watching us, the water can in her hands, but forgotten. Pipe came out on her porch too, as if to complete some needed symmetry. Her screen door slammed shut behind her. No water can in her hand—instead, she had a baseball bat casually propped over one shoulder. She looked like she'd be good with it. She was looking unswervingly at Daniel. He glanced over at her, then back at me.

"I assure you, Miss McPeake—"

"You assure me what?" I interrupted him, my blood still boiling at his outrageous statement.

"Like I said, Brother James left everything to the Church. Everything. All his property."

"Katie is not property." My words were icily spaced apart so there was no misunderstanding between us.

"We believe differently. Children are the vassals of the Lord and the lambs of the Church. James wanted it so. He *willed* it so," he said, with emphasis.

He was still backed up against his car. I could only think of one thing to say. I took another step forward so I was right up in his face.

"Get the fuck out of here. I'll see you in court."

"I have the right to—" he tried to say.

"You have the right to drive away before I beat you to death with my friend's baseball bat," I said. "I'll see you in hell before you lay a finger on that child."

His face darkened. He'd been halfway trying to placate me before. Like a switch had been flipped, I saw him summon his own anger as he loomed over me. He seemed to swell and grow another six inches. His shadow crossed over me.

"You will see us. In court. That child is ours now, by law. We've won this fight before," he said, chillingly.

Pipe came down her steps. I paused her with a flick of a glance.

"Beat it," I said to the man.

He went around to the other side of the car and opened the driver's door. He pointed a long finger at me over the top of the car and couldn't resist a doleful parting shot. "The wages of sin

146

are death, missy."

I was so angry I was spitting. It would have been great, no doubt, to come back with some devastating Bible quote, but I was fresh out. Clearly, there was no choice but to cuss him up one side and down the other.

"Go fuck yourself, you self-righteous vulture of a bastard."

He stared at me for a minute, but got in the car and slowly drove off up the hill, the automatic transmission downshifting as the big vehicle labored to ascend the steep incline.

Katie ran down to my side and grabbed my leg like she'd never let go. I put my hand on her head, murmuring "It's okay, it's okay…"

Pipe crossed over too, dropping the bat as she reached my side. "Jesus H., Mad…" she said. "You're shakin'…"

I turned to her blindly. And found myself in the fierce protective clasp of her embrace, Katie still glued to my right leg. I wanted to melt into Pipe, it felt so good. So right. Her face was in my hair, whispering words of comfort I couldn't quite catch. I held onto both of them for dear life, for I don't know how long.

Chapter 18

The afternoon had turned cold, the fog rolling in out of nowhere. Pipe let me go and brushed a strand of hair off my forehead, her hand lingering warmly on my cheek for a moment. She smiled into my eyes and after a second, I gave her a feeble smile back. She pried Katie off my leg without too much problem and swung her around in a circle, which immediately brought out the giggles, as I'm sure she planned. Set back on her own feet, Katie grabbed Pipe's hand and mine and declared "tea party!" in a tone that brooked no argument.

The three of us trudged up to the porch and took our places around the upended milk crate doing duty as a table. Katie resumed her own seat, Pipe shared a chair with Babs and I was surprised to find there was another guest present in my chair—a little plastic baby doll, maybe four inches long, with unblinking blue eyes and long lashes. And dressed in a deep red velvet dress, a hair ribbon of the same material and black leather shoes that would require a buttonhook.

"Oh, shh…oot," Pipe said, half laughing as I held it up for her to see, Babs on her knee.

Katie was busy pouring tea into our shells and didn't look up until I spoke to her.

"Katie."

"Huh?" She saw the baby doll in my hand. "Oh."

"Yes, oh. Where did you get this doll, young lady?"

"I…phunumph…" Her words were muffled as she turned her head away from me.

"Katie," I said, lengthening the syllables to about three seconds apiece.

Suddenly struck by inspiration, she turned brightly back to me.

"I borrowed it!" she said.

"From whom?" I inquired.

"From Mr. B."

I glanced at Pipe, who seemed to be having trouble repressing a large amount of laughter. Her eyes sparkled as she told me, "He's gonna be peeved."

I shook my head at both of them wearily. Great—crazy aunt and klepto kid. Just great. Sensing she was off the hook, Katie leaned forward and plucked the doll out of my grasp, crooning to it as she smoothed the tiny skirts and made a minute adjustment to the ribbon. I shrugged it off as too far down the list of problems to deal with now. I'd get Pipe to return it to Bohannon later, hopefully undamaged. In the meantime…

Five minutes of tea party was enough to make me wish one of those famous California earthquakes would open up the ground and swallow us whole, but no such luck. I sat across from Pipe, not touching, but so close. I felt torn in several different directions. I needed a minute to catch my breath after the encounter with Daniel, but I hadn't forgotten my vow to get Katie and myself off the Point as soon as possible. I knew she was going to throw a total wingding when I not only declared the tea party over, but that we were leaving. And every second was a tick of the clock that brought me closer to parting from Pipe, perhaps forever. I felt weak for a moment, drained of the strength I needed to make that break.

Pipe glanced at me, then made a show of draining her seashell. She stood up and said, "Well, thanks a lot, Katiekins, but I've got some work to do up at the lab."

The wingding started to kick in, but I temporarily diverted the kid by suggesting she make up imaginary doggie bags for Babs and the doll while I said goodbye to Pipe.

Goodbye. The word had an awful finality about it. The two of us walked down to the end of the sidewalk.

"I guess you two will be taking off now," she said. She gazed past me to the porch, where Katie was roundly berating Babs for taking too big a piece of cake. (For gosh sakes, girl, she's an elephant!)

"Yeah," I responded, "I need to find a hotel…" My voice trailed off, my voice suddenly small and choked.

Pipe had turned to stare off toward the fog rolling down the hillside toward us. Her profile was expressionless, dispassionate even. Why wouldn't she look at me?

"Pipe," I said. She flicked me a glance. I stumbled on. "I…I…"

She finally turned to face me, but I didn't know what to say. Say what's in your heart, stupid, the little voice in my head ordered me. But I always screw that up, I said back. Too bad, it said. Scathingly, I might add. End of transmission from the little voice. I folded my arms. It really was getting cold now with the fog rolling in ever more heavily.

I tried again. "Pipe, I…I guess I don't want this to be goodbye," I finally blurted out.

She smiled at me then. Slowly, at first and then the full effect with the eyes and everything. Only the greatest smile ever.

"You guess?" she said. Somehow, it was easier with her mocking me.

"Well, no, I don't. In fact, I'm quite certain I *know*," I said, much more definitely.

"Well, then, that's all right," she said and pulled me in tight for a serious kiss.

I hadn't really made my mind up about the decorum of public displays of affection in front of the child, never having had to consider that issue before, but frankly, that part of my brain flew right out the window when she put her hands on me, so I didn't really get a say in the matter. A little flustered by the unexpected PDA, I cast an eye over at Katie, but she was merely incuriously watching our exchange as she cleared the table by throwing everything except the two toys into the bushes.

Pipe reached into her back pocket and pulled out a slip of paper. Handing it to me, she said, "You can reach me at this number up at the lab. Why don't you give me a call once you're settled at the hotel? Maybe we can get together before you guys go back to Boston."

Get together—I liked the sound of that. I assured her I would phone. She called out a farewell to Katie, waving goodbye as she headed for her truck. Katie waved back, running down the sidewalk to stand beside me as we watched Pipe disappear into the thick, gray-white fog which almost immediately muffled the sound of her engine.

Chapter 19

Fortunately, we didn't have that much luggage, so it was relatively easy to unearth our denim jackets and my Niners cap from the bags in the Jeep. I mentally swore as I realized I should have enlisted Pipe's help to put the top up on the vehicle. Dang. Another freezing ride in the mist, with that foul odor also now returning to light our way. Well, hopefully, we'd be back in the sunshine and fresh air once we got off the Point. Katie was up for a ride in the car, although she wasn't so sure about the hotel part.

"'Cause we're coming back later, right?" she kept asking me. My ambivalent non answers were making her suspicious, but I played the ice cream card again to good effect. Great, that ought to get me through the elementary school years, then I could promise her a pony or a car... I put aside the question of my low character (easily done, as always) and focused on the task at hand. Getting the two of us up the hill in a dense fog and off this godforsaken peninsula forever.

I made sure we were both securely strapped in, adjusted the

rearview mirror slightly and turned the key.

A low grinding noise was the only result.

I tried it again, with the same outcome. Crap. I called upon all the powers of Heaven and Earth, made several exceedingly rash promises to the Almighty and begged for it to start. Please please please.

I turned the key. Nothing at all this time. Nothing.

"Are we going?" said my passenger.

Think, I told myself. It's just a dead battery—happens all the time. So how do people solve this problem? Duh, they call Triple A. Except my cell phone didn't work out here. I looked longingly over at James's vehicle, but I hadn't ever come across his keys. They were probably at the bottom of the ocean somewhere. His car no doubt had a perfectly good battery in it...if I could pop the hood, I could swap it with the Jeep's...except I'd have to break the window to pop the hood. Pipe's Louisville slugger was still laying in the yard, but I doubted my ability to break safety glass with a wooden baseball bat. Plus, what did I know about car batteries? I'd no doubt electrocute myself just trying to get it out of James's car, let alone install it properly in the Jeep. It might not even be the right kind. Do those things come in different sizes?

"Madison?" The peanut gallery was restless.

"Just a sec, kiddo, let me think..."

I tried the key again, but it was dead as a doornail. The fog was swirling so heavily around us, it was hard to tell what time of day it was, but I knew the sun had begun its westerly descent. I had to get us out of there before dark, I knew that much. I could wait until Pipe came back and have her jumpstart the Jeep (assuming she had cables, but she seemed like the kind of girl who would), but who knew when she'd be back? The clock was ticking. I could only think of one thing to do.

I undid my seat belt and twisted around in my seat to face Katie, who was waiting expectantly for me to be the adult and fix everything.

"Come on," I said. "We gotta walk."

Chapter 20

The tramp of our footsteps was the only sound in the fog-deadened landscape. The only direction I needed to know was up, which was good, as I had no idea about left, right, north or south in the pea soup we now found ourselves in. Occasional missteps into the bushes that lined the sides of the road let me know when we were off track. Katie didn't want to hold my hand after the first minute or two, but I made sure she was close so I didn't lose sight of her.

I hadn't even bothered with any luggage beyond our toothbrushes, my purse and Katie's little backpack, in which she was transporting Babs.

Up we climbed the weary winding road. I checked my watch to see how long we'd been walking, but beads of moisture inside the face told the tale. The watch had stopped at 2:47 and was as dead as the car battery. Damn.

Katie was prancing a few steps ahead of me, just about merging into the mist. At first the fog had seemed solid and impenetrable, but as we advanced, it took on a different character. There were currents and eddies inside it, though I felt no breeze. If I looked straight at it, all I saw was white, but there were wisps and swirls of unseen figures moving just outside my peripheral vision... I knew it was just the fog playing tricks on my eyes, but still...

Sound was odd too. It was like being in a jar of cotton balls—hard to tell which direction sounds were coming from. At first, the only sound was our own footsteps, but as we climbed higher, I could hear...something. Something like the muffled sibilance of the voices I'd heard the first night outside the cabin. Never quite close enough to make out words or intent, just tantalizingly beyond the limits of my hearing. The fog owned the sights and sounds. And the clammy coldness of it was creeping into my chest.

Katie stepped into a big white puff of it and disappeared from view.

"Katie!" I called out. She shrieked, once, then was silent.

"Katie!" I yelled, leaping ahead to get to where she was. I almost missed her since I was smack in the middle of the road. She was off to one edge, tangled up in a pricker bush that had snagged her hair, her backpack and her jacket. I extricated her with some difficulty and we both ended up with an "Oomph," me on my backside, her on top of me.

"Are you okay?" I asked, dusting her off as best I could. She nodded, holding tight to my lapels. Apart from a few scratches on her hands, she seemed unhurt.

"Madison," she said.

"Uh-huh," I answered, doing the classic Mom lick-the-ball-of-the-thumb-and-apply-it-to-the-dirty-spot-on-the-kid's-face thing. When she didn't respond, I stopped and gave her my full attention.

She stared straight back.

"Well, what?" I said, patiently.

"He pushed me," she said. "He never pushed me before, but

he pushed me right in that pricker bush." She wasn't frightened or injured, just…miffed.

Startled, I looked around, but could only see a wall of white. I stood up. This time, she took my hand with no complaint.

"Who?" I said, although I had a fair idea of the answer.

"The man from the porch," she said.

"Is he still around?" I asked.

"You never know," she said, unnervingly.

Great. Well, malevolent phantoms aside, we still had to get to the top of this hill and call a cab or Triple A or the cavalry or somebody. If I'd been by myself, I would have succumbed to total panic long before then, but with Katie to take care of, all I could think was we had to make it topside. I got us moving again, although it felt like we'd been hiking for ages already. Where was the top of the hill? It couldn't be that far. Even if hadn't been for Delgado's snake warning, there was no question of leaving the road in such poor visibility.

Up we climbed. My legs felt like lead. But my breath was coming a little easier. At least I wasn't missing any workouts on this trip. Sheesh. I realized the road was flattening out. Was that the kiosk up ahead? I squinted, trying to make out shapes in the fog. Was that the Latina with her rifle slung across her back? Why didn't they have any lights on?

"Hello?" I called out, but the fog threw the word right back at me, dull and quiet and insubstantial. A hundred more paces, but whatever I thought I saw was no closer and no clearer. Plus the road hung a curve and started going up again.

And where was the foghorn? Wasn't this exactly why they built such a contraption in the first place? As soon as I thought that, I heard its plaintive bellow. It sounded close. It mooed again, even louder this time. Its light swept above us, momentarily illuminating the drops of moisture in the mist. The stench was thickening too, to match the fog. The wetness seemed to bring it out.

"Man, what is that smell?" I said in exasperation, not really expecting an answer from Katie.

"It's the dead people," she said.

"What?"

"All the dead people. In the graveyard, on top."

I caught a vivid mental image of all those clean symmetrical rows of white crosses on green grass.

"No, sweetie," I said, though. "I don't think that's it."

"It is," she insisted. "That's what all the kids at my school say. It's The Dead Bodies Rotting In San Cerros," she said, obviously reciting a line she'd learned by rote. I gave it up. It didn't seem like the time to argue the point.

Could we possibly be going in circles? Surely I would notice if our steps were headed downward... Katie shrieked again, pointing at me.

"*What?*" I cried, then realized she was pointing at my sleeve. I sensed, more than saw, the good-sized spider just above my wrist. With a strangled squawk, I brushed it onto the ground. Where it lay still and unmoving. It had been dead before I touched it, I realized. We both stood and gawked at it for a second, then silently moved on.

Other small dead things began to appear in the road every few feet. Bugs. A sparrow, its wings broken and awkwardly unfolded. Two lizards with their tails missing. A possum, its neck at an impossible angle. Then we saw the snake.

I took Katie's hand as we abruptly stopped. The smell was bad now. The snake was partly on, partly off the roadway, its head in the bushes. It was a dusty brown, with lighter markings and underbelly, about as big around as my wrist. I couldn't tell how long it was, but a good three feet of it was on the road. Was it dead? I tried to get Katie moving to the far side of the road so we could pass, but she didn't want to go. We struggled, silently, her doggedly and me gently, for a few seconds, then I let her go.

Maybe we should just go back, I thought.

The fog stirred and roiled ahead. For a fleeting second, I thought I saw two men walking toward us...with short pigtails, bare feet and pants cut off just below the knee…the figures dissolved into white. Just more fog, trying to mess with me, right? The sibilance grew louder, a crescendo of white noise heightening to a deafening growl as the lighthouse pinned us with its deadly beam—

I grabbed Katie and threw her sidelong into the bushes, then dove after her desperately as a vehicle suddenly roared out of the mist, mere feet from mowing us down.

Gravel sprayed us as the driver hit the brakes, the backside spinning around within inches of my feet. The violence of the sudden attempt to stop wrenched it completely around, headlights pointing up the hill, the back in the ditch on the far side, the whole thing precariously balanced on its two right tires for an eternity of a moment, then with a screeching crash it toppled over into the bushes off the road. The engine roared for a second and then cut abruptly. The only sound in the cold white silence was the ticking of hot metal and the smashing of my heart against my ribs.

Chapter 21

"Katie!" I cried, pulling myself off her. She was staring right back up at me, her face white and her eyes as big as saucers, but she didn't say anything.

I did a quick check for broken bones and missing limbs (both hers and mine), but we were both more or less intact. No blood that I could see either.

"Are you okay?" I said to her. I could smell gasoline. I heard a muffled thud from the wreck as if someone was trying to kick the door open from the inside.

She nodded, mutely, then said something I couldn't make out. She struggled to arise.

"What, sweetie?" I helped her sit up and put my ear to her lips.

"Pipe…" she breathed.

Holding her tight, my head swiveled back to the wreck. Jesus, she was right, it was Pipe's truck. The muffled thud came again, more insistent this time. I hauled myself to my feet, picking up Katie at the same time and ran over there, adrenaline pumping.

"Pipe!" I screamed. The gasoline smell was strong enough now to block out the stench.

"Pipe!" Her truck was completely flipped over, one tire still lazily spinning as the fog swirled about it. It lay at an angle, with the passenger side propped up on the edge of the roadway, the driver's side down into the brush which sloped away from the road. Every instinct told me to get Katie away from such a dangerous scene, but there was no way I was letting her go in that fog again alone. But Pipe was stuck in there…

"Madison? Is that you?" she yelled out. "Are you okay?"

"We're fine, but we've got to get you out. Where are you?"

"If you can get the passenger door open, I think I can wriggle out. You pull and I'll kick, okay?"

At least she sounded okay. But I'd have to put Katie down to pull on the door. I turned to her.

"Katiekins, I'm going to set you down, but you hold tight to my leg, all right? You got that? Don't let go of my leg. We're going to get Pipe out of here right now, okay?"

She looked about as okay as I felt, but slid down the length of me and grabbed my leg as tight as she could with both arms. I smoothed the hair on top of her head and told her she was doing great.

I yelled encouragement to Pipe, who was kicking away with gusto and heaved on the door handle with all my might. It took a few tries, but I finally managed to pull her out of there like a breeched calf. We all three stumbled back to the road and downhill a good fifty feet or so before collapsing in a pile. All three of us were covered in dirt, streaked with oil, wet with fog and in general, a mess. Pipe had a small cut near her hairline that had bled a bit, but didn't look too serious.

The fog, if anything, had intensified. When I looked back up the road toward the truck, I couldn't see a thing—just a solid wall of white. It seemed slightly less impenetrable down the hill. We took a minute to reassure ourselves we truly all were in one piece and assess the situation.

I tried to explain to Pipe about the dead battery and walking up the hill, but didn't get more than two sentences out before I found myself sobbing like a child, knowing she'd think I was a lunatic but unable to control myself anyhow.

"Hey, hey now," she said, sounding a little alarmed as she cradled my head on her shoulder, her other arm around Katie, who still hadn't said a word out loud.

One or the other McPeakes was always crying on her, she must have been thinking. I struggled to regain some semblance of composure. A few more gulps, snorts and ragged deep breaths brought me back to the other side of the brink. I wiped my nose on my sleeve (a lot of that going on this weekend too) and sat up.

She tucked my hair behind my ear, then ran her fingers down my cheek. "Better?" she said.

"Sorry. I'm having a…a really bad week," I said seriously.

To which she laughed out loud. "You think?" she said.

And I couldn't help but laugh too.

"Fuck…" It got away from me before I could engage the censor. Oh, well. Somebody take ten points off my score. I glanced at Katie, who was kneeling, kind of rigidly, with one hand on my shoulder and the other on Pipe's sleeve, her gaze pinned uphill on the fog.

"Y'all right there, Katie cakes?" Pipe said to her.

She dragged her gaze back to Pipe.

"There's blood on your face," she said, her voice tight and small.

"Shoot," Pipe drawled. "That ain't nothing, Katie Lou. One time I was out there surfin' and my board broke in two and it smacked me right…in…the….*butt*!"

The dramatic emphasis employed by the speaker on the last word of the sentence greatly added to the effect. In any event, it reassured Katie enough to produce a half-hearted smile. Pipe reached out to hug her and she reciprocated. Pipe gave me a

161

mock grimace over her shoulder and tested the now tacky blood on her forehead with her free hand, then wiped it on the back of her jeans as she stood herself and Katie up.

"I believe it's about time we headed home, don't you think?" she said to me, extending a hand to pull me up. She pulled a tissue out of her pocket, spat on it and began dabbing at her forehead.

"Uh…no," I said, as I semi-gracefully rose to my feet. "We're going to a hotel," I said, a little more shakily than I'd hoped to. When I make a plan, people, I'm telling you, It's A Plan.

"Madison," she said, in a tone that said I Just Wrecked My Truck In The Impenetrable Fog For You And Nearly Killed All of Us, Dumbass. And also somehow said…well, I can't really tell you, but it was kind of dirty in a nice way, if you know what I mean.

I would've argued a lot longer, but I couldn't help but notice that solid wall of fog was inching ever closer to us and besides, she was right. Where the hell did I think I was going with her car wrecked and mine dead? Walking was clearly not an option, what with the dead stuff and the ghosts or visions or whatever I'd been seeing in the mist. The light had grown noticeably more dim since we'd started up the hill, so sunset couldn't be too far away. Something told me we'd better be back inside Pipe's cabin before night fell.

Chapter 22

Strangely, it only took us about twenty minutes to walk back down to the cabins once we pulled ourselves together. It was as if Pipe's return brought time back to normal too. With her accompanying us, the walk back down was uneventful. The fog was still thick, though. I was sick of it—sick of its whiteness, its wetness, its clammy suffocation of the landscape. I longed for blue sky and a return to feeling like I was at least halfway in control of things.

I tried to apologize to Pipe for wrecking her truck, but she waved that off. I thought that was amazingly gracious of her, considering it was probably totaled. I vowed to pay her back, nonetheless.

"Oh, heck, I never thought it was going to make it all the way to Frisco anyhow," she said.

"Uh…Frisco?" I said.

"Didn't I tell you?"

By now, the three of us were striding abreast down the dirt road with Katie in the middle. We took an easy pace to accommodate Pipe's new limp, which she claimed was nothing.

She continued her explanation. "Well, I told you my year here is just about up, right?"

I nodded.

"Well, lucky for me, I got a new job lined up that starts next month in San Francisco. Steinhart Aquarium, as a matter of fact."

"Wow!" I was impressed. Steinhart's a big deal in San Francisco.

"You've heard of it?" she asked.

I could tell she was pleased, but didn't want to act like she was bragging. "Yeah, I've heard of it! I'm *from* San Francisco," I told her.

"I thought you were from Boston."

"I live in Boston, but I grew up in San Francisco."

"Huh," she said—an exhalation that seemed to cover the "small world" and "whodathunkit" bases equally. She gave me a sidelong glance before asking her next question.

"You ever think about moving back?"

I looked over at her. Her eyes were pinned to the road ahead. Katie was bopping along between us, no worse for wear despite the various tumbles she'd taken and seemingly not paying any mind to our conversation. I decided to play it cool.

"All the time," I said, as nonchalantly as I could manage. She gave me a quick and indecipherable smile.

The cabins were still hidden by the mist, but the road ten feet ahead of us was petering out into the gravel parking area. For lack of a better word, we were home.

Chapter 23

The darkness was gathering under the trees and in the shadows. The Explorer was still there, but my rental Jeep had rolled backward into James's front yard, slamming into the side of the house with enough force to knock one of the porch pillars askew. The fog crept up the steps in tentative tendrils.

Had I left the brake off? Left it in neutral or reverse? I didn't think so. As I recalled, I couldn't even get the damn thing to turn over, much less have a reason to shift it out of first, the gear I'd left it parked in.

I could feel Pipe looking at me. Sideways. But not saying anything.

"We're not going in there," I said. We stood on the gravel between her cabin and James's, eyeing the damage to his place.

"No reason," she agreed. "We can all stay at my place tonight."

I looked at her. She looked straight back.

"I left the brake on," I said.

She nodded.

"You guys need anything out of the Jeep?" she asked.

I didn't even want to set foot in the yard. I looked down at Katie, who was holding my hand tightly. She shivered and shook her head.

"Not as long as we can borrow some pajamas and toothpaste," I said to Pipe.

"Oh, I got toothpaste," she said, with that devilish glint in her eye.

Chapter 24

The clock said six thirty-six when we trooped into Pipe's cabin. Both the fog and the darkness swirled about us as we climbed wearily up her steps. I couldn't recall the last time I'd felt so tired. I dreaded spending another night on Shadow Point, but was trying to keep a brave face for Katie.

She, on the other hand, was fucking thrilled to be doing a sleepover at her best friend Pipe's house. Which she'd apparently never done before. I'm sure James would have never allowed that. Katie was full of energy, zipping from spot to spot, room to room, touching all of Pipe's possessions and brimming with a zillion questions.

"Sorry," I said to Pipe in the kitchen, whilst Katie was rummaging through her stuff in the living room.

"It's fine." She laughed. "I got nephews and nieces and they're all the same."

The cut on her forehead had been addressed with a small

bandage. All three of us having washed our hands and faces, we were now working to come up with an evening meal. And by we, I mean her, since I was worthless in the kitchen unless it involved a corkscrew or a microwave and Katie was busy doing her Tasmanian devil routine.

"Pipe!" Katie called.

"Yes, ma'am," she responded, looking up from the potato she was peeling in the sink.

Katie appeared in the doorway of the kitchen, vibrating with excitement. It seemed she had found Pipe's meager supply of DVDs on the bottom shelf of the bookcase in the living room. I knew she and James had had no TV set in their cabin. Even if reception were possible, I guessed James would not have owned a TV with its nonstop cavalcade of sin and vice. But Katie had apparently seen some TV or videos in nursery school, because she knew exactly what the DVDs were.

"Can I watch a movie?" she asked, already hyperexcited. Oh, Lord.

Pipe turned and gave me the arched eyebrow, so I joined the two of them as they sat down on the living room floor to investigate her find. Which was an interesting mix of R-rated post-apocalyptic action movies and romantic girl-meets-girl thrillers, none of which were suitable for a five year-old.

But, thank God, further investigation revealed one last DVD that was a compilation of some old Jacques Cousteau National Geographic specials. We set Katie up with that one on Pipe's laptop, after extracting severe promises to not touch anything on the computer. She was immediately enthralled and completely lost to us. We propped her up on the chair by the corner table, with the help of a few cushions to achieve the needed height. Her mouth open, she was entranced by Jacques and the rest of that crazy Calypso crew. I made a mental note to cancel everything except basic cable back in Boston.

Back in the kitchen, Pipe now had the spuds merrily boiling in a saucepan on the stove. To go with those, we had hot dogs and buns left over from the night before, some watermelon and half a carton of Neapolitan ice cream. What more could an unanticipated houseguest hope for? A cigarette and a glass of wine, that's what, but I was trying to deal with both of those cravings by frenetically crunching on the ice left in my glass of Coke. I could not stop thinking about the wine coolers and beer I'd seen in her fridge the night before.

Jacques's unmistakable nasal monotone was droning on in the adjoining room, but the silence, I thought, was becoming a little awkward in the kitchen. Besides my serious jonesing, I was (a) totally freaked out by our walk-in-the-haunted-fog slash brush-with-death slash poltergeist-Jeep-crash, you name it, not to mention (b) nervous as hell about spending the night. Where exactly was everybody going to sleep?

Pipe turned the heat down on the stove and put the lid on the saucepan and told me we had about another ten minutes or so until it was time to fire up the wienies. I'd gone back to sitting on the opposite counter and chewing my ice, ignoring the refrigerator with all my might when she opened it to retrieve the watermelon. I felt exhausted and keyed up at the same time— what do they call that? Oh, yeah. Strung out. Great, Mad. Just fucking great.

I crossed and then uncrossed my ankles to keep myself from drumming my heels on the cabinet doors, contenting myself with more ice swirling instead. Pipe had her back to me again, slicing the melon into a bowl in the sink. She'd taken her hoodie off when we came in, revealing a threadbare, form-fitting, John Deere T-shirt. On her, threadbare and form-fitting were definitely good things. The backs of her arms were slender, yet defined. All that surfing, no doubt. I decided it was nice she was domestic. Very unlike the kind of girls I usually ended up with, though. They were, well, more like me. And since I kind of hated me, it was nice to meet somebody different. I couldn't recall the last time someone had peeled and boiled a potato for me. Great ass too.

As if reading my thoughts, she turned around at that very moment, drying her hands on a kitchen towel and said to me, "Are you staring at my butt?"

But she was smiling. I couldn't think of a thing to say. Damn, she was cute. And there I was, dumbstruck, swirling my ice like a madwoman.

She walked up to me and pried the glass loose from my hand, setting it down on the counter. I could hear Jacques talking about kelp. I put both hands down on the countertop for support since I was feeling a little dizzy anyway. She put one hand on the counter too, the other on her hip. Her face was tilted up toward mine as she gazed at me assessingly. She wasn't touching me, but there were a lot of body parts in awful close proximity. But. Not. Quite. Touching. I thought I might implode. My thighs were on the verge of trembling. She seemed to sense that and put her right hand on my left knee, watching me carefully all the while. The slight, deft pressure of her thumb on the inside of my leg afforded a small opening into which her body insinuated itself. The hand slid up my thigh, the other one somehow now at my waist, warm fingertips just under my shirt. I felt liquefied, feverish, paralyzed with my desire for her.

Her lips brushing my throat, she spoke a few inches below my ear.

"I'm gonna go jump in the shower now."

A quiver shook me as the hand at my waistband delicately ventured south a quarter inch or so.

"Don't."

"Don't...what?" she breathed, those fingertips now slowly wending their way up my lumbar spine.

"Don't leave us."

She backed off a whole two inches so she could tilt her face up to mine again, quizzically. I took advantage of that partial withdrawal to slide myself forward and down off the counter, forcing her to back up another step. I planted my feet as firmly as I could on the kitchen floor, my butt braced against the counter.

The light-headed feeling persisted. My hands at her waist, I drew her in. Her hands went gently around my neck.

"Madison…" she said.

I couldn't help it. I felt safe when she was with me. The bad things happened when she wasn't. I was keenly aware how the small lighted square of the cabin must appear within the wilderness of Stygian darkness and impenetrable fog and the burnt-out hulk of the lighthouse not far off in the blackness.

I was so tired. My hands, of their own volition, slid up to the small of her back. I laid my head on her shoulder. Her neck smelled nothing short of wonderful.

"Don't go," I whispered.

She pulled me tight.

"You're safe here, Mad. You and Katie both. The door is locked. The windows are locked. We're okay, baby," she said, rocking me gently.

And I believed her.

Chapter 25

The fog turned to rain sometime in the night.

I heard it pattering on the roof when I awoke somewhere around two or three. Pipe's naked body felt soft and warm and strong in my arms. I could feel her steady breathing.

The rain had washed away the foul odor. Her bedroom smelled like a combination of all the good things I've ever smelled. Like peach upside down cake...and Coppertone...and leather...and my favorite pineapple cilantro candle...and clean laundry and ocean air...

We'd got through our makeshift dinner without incident, especially since we let Jacques continue to roll throughout. The kid was freaking mesmerized by a 1969 National Geographic special about freaking seaweed. Maybe it was in the genes.

Katie was fully crashed by eight thirty and passed out in the loveseat with a chenille throw tossed over her for comfort as much as warmth, Babs by her side.

I tried to be a good guest and do the dishes, with Pipe drying, but the dishwashing kept getting interrupted by French kissing and other immodesties. By the time I got her T-shirt peeled off and the first two buttons of her 501s undone, we abandoned the dishes and made our way to her tiny bedroom. Somewhere in the night, she'd slipped in there to light a couple of candles and put a CD in the player with the volume way down. She stretched up to hit play as she arched her hips for me to slide her bikini briefs off.

Chapter 26

Monday morning was painfully bright and clear, with water dripping off the eaves and the sunlight dazzling as it reflected off the dew in the grass. It was almost like Mother Nature was playing a little joke on us, acting like none of that stuff had happened on Sunday. Fog? Stench? Paranormal occurrences? Nahhhh…

The Jeep was still in James's front yard, though. I gazed at it soberly through Pipe's front window as I sipped one of her Cokes. Katie was still asleep on the loveseat, but I knew that wouldn't last much longer. And then I would have to have a plan.

I guessed the plan was the same as yesterday's—get the heck off the Point and check into a hotel. The question was: would we be allowed to leave this time?

I'd been up since before sunrise pondering that very question and watching over Katie's slumbers. Despite the feeling of security Pipe's abode and presence engendered, the worrying part of me wondered if it might not be a false sense of security. Thus my predawn vigil over the kidlet. Even a warm and welcoming Pipe in her bed wasn't enough to overcome my anxiety. Something was wrong in this place. I knew that in my gut.

Katie stirred, shrugging the chenille throw off her and pushing the long-suffering Babs onto the floor. I put the toy back on the couch as Pipe emerged sleepy-eyed and tousle-headed from the bathroom. She was alluringly garbed in flannel pajama pants (fluffy white clouds on a sky blue background) and a much worn white UCSD sweatshirt.

I smiled at her, but her response was a huge jaw-cracking yawn. Seeing Katie still asleep, she nodded toward the kitchen and we moved there in unspoken accord. She went straight to a little coffeemaker on the counter and started fiddling with it, her back to me.

Uh-oh. Awkward alert. I'm no good at those morning-after tête-á-têtes. I never know what to say. Thanks for the orgasm? Really enjoyed the ecstasy? God, why am I such an idiot?

I wanted to come up behind her and put my arms around her waist, but her single-minded focus on the coffee preparations made me hesitate.

Having set the coffeemaker to her satisfaction, my hostess solved the dilemma by turning around and kissing me with the same deliberation which she had just applied to the java. Maybe it's a scientist thing. That girl could concentrate the ass off a thing.

In any event, the resulting clinch led to my discovery that there was nothing under those PJ pants or the sweatshirt. More explorations might have followed, but a thump from the living room indicated some five-year-old feet had hit the floor. I had barely disentangled myself before she padded into the kitchen, looking bright-eyed and bushy-tailed.

"Hey," was the economical greeting she democratically bestowed upon both of us.

"Hey yourself," I managed, the minty taste of Pipe's toothpaste

175

fresh in my mouth. Pipe pulled a carton of orange juice out of the fridge and proceeded to pour three tots of it. Katie accepted hers and drained half of it in one slug. Wiping her mouth with the back of one hand, she put the cup down on the counter and headed for the bathroom, calling back over her shoulder, "So what are we doing today?"

Good question. Pipe and I exchanged a look.

"I guess we're walking up to topside," I said. "Again."

"I'm in," Pipe said. Two little words and yet my heart had to skip a beat. I smiled at her. She smiled back.

"Actually, I had a thought," she said. "I bet James had a spare set of car keys somewhere in his cabin..."

I was shaking my head. "No. I don't want any of us going back in there."

"Mad," she said, in a tone a little too understanding. She went on, "Look, I know things have been a little weird down here and I know it can't be easy for you losing your brother and having to take on Katie..."

At this point, Katie marched back into the kitchen and held her arms up to Pipe, who lifted her up to sit on the counter. She looked at the two of us expectantly. Breakfast, salvation, first day of the rest of our lives. Something along those lines was clearly on her agenda this fine morning.

And, to my dismay (which I wasn't proud of), she had adorned herself with my precious Niners cap (only my all-time favorite hat ever!), which I had foolishly left out somewhere. It was way too big for her and slid down over her eyes as she wiggled on the counter. She tipped it back up with a rakish grin. Arrrgh! My hat! I knew she was five and I was twenty-eight, but...I couldn't stand it—she was wearing my hat!

I handed her the cup of juice as a distraction, then casually slipped the hat off her head and took it out into the living room to stuff in my purse. Ashamed, but unrepentant (my hat!), I could only hope my fatal flaw had passed unnoticed by the both of them.

Pipe was getting some bread and butter out of the fridge as I rejoined them. She handed me the bread with a knowing look, but merely gestured toward the toaster behind me. I put two slices in and pressed the lever. I hoped Katie liked toast for breakfast.

"Anyhow," Pipe continued, "we could be in and out of there in two minutes and get the keys, I bet. *I* could be in and out of there in two minutes, easy. You don't even have to go in."

"You don't understand," I started to respond, but Katie simultaneously said, "What keys?"

We both looked at her. Pipe said, "Your daddy's spare car keys. Do you know where he kept those, kiddo?"

Without a moment's hesitation, Katie said, "In the purple pot."

"By the Bible, on the foot locker?" I clarified.

She nodded as she gulped down some more OJ. Now why in the world hadn't I thought to ask her that like two days ago?

Pipe gave me a look like, "See?"

"You don't understand." I tried again. "Something is going on down here. The fog…"

"I know it was bad yesterday, but—it's the beach, Madison. It gets foggy sometimes. Really foggy, like yesterday."

I couldn't believe what I was hearing. Did she seriously think that was normal fog?

Or…was I the only one seeing the weirdness? God, maybe some of this was in my head. I hadn't had a decent night's sleep in I didn't know how long, that was for sure.

Pipe was giving me the concerned look again. I tried one more time.

"I left the brake on, Pipe. I know I did."

"Well, brakes fail sometimes…it could be just an accident. Right?"

I didn't think so. But I was so tired. The maybe four hours of sleep I'd gotten the night before suddenly rose up and washed over me. My whole body ached.

The toaster popped behind me and I jumped, which made Katie giggle. Pipe swept her off the counter and got her involved in buttering the toast. She found a couple of those restaurant packets of grape jelly in a drawer and turned Katie loose on those too. I put more bread in the toaster as Pipe filled her extra large coffee mug. I grabbed the last can of Coke out of the fridge. Well, I guess that settled it. We had to get off the Point that day—we were out of Coke.

Katie was fine with us eating breakfast standing up in the kitchen. In fact, she seemed fine with the whole unorthodox turn her life had taken. On a normal Monday, I guessed she'd be in day care. This was supposed to be the day I was making all those calls to the attorney and everybody else. Well, maybe I still would, I thought—just get us out of here first. Maybe Pipe didn't believe there was anything strange happening, but as long as she was with us, we would surely make it to topside today. Anything else was unthinkable.

Chapter 27

At least we all agreed the first order of business after breakfast was to get dressed and pack for the hike. That didn't take long for me and Katie. All three of us ended up wearing the same clothes we'd had on the day before. Pipe then packed a backpack of her own, humoring my requests to add food, bottles of water, her lighter, a flashlight, binoculars, a small first-aid kit, twenty feet of clothesline and a tarp from her heretofore unseen collection of camping gear in the bedroom closet. Katie helpfully contributed a bag of marshmallows she'd found in the kitchen.

Well…if we walked right up there in thirty minutes and never needed any of the stuff, then (a) good and (b) I would apologize and plead stress and lack of sleep. "Be Prepared," I'd once heard someone say. But how do you prepare for the evil presence of a long dead madman?

I could tell Pipe was not buying into my fears. I didn't know how to convince her something was wrong. If she didn't see it, how could I explain it? But if she didn't believe me, why was she even bothering with me? For a one-night stand? Because of her affection for Katie? I was starting to get that "oh my God this is a huge mistake" feeling in the back of my mind and I didn't like it. Not one bit.

I slipped a steak knife in my back pocket when she wasn't looking. No good against the supernatural, but it still made me feel a little better. A little.

Pipe had left her baseball bat in James's yard, so it was off limits as far as I was concerned. I remembered her golf clubs in the bedroom. I can't say I know a mashie from a five iron, but I selected two good ones for me and Pipe anyway. Lightweight, not bad as walking sticks and they'd leave a wicked mark if we connected with anything.

We still hadn't resolved the question of going back into James's cabin for the spare car keys. I was still against it, but I knew she wanted to give it a shot. Was a two-minute risk worth the possible gain? I didn't think so, but I hated arguing with her. I was brooding over this while sitting on the loveseat. Katie was at my feet, on the rug, playing with Babs. Pipe came out of her bedroom with the full backpack and sat down next to me to zip it up. Her jean-clad thigh brushed against mine—even that minimal contact got me feeling all warm and fuzzy, with pleasant memories from the night before dancing like sugarplums in my head. Super hot naked girl sugarplums.

Suddenly, she paused and looked over at me with her mouth open.

"What?" I said. Katie looked up at us from the floor.

"Oh my God—I am so stupid," Pipe said. "I just remembered—Bohannon has a two-way radio down at the lighthouse. We can call topside on that."

When she said that, I remembered seeing the radio setup on the cluttered workbench at the lighthouse, amongst the boxes and food wrappers.

"It's two-way?" I asked her.

"Yeah, it's his own personal radio, but I've seen him talking to his buddies topside on it. All we need to do is walk down there and call Delgado and he'll send somebody down pronto!"

She was acting like this was great news, but somehow anything other than an immediate jaunt up the hill seemed like a step backward to me.

"How long should it take us to walk up the hill?" I asked her.

"Longer than it will take us to walk to the lighthouse and get one of the guys to come down," she said. "Come on, Mad—this is the quickest solution."

"But do you know how to work the radio? And isn't the lighthouse locked?" I persisted. I knew for a fact neither technology nor lockpicking was my strong point.

"Trust me," she teased. "I'm a doctor."

When she saw the look that earned, she reached into her jeans pocket and pulled out a small ring of keys.

"And, besides," she said. "Walter gave me the spare."

Chapter 28

Well, it beat going back into James's cabin. I still felt like we should just head straight up the hill, but with no logic to support that, I bowed to Pipe's desire to try the lighthouse first. It is a continuing mystery to me why I always seem to be too forceful in the workplace and not forceful enough in my personal life, with Messes & Complications the common result in both spheres.

The sun shone brightly upon us as we made our way down the path to the lighthouse. The warm smell of the earth, the sea and the brush was pleasantly pungent. Pipe and Katie had their backpacks. I, wondering how in the hell I'd been cast in the role of Loser Mom/Pack Mule, brought up the rear with my voluminous purse, our three jackets, the two golf clubs and a plastic bag full of miscellaneous crap that didn't fit in the backpacks. Pipe was still limping a bit from our misadventure the day before, but not too badly.

The first thing that looked wrong to me was Bohannon's

truck parked not far from the foot of the stairs. Pipe saw it the same time I did and stopped.

"Oh, good, he's here!" she said, turning around to me with a smile.

"How the hell did he get down here?" I asked, my tone equal parts incredulous and exasperated, my inner voice condemning me for swearing in front of the kid.

"There's an old service road he sometimes takes. It goes all the way around the base of the Point, from the bay side to here. It's a lot rougher and longer, but he likes the challenge of off-roading it from time to time. He's a pretty tough old dude, you know. He still scuba dives, believe it or not." There was admiration in her voice.

"So, can he give us a ride?" That was all I cared about. He could run marathons and bake pies from scratch, for all it mattered to me. But if he'd gotten *in* via the service road, surely we could get *out* the same way...

"Absolutely," she said.

"Are we going to see Mr. B.?" Katie asked.

"Yeah, baby," I answered, taking her hand. "And then we're getting out of here," I added, with grim determination.

"Pipe too?" she anxiously inquired. I looked at my new favorite surfer girl.

"Pipe too," she answered with a grin.

The lighthouse door was open, just like the day before. As we approached, its interior looked just as dark and foreboding as it had to me yesterday. I was loath to encounter Bohannon again after our previous conversation. I think Pipe sensed that. As we neared the door, she suggested we wait outside while she went in to talk to him. My instincts told me the three of us should stick together, but an involuntary shudder shook me at the thought of reentering the lighthouse. I looked up at the sky, which was a perfect clear blue. No sign of the foul stench either. Katie tugged on my back jeans pocket and said she wanted to go see if Henry the Eighth was in the truck, so that clinched it.

Pipe gave me a nod. "I'll be right back," she said and turned to go inside.

"Wait," I said, urgently.

She inquiringly turned back. Her blue gray gaze held mine for a long moment.

"Take this," I said, handing her one of the golf clubs. "Just… in case."

She smiled at my foolishness, but took it anyway, her fingers brushing mine. Then stepped right up close to me to whisper in my ear, "I'll. Be. Right. Back." and finished with a quick soft kiss on my neck, right under that ear. I couldn't tell if my shiver was lust or premonition. Or both.

She sauntered into the lighthouse with the golf club over her shoulder as I came to the realization that, despite my newfound responsibilities, despite the strange and terrifying circumstances, I was totally and irredeemably falling in love with Dr. Alice Piper from Austin, Texas.

Katie brought me back to my senses by tugging on my jeans pocket again, with a look that said "Come on!" as clear as day. The truck squatted awkwardly near the foot of the stairs, but I figured that was due to the uneven ground on which it was parked. There was no sign of the dog, not even when Katie called out his name. We walked along the passenger side. I could see there was nothing in the cab or the bed, although I was happy to see the keys in the ignition. Katie wanted me to lift her up so she could see for herself. I complied, all the while keeping an ear cocked toward the lighthouse—where was Pipe? Where was Bohannon? When could we get the fuck out of here?

Not soon, was the answer I found when we walked around to the driver's side. Both of the huge tires on that side were flat. Not just flat, but slashed as if with a machete or some other violent instrument. The force needed to render such damage was unimaginable to me. And horrifying.

I grabbed Katie and whirled toward the lighthouse. "Pipe!" I screamed.

But she was coming out of the doorway, the golf club and something else in her hands. Katie and I ran toward her as she staggered, dropped to her knees, then all fours and vomited on the ground.

"Oh my God, Pipe!" I cried as we reached her. I cast a fearful eye at the open maw of the lighthouse, but no sound or movement emanated from within. I put a hand on Pipe's back, but she was already back up on one knee, shakily wiping her mouth with the back of one hand.

"I'm okay," she whispered, but she was white as a sheet, her breathing labored and shallow. I pulled a bottle of water out of my purse and offered it to her. She pushed it away and somehow got to her feet, leaning heavily upon me for support. Katie was wrapped around my leg, looking scared to death. I took a deep breath and stroked Katie's hair, telling her everything was all right, in as calm a voice as I could muster. Not one of the three of us believed that, but Katie relaxed her hold on my leg a fraction.

I turned my attention back to Pipe, who had regained some of her color and was urging us down the path back toward the truck. She stopped after a few steps, however and went back for the golf club and the other item she had dropped, which turned out to be a walkie-talkie.

Rejoining us, she said urgently, "Come on, come on—we have to get to the truck!"

We were at the foot of the stairs. I stopped us. "The truck's no good, Pipe—two of the tires are flat!"

She looked at me wildly, then hurried us all up the steps at top speed. I tripped at the top, bringing us all down in a heap. Pipe was already scrambling to her feet, but I grabbed her, gasping for breath. "Pipe, wait…stop…what happened?" I panted.

The top of the staircase at least had the benefit of providing a vantage point in three out of four directions. Pipe cast a quick glance around—no one or thing visible coming up the stairs, up the path or down the path. The scrub brush up the hill in the fourth direction didn't appear to be concealing anything, either.

I struggled to a sitting position as she crouched over me. Katie was on her feet beside me.

"Bohannon…" Pipe said to me. Our eyes met. She shook her head, once. A smear of blood on her T-shirt caught my attention.

"Oh my God, are you hurt?" I cried.

"No, no," she replied, "it's from my hand—just a cut, from the radio."

We all three looked at the radio/walkie-talkie, which was in far from sterling shape. Its yellow plastic casing was cracked in multiple places and its antenna was all but snapped off and hanging by a thread.

"We have to call the police," Pipe said grimly. "We have to get topside."

"Does it work?" I asked, pointing to the walkie-talkie.

"Let me try," she said. "You keep a lookout."

I was too scared to ask, for what? But I did as she said, rising to my feet and pulling Katie in tight as I did so.

"Mayday, Mayday," Pipe was saying. Crackling static was the only response. She tried again, apparently calling on the channel set aside for communications with topside. More static. She made an adjustment to a knob. Suddenly, a woman's voice burst through the static—all I could catch was the last bit: "…do you copy? Over."

"Torres, it's Pipe," Pipe said. "Can you hear me? We've got an emergency down here and need immediate assistance."

More static. Pipe again asked if Torres could hear her. Another burst of white noise, with a few scrambled words. "…not copy… repeat…" The signal seemed to be growing weaker or maybe the mangled walkie was just giving out. Pipe tried one more time, but this time there was not even static to be heard. She pressed some buttons and turned the knobs, but it was clearly dead.

Dead—like Bohannon? I could hardly quiz Pipe for details with Katie there, but it seemed obvious from her reaction that he must be dead. And between her reaction and the slashed tires, natural causes didn't seem likely. With the radio not working, it seemed we were back to the previous plan of trying to get James's car keys out of the cabin. Pipe seemed to reach the same conclusion at the same time.

"Let's go," she said abruptly to me and Katie. "We'll get James's keys and be on our way." She stuck the walkie-talkie in her backpack.

Her uncharacteristically severe manner was scaring Katie, who looked from me to Pipe and back again, on the verge of tears. "But what about Mr. B.? What about Henry the Eighth?" her voice crescendoing up the scale toward a wail.

Pipe held out her arms and Katie launched herself into a tight hug, her arms wrapped around Pipe's thighs. Pipe took the opportunity to cover the little girl's ears and say quietly to me, "Whoever did that down there may still be around. We need to keep our eyes and ears open and get ourselves topside pronto, Madison."

I couldn't have agreed with her more.

Katie pulled Pipe's hands off her ears and demanded to know what we were talking about.

Pipe said, "I was just asking Mad if she's got any gum in that big ole purse of hers."

The tight little smile she gave me reminded me we had to keep it together for Katie's sake. The depths of my purse hid my shaking hands as I searched for gum, finally unearthing some breath mints instead, which I doled out to the both of them. Katie was temporarily mollified by that and Pipe's quick squeeze of my shoulder helped me to summon the strength for the walk back to the cabins. Every rustle in the undergrowth or screech from a gull had my heart in my mouth.

Pipe stopped us just before we emerged from the path into the gravel area. We crouched down, taking advantage of the cover afforded by the bushes while she dug the binoculars out of her backpack. I was having a weird flashback to a childhood game James had invented that we used to play with the neighborhood kids—combat patrol, he called it. The sick thrill of figuring out whether you were the hunter or the hunted was coming back to me now in far too real a fashion.

Pipe brought me back to the present by asking me to keep an eye on the path behind us while she scoped out the cabins. I did so, with a quick glance every few seconds at either her or Katie, who as usual was captivated by Pipe and her actions. Concentrating intensely, Pipe looked carefully all around in every direction with the binoculars, checking out the cabins, James's Explorer and everything else in sight.

"Everything looks okay," she reported. I nodded my agreement. We both knew, though, that not seeing—or hearing or smelling—anything didn't mean we were alone.

Pipe said in a low tone, "Okay, you guys wait here. I'll be in and out in thirty seconds. As soon as you see me come out, you run and meet me at the Explorer, all right?"

"No," I said.

She looked at me, surprised.

"This time, we stick together," I told her.

"Mad, we don't know what's in there," she said.

"And we don't know what's out here," I replied. "We stick together," I finished, firmly.

She looked at me assessingly, then nodded, holding out her hand to Katie for a high five.

"Three Musketeers?" she said.

"Three Muffadeers!" Katie replied, slapping Pipe's hand with gusto. Oh, well. Maybe math would be her best subject.

A cloud passing in front of the sun momentarily darkened the dell. I looked up—the sky, which had been perfectly clear and blue just a few minutes before, was now dotted with wispy white clouds. June Gloom was reasserting itself.

With Pipe leading the way, we moved cautiously forward to the foot of the sidewalk in front of James's cabin. All looked serene there—the red trike in the front yard, the wind chimes on the railing, the baby doll still in the chair on the porch where Katie had left her. No muddy footprints on the sidewalk or the porch. The rental Jeep crashed into the side of the house was the false note, but at least that too, was still the same way it had been the night before.

We went up the path and onto the porch, me with a tight grip on Katie the whole way. All was still quiet. Unnervingly so. Pipe motioned to me to unlock the front door. As soon as I let go of Katie, she took a step to the side and scooped up the baby doll in her arms. Pipe gathered her in. I fumbled for the keys in my purse and managed to unlock the door despite my shaking hands. I turned the knob and pushed the door open. Slowly...

I don't know what I was expecting, but it was kind of an anticlimax when everything looked fine. Just as we had left it. Even the foul smell I'd come to associate with Shadow Point was nowhere to be sniffed.

The three of us slowly shuffled into the living room. Pipe left the front door open behind us. Her head was on a swivel, checking everywhere for danger, but all was quiet in the cabin. The place had that empty feeling. Everything was the same... except...

"Where's the purple pot?" Pipe asked me in a low tone.

I looked at the room. Footlocker—check. Bible—check. Purple pot—gone. I didn't remember moving it anywhere. I didn't even remember touching it after I'd picked it up that first night.

"I don't know," I stage whispered back. "Katie?"

She looked up at both of us with a "who, me?" face of total innocence, but it seemed to be genuine this time. Maybe in the flurry of packing up our stuff, I'd stashed it somewhere... I shrugged my purse off my shoulder and dropped the rest of my burdens in a heap by the front door.

"Let's look," I said to Pipe. "It's gotta be here somewhere."

She put a finger to her lips, then held up her hand, indicating Katie and I should wait a moment. Gripping her golf club tightly, she slunk over to the kitchen doorway, then snuck a peek inside. All clear, her look told me. She then headed for the hallway.

Katie was grabbing my hand so hard it almost hurt, but when I looked down at her, she was staring at the old piano, not at Pipe's retreating figure. I couldn't see what had captured her attention—the purple pot certainly wasn't on the piano.

Pipe returned from her search and gave me a thumbs-up. She went past me to close and lock the front door, then started combing the living room for the purple pot. Katie let go of my hand, dropped the baby doll on top of my pile of stuff and went over to the piano stool. She agilely climbed up on it, then sat slowly twirling with one hand on the keyboard as needed for balance. That was as good a place as any for her to be safe and out of the way, I thought.

"I'll check the back," I said to Pipe, who gave me a nod without interrupting her hunt, which had now expanded to the inside of the footlocker and underneath the couch.

I have to admit I had an ulterior motive for volunteering to look in the back of the cabin, one which was more pragmatic than heroic—I really had to pee. I took a quick glance in each of the bedrooms on my way back to the bathroom, but didn't spy the purple pot. I'd investigate more closely on my way back.

The elusive purple pot didn't appear to be in the bathroom either as I closed the door behind me and took advantage of the facilities. Ah, blessed relief! I jumped a bit as the pipes shrieked when I flushed, but then steadied myself—just super old plumbing, Madison, not supernatural. Nevertheless, I opened the door before I washed my hands to reestablish contact with my comrades in the living room. Opening the door made the grubby once-white shower curtain billow a bit—after my shower on Saturday night, I'd pulled it open to its fullest extent, enclosing the bathtub, hoping to avoid more mildew growing in its folds.

I briefly examined myself in the shadowy mirror above the sink as I washed my hands. The elderly pipes shuddered and moaned. My hair in particular looked like something out of Crazy Persons Quarterly. I resolved to put my Niners cap on at the first opportunity.

The shower curtain trembled again. I heard Katie strike a note on the piano, somewhere around middle C. It sounded fractured, like it had hurt the aged instrument to produce the sound. She played a higher note, then one in the middle. A less musical combination was hard to imagine. It was like nails on a chalkboard. Katie repeated the three notes. I heard Pipe murmur something to her, but Katie played them again. Pounded them, really. And again. The same three dissonant notes. Low, high, medium.

Pipe said, "Katie!"

The cold water tap snapped off in my hand as I tried to turn it off. The paradoxical spurt of water from the faucet was accompanied by a burst of rotten egg odor in my face, coming up from the drain. From all the drains. As I wheeled to face the doorway, I almost gagged on the stench emanating from the tub. The shower curtain rippled and shook. I suddenly thought I knew where the purple pot was. Behind the curtain, in the tub. The only question was, what else was in there?

I heard Pipe calling my name from the living room and the continuing cacophony of Katie banging out those same three harsh notes, over and over, but, for a moment, time stood still in that awful bathroom.

I need the keys, I told myself. For Katie... I stretched a shuddering hand out toward the undulating curtain. Before I could draw it back, something reached around at tub level. A strangled noise got no further than my throat. A long spindly whitish stick thing was groping its way out of the tub. I threw back the curtain with a yelp. No purple pot—just the nightmare crab from my dream, slipping and sliding on the porcelain as it blindly waved its bleached limbs at me.

I banged off the doorway hard as I bolted from the bathroom with a yell. Pipe reached out and grabbed me around the waist with one strong arm, the other being locked around Katie who was still trying to pound out her devil's triad on the ancient piano. It *was* middle C, I could see in those brief moments of struggle.

C...B...F...

"What the *hell*?" Pipe said to me, having finally pulled all three of us down on the floor. Katie lay absolutely still, like someone in the aftermath of a seizure. Her face looked waxen and pale, her eyes still unwaveringly fixed on the piano.

I scrambled to my feet, doing my best to pull her and Katie along with me.

"We've got to get out of here!" I yelled at them. Volume control is always the first thing I lose under pressure.

Pipe's face was taut. She reached down and picked up a more or less limp Katie in her arms.

"The keys! We've got to get the keys!" she yelled right back at me.

"We'll never find them, Pipe! Can't you smell that?" I was coughing now, hardly able to catch my breath in the intensity of the reek. Katie stirred on her shoulder, only to start coughing and gagging as well. Only Pipe seemed unaffected. I took a fleeting look back toward the bathroom. A thin trickle of water was worming its way down the hall toward us.

"Pipe, come on!!!" I told her urgently. "We've got to go now!"

She seemed to finally be infected by my urgency. As I ran the few steps toward the front door and gathered up all the stuff there, she went out the front door onto the porch, a groggy Katie still in her arms.

The day had darkened considerably. The top of the hill was obscured by fog, which seemed to be rolling in from both the bay and ocean sides. The distant bleat of the foghorn was a reminder of how far we had yet to go. A cold wind was in our faces, yet welcome as it blew away the noxious fumes from inside the cabin. My flight instinct was fully engaged, but Pipe wouldn't let us move off the porch until she had scanned the four corners of the dell for God knows what. Seeing nothing, we made our way off the porch into the yard.

Katie was restless in her arms, fully awake now and Pipe let her slide to the ground. The little girl promptly turned around and plucked the baby doll out of my arms, cradling it in her own. More importantly, she stayed close to my side of her own volition. She looked a little shaky, not like her usual self. She shivered as the wind blew across us and I pulled her close, shivering a bit myself.

Pipe crouched down at the end of the sidewalk, motioning us to join her. "All right," she said in a hoarse whisper. "The car's out, so we've got four options: wait here for somebody to check on us, take the long way 'round via the old service road, cut through the brush straight up the hill or take this road up to topside."

I wondered why exactly we were whispering, but couldn't help but join in. "Let's take the hill," I pitched. "That's the quickest."

"Yeah, except for the snakes and the rough terrain. It's practically a vertical climb, Mad," she whispered back.

Oh, yeah.

Pipe was still going. "Do you really think all three of us can make it up the hill?"

Clearly, she meant Katie. And maybe Feeble Ass From Boston.

"Our best bet is the road, all right?"

Pipe posed the question to me, but then seemed distracted by something she'd spotted near the sidewalk. It was her baseball bat. Or what was left of it. She leaned over and carefully picked it up out of the scraggly grass. The base of the bat, with its taped handle, was intact, but the rest of it had rotted away to nothing in the less than twenty-four hours since Pipe had dropped it there. She looked at it strangely, then at me. She dropped it then, like it had suddenly grown hot. She stared at her hand, then shook herself like a dog.

"Stay right there," she said intensely to me and Katie. "Don't move."

"What…" I started, but she was already running across the way to her own cabin and in the door. She came right back out in less than thirty seconds and sprinted across to us, with—of all things—a large book in her hands.

193

"Here," she said to me. "Put this in your purse."

The unwieldy hardcover book was *A History Of Bly Point* by Jude Baskett, with illustrations by Delta D. Rugg. Not wanting to argue the point, but not that thrilled about adding a five-pound historical text to my load, I silently stuffed it in my purse. I pulled out and donned my Niners hat while I was at it. Why would that make me feel marginally better? I don't know, but who wouldn't feel better with Joe Montana on her side?

"Now…" I started to say, but a softly sinister sound made me stop. I could see that Pipe heard it too, but neither one of us could identify the source. It was like white noise, almost like the sound of the sea, but it was growing louder and louder.

As it intensified, we realized it was coming from up the road. And headed down our way.

Fast.

"What is that?" I cried to Pipe, but she shook her head. We all three rose to our feet, looking about wildly as to which way to run from this new threat. As we dithered, Daniel The Church Guy's car—clearly driverless—sailed majestically past us at about twenty miles an hour, straight down the gravel stretch and then off the road into the bushes to the right of where the path took over.

I looked at Pipe, my mouth open.

"Fuck the road," she said. "We're taking the hill."

Hand in hand, the three of us ran toward the trees. In the gathering darkness, I glanced over my shoulder for what I hoped would be my last look at James's cabin.

The wind chimes were gone from the porch railing. Despite the stiff breeze, they hung still and unmoving in the unnatural twilight, making no sound as we fled the dell.

Chapter 29

As we ran off into the brush, I couldn't help but wonder if we were somehow being *herded* toward a specific destination.

"Come on!" Pipe panted. "I know a place…"

With branches and brambles clutching at our every step, progress was difficult. The abnormal twilight was no help either. How could it be getting dark when it was barely midday?

Pipe was getting farther ahead of me and Katie, almost out of sight.

"Pipe, wait!" I called, but to no avail. Her back disappeared in the deepening gloom uphill as I tripped on a rock or a root. Something big enough to bring me and Katie down in a jumble. My overloaded purse swung around and caught me right in the solar plexus, with the ground breaking my fall and Katie landing on top of me.

I labored to get my breath back while Katie surged to her feet, my hand on her wrist.

"Pipe!" she called out shrilly. "Pipe!"

I managed to sit up as oxygen reentered my system in a most welcome manner. Pipe came running back into the clearing where we'd fallen, then stopped in apparent amazement.

"What?" I said.

"That isn't supposed to be here…" she said, her voice tapering off with each word.

"What isn't?" I said, but then I saw it.

I couldn't really call it a "clearing," the place in which I'd stumbled. It was a roughly circular spot about ten feet in diameter. The interlaced branches of the trees overhead kept the light from shining through except in an offhand manner. The cool sandy soil amongst the tree roots supported no other growth. So, I guess, in a way, it was a perfect spot for a grave.

The crumbling tombstone was about a foot long and no more than three inches high—just the right height to trip up the unsuspecting hiker. I stood to read the inscription:

Beloved Wife And Mother
Rachel Bly
November 11, 1911—September 6, 1929
"Gone Forth Into The Darkness Until That Day When All Sorrows Are Forgotten."

Not a real pick-me-up, if you ask me. Katie leaned forward as if to brush some dirt off the stone.

"Don't touch it!" Pipe and I yelped in unison. Katie jumped as if stung, then gave us a reproachful look.

"Let's get out of here," Pipe said.

The place was clearly giving her the willies. Me too. The three of resumed our march up the hillside, following her lead as there was no path. We were freestyling it through the bushes now. I tried not to think of things slithering nearby. To take my mind off that, I asked Pipe why she had said the grave wasn't supposed to be there.

"Because it's not," was her reply. She glanced back at me over Katie's head and saw that further explanation was needed. She kept moving, but said over her shoulder, "Rachel Bly wasn't buried on the Point. She came from a well-to-do San Diego merchant family. They buried her in the family plot at their mansion in Old Town San Diego. It's still there—the mansion, I mean. It's called Lowe House. They give guided tours of it for the tourists and history buffs."

She looked back to see if I was still following, both literally and figuratively, then added, "And I never heard of any gravesites on this hill before, so I don't know what the heck that was…"

Something she had said rang a bell somewhere in my mind, but I couldn't think what it was. I'd figure it out later. Right now, I needed to concentrate on my breathing. I was already huffing and puffing as we laboriously made our way up the hill. Between the brush and the ever-increasing fog, I often could not see the top of the hill, but I trusted Pipe to lead us in the right direction. I'd bet she'd been one hell of a Girl Scout. Me, I'd been kicked out of Brownies for cracking wise one too many times with Rhonda Sue Oglethorpe in the back row of the troop meeting. Never been much of a joiner since, either.

"Come on," Pipe encouraged us. "We'll find a place where we can catch our breath."

The good news was there was no sign of any pursuit behind us. The bad news was—there never had been any sign of anything, if you know what I mean. Nevertheless, the thought of stopping to rest, no matter how brief, was a welcome one at that point. Katie was trucking away with no problem, but I looked forward to rearranging my various burdens in a more efficient manner. My purse was driving me nuts, either bashing me in the ribs or slipping off my shoulder.

The place Pipe stopped us in a few minutes later was a natural lookout spot—a cluster of three big boulders overlooking the currently obscured Pacific. The part of my brain responsible for odd random thoughts noted that one of the boulders kind of looked like Bing Crosby. I decided not to share that. Throughout my life, I'd made the mistake many times of sharing such random thoughts with other people. Let's just say it never went my way.

We'd been following a rudimentary trail up the hill. Even I, with my complete lack of woodlore, could tell it was a path created by animals, not humans. The trail curved around the boulders and on up the hill. We took shelter in the lee side of the boulders, which took us out of sight of the cabins below but allowed us to spy down upon them. The lookout spot probably offered a splendid vista of the Pacific on a normal day, but what with the fog and the strange gloom, we couldn't see the ocean at all. I could see the cabins and cars, but barely—white wisps of fog kept drifting in between us.

Katie and Pipe took a few sips from a bottle of water while I readjusted my load. Pipe was doing her eternal vigilance thing, casting glances this way and that.

"You ready?" she said to me.

I started to nod, but then we all froze at a loud rustle in the bushes. I grabbed Katie and took a step back. Pipe turned to face this latest menace with her golf club upraised. I held my breath. There was a sickening pause, then even louder rustling as whatever was in the bushes rushed upon us.

Pipe checked her swing just in time to avoid clocking Henry the Eighth, who ran out of the bushes and right up to Katie, wagging his stumpy little excuse for a tail like there was no tomorrow. She twisted out of my grip and fell to her knees, accepting his sloppy kisses and throwing her arms around him in a tight embrace.

"Can he come with us, Madison?" she implored me.

Uh… I looked at Pipe, who shrugged.

"If he wants to walk with us, he can come," I temporized. "But we can't be chasing after him if he takes off into the brush."

She was already giving him some water from the bottle, which he attempted to slobber into his mouth with limited success.

"Okay, okay," I said, handing the bottle to Pipe and raising

Katie to her feet. "We gotta get going now."

As fat as he was, the pooch kept pace with us with little effort. Perhaps he was as anxious to exit the Point as we were. We had no leash, of course, but he trotted along at Katie's side as if that were his rightful spot. Occasionally, he'd eyeball me doubtfully over his pudgy shoulder, but apparently my rightful spot was bringing up the rear, in his opinion. Following a bulldog butt uphill was not adding to my experience, but on the scale of unpleasant things, it was better than a staff meeting, I guess.

We trekked along for quite some time. After a while, Pipe seemed to be leading us more laterally than vertically, but I trusted her sense of direction and knowledge of the terrain a great deal more than my own. All the same, I was beginning to wonder a bit by the time we made our next rest stop. We didn't seem to be making much uphill progress. Did she have a specific destination in mind? Why weren't we heading straight up? I determined to ask her as soon as we stopped, hopefully when Katie's attention was focused elsewhere.

It felt like an hour or more, but with my out of commission watch, who was to say? With the gloom hanging heavy over our heads, it could have been six a.m. or six p.m., although reason suggested it was likely still on the morning side of noon. The air felt heavy, almost as if it was going to rain again. And they say it never rains in San Diego.

Finally, Pipe called us to a halt. No clearing or outcropping of boulders this time. We stopped where we were, in the midst of the brush. Pipe dropped to one knee and pulled a bottle of water out of her backpack. Katie sat down, Indian style, with Henry the Eighth panting under one arm. I too, flopped down and took advantage of the timeout to remove an irksome pebble from my shoe. We passed the water around. I'm pleased to say I was number three out of four.

"We're not lost," Pipe said.

"Never thought we were," I replied, with a stab of anxiety running through me.

"There's a path that leads up the hill to the back of the new lighthouse, the one on top. It might be a bit overgrown, but it's there." She looked troubled, however.

"Great," I said. "How far?"

She grimaced and took another sip of water as the bottle made its way back to her. "That's the problem—we should have already crossed it."

We exchanged worried looks as Katie stroked the bulldog's head. He licked his chops and waited for us to make up our minds.

"So…do we go on?" I asked. "Or just head straight up?"

"Straight up is through heavy brush," she said. "Rough going. If we can find the path, it shouldn't take us more than half an hour to get up there."

We both thought about that for a moment.

"Let's give it another thirty minutes," Pipe said. "It's hard to tell in this gloom…what time do you have?"

I wordlessly showed her my stopped watch. Why was I even wearing it? Habit, I guess and the hope that—maybe—I could get it fixed someday soon.

"Mine's stopped too," she exclaimed. Indeed, her fancy digital diver's watch was nothing but a blank screen.

"Shit," she said under her breath. "I don't like the look of those clouds either."

I hadn't noticed the changes above us. The day had continued to grow ever darker, but I hadn't realized before then that the clouds were looking so black and ominous. Like thunderclouds, massing in big clumps over the ocean and moving ever closer to us with each breath.

The wind was picking up too. It quietly ruffled the brush around us in a chilly embrace. Great, more rustling noises in the undergrowth—just what I needed. I almost thought I could hear the wind chimes tinkling in the distance. Or was that in my head? Nobody else mentioned it, so I kept my trap shut. A policy I should no doubt apply more often.

"I'm hungry," Katie announced. "And I think Henry the

Eighth is too."

I was pretty sure that dog was always hungry, but I again kept my thoughts to myself. Pipe rummaged in her bag and came up with a granola bar. She gave Katie half, then held it out toward me. I shook my head, so she bit into it herself.

"That's for you, Katie pie," she said once she'd swallowed, "and not the dog. He'll find his own food out here—bulldogs are excellent hunters."

Her glance at me dared me to rebut. Far from arguing, I added, "And I'm pretty sure granola makes dogs sick."

Henry the Eighth was watching every morsel move from Katie's hands to her mouth. Catching my eye, he quickly looked away, snorting and licking his nose. Did I detect a note of scorn in that look? Anthropomorphism's a bitch.

Having finished her snack and washed it down with the last sip of water from the bottle, Katie said, "Is that it? When are we going to have lunch?"

When, indeed? A few stray raindrops scattered the area as Pipe rose to her feet, with the rest of us following.

"Come on, troops," she said. "We'll find the path and have our lunch topside."

"Yay!" Katie responded. "Topside, topside, topside…" As she began singing her own newly invented, completely tuneless and frankly annoying song under her breath, we set out once again to find our way.

Those few random raindrops were not as random as I'd hoped. As we struggled along, they quickly multiplied until they were a veritable downpour. We really weren't dressed for that, even after I doled out the jackets. I had my denim jacket and my ever trusty Niners hat, with beads of water now forming and dripping off the rim. Pipe had her Mexican hoodie, which wasn't too water resistant, but at least gave her head and body some protection. Last, but not least, I had somehow remembered I still had Katie's massively wrinkled windbreaker in my purse and got that added on top of her little sweatshirt jacket and denim jacket.

It was a tight fit on top of the other two, but we got it zipped. The hood of her sweatshirt jacket afforded her some protection as well. Its bright goldenrod color stood out sharply amid the dull hues of the hillside, but at least she'd be semi-warm and dry.

"All set?" I said to her, pulling the drawstrings of the hood. Her little face looked serious and intent.

"All set, Mad," she replied like a good little soldier, warming my heart. I gave her a quick hug and we were ready to go.

Thunder rumbled out at sea. The wind was picking up, whipping the rain at us from every which way. The only member of our party seemingly unbothered by the storm was the stupid dog, who snapped at errant raindrops from time to time. We stumbled along as best we could behind Pipe. The ground had been uncertain before, with lots of tricky little pebbles and larger stones to trip you up, but now it was turning to a sticky mud goulash beneath our feet, significantly hampering our progress.

Lightning clashed overhead. The thunder followed hard upon its heels, so loud I involuntarily cried out. I could feel the very bones of the earth shake underneath us. Katie turned and grabbed me. The dog shot off into the undergrowth.

"Pipe!" I shouted. "Pipe! Wait up!"

She came back to us and we huddled in a small wet circle, the cold rain drenching us as more thunder shook the hillside.

"This is crazy!" I yelled above the clamor. "We're soaked and freezing and I can hardly see where we're going!"

I could feel Katie's small body trembling against my leg. I pulled her in between me and Pipe, to better shelter her against the buffets of the storm.

"I know," Pipe shouted back, "But where can we go?"

I looked around us wildly. The chill wind, gusting fiercely, threatened to take off my hat, but I held it firm with one hand. All around us was the murk of the day, with vision further reduced by the torrents of rain. Down the hill, I saw only brush. To either side, more brush. Fifty feet above us and slightly to the left, however, I saw—what? Something shiny... A momentary gleam of light on a wet metal surface? Something that—oddly—looked like a manhole cover out here in the middle of nothing? Something…

"There!" I pointed it out to Pipe. "Up there!"

She saw it. And turned to me with a smile.

"Come on, Katiekins!" she cried to the child, who grabbed her hand as Pipe set off straight up the incline. I followed close behind, making sure she didn't slide if she fell. A hard-fought couple of minutes later, we all three were clustered around the manhole cover, which I could now see had some kind of handle in its center. Close up, it was more like a hatch than a manhole. A metal hatch set in concrete. A few weeds grew in the dirt around it, but it looked like someone (Uncle Sam?) had taken at least a desultory interest in keeping it from being completely overgrown.

Pipe grabbed the handle and turned, straining with all her strength. No luck. And no movement. She tried again as thunder boomed. I looked around to see if there was any stick or rock or something we could use as a tool to open it up, but saw nothing useful.

I felt Pipe's hand on mine. I looked down, into the endless clarity of her eyes.

"Help me," she said.

We both gripped the handle and gave it the old heave-ho. No go. Pipe sat back, on her heels, panting.

"One more time," she said to me and grasped the handle.

I did too, my hands touching hers. From the department of monkey see monkey do, Katie knelt down and put her hands on top of both of ours. Pipe looked over at me and gave me that million-dollar smile.

"Fourth time's the charm," she said and we struggled to turn it with all our might. I was pushing so hard I was seeing little black dots before my eyes, but just when I thought I couldn't go a moment more, we felt the handle give with a low groan. I let go and grabbed Katie in surprise and also to keep her from popping down any rabbit holes that were about to open up. Pipe turned it again, this time with obvious results. Another go-round and she was able to pull the hatch open, although it was clearly quite heavy. A dark circular shaft was revealed. The top two rungs of a rusted metal ladder were just visible in the waning daylight.

Pipe slipped out of her backpack and pulled out her flashlight. She shone it down the concrete shaft. It extended down about twelve feet. The rest of the ladder was visible in the small beam from the flashlight, as was a concrete floor. I moved Katie and myself around to her side of it.

"Is it safe?" I said in Pipe's ear, raising my voice above the storm.

"I think so," she said. "It must be one of the old Navy machine gun nests."

Oh, yeah. Machine guns—that sounded safe. As she saw the apprehension on my face, Pipe said, "Don't worry—the guns are long gone. It's probably just an empty bunker now. At least it'll get us out of this wind and wet."

I couldn't argue with that, especially as she volunteered to go check it out first. The light from her flashlight disappeared down the shaft as she agilely climbed down and then moved into the bunker. She was back in a few moments, at the bottom of the ladder, looking up at us.

"Come on!" she said. "It's fine."

One by one, I dropped the backpacks, my purse, the plastic bag and the two golf clubs down to her. She neatly caught all the items and stowed them away in the unseen bunker. She returned to the foot of the ladder as Katie started her climb down. My heart was in my throat the whole way, but the kid was a natural, clambering down with grace and athleticism. She and Pipe then looked up to me, awaiting my descent.

A strange feeling of remoteness, of disconnection overcame me suddenly. Who were these people? I'd never seen them in my life before a few days ago. What the hell was I doing out here, freezing my ass off on a windswept hill in a thunderstorm?

I looked up at the sky, at the black swollen clouds looming above. Cold rain bit at my face.

"What are you doing to me, James?" I yelled.

There was no answer. Just the wind and the rain and—maybe—the far off whisper of wind chimes.

Katie's voice came to me from below. "Madison? Are you coming down?"

I set aside my doubts and confusion and stuck a tentative toe down the shaft. My foot found the rung, but I was keenly aware that the ladder was slick with rain, decayed with rust and who knew how decrepit. I inched downward slowly and fearfully, with none of the agility of my companions. Oh, well. I made it somehow to the bottom, but wasn't looking forward to the climb back up. Another of life's questions that are best not asked or answered: Does my butt look big when I'm climbing down the shaft of a machine gun nest?

Having made it to the bottom, the three of us then looked up to the top. Where the hatch was still wide open. Oh. Duh. Maybe I should have closed that, being the last one to come down. On the other hand, if we closed it, would we be able to reopen it?

Sensing my thought, Pipe said, "Let's check out the bunker first. If we decide to stay, we can deal with the hatch then."

So sensible, that girl. She led the way with the flashlight through a short passage into the bunker, which, surprisingly, was not completely dark. Weak daylight straggled in through a rectangular slit cut high in one wall. It wasn't a window with glass in it, it was an opening to the outside which, I tardily realized, must have been for the machine guns to poke out of. I imagined, on a clear day, a clear view of the Pacific and the slope in between. On the outside, vegetation had sprung up to partially obscure the opening, which was a good thing for us—it was mostly keeping the rain out, but letting in some air and light. A long, narrow puddle of water had formed at the base of that wall.

The entire space was about ten feet square, I guessed. With a ten-foot ceiling. A cold, dank and dim concrete cube, but at least we were out of the rain. As my eyes adjusted to the dimness, I saw that it was not entirely empty. My heart leapt for a moment when I saw the outline of a door leading into the side of the hill.

"Pipe, look!" I exclaimed, grabbing her arm to steer the flashlight beam in that direction.

"Yeah, I know," she said. "But they've sealed it."

Sure enough, the outline of the door remained, but that was all. The door handle had been removed. As best as I could tell in the sketchy light, they had poured concrete right over it to completely close up the opening. God knows why. Maybe the tunnel behind it had collapsed... There was no point even speculating. I turned my attention to the rest of the small space. There was nothing else except the growing puddle of water, dirt and minor debris on the floor that had blown in from the gun slit and a shadow in the far corner, which turned out to be a four drawer metal filing cabinet, government issue.

It was dark green and way older than me. Why had they left it behind? Who knows... The top two drawers were hard to open, but empty. With a perversity and sloppiness I can only ascribe to our federal government, the bottom two drawers of the file cabinet were filled with mildewing San Diego area phone books from the seventies and binders full of outdated regulations for civil servants, as well as several *Sports Illustrated* swimsuit issues from years gone by. Clearly, the bunker had seen some kind of use by the Navy since World War II (storage?), but what that might have been I could not tell. If, indeed, it was a machine gun nest—who knows, maybe it was some top secret Navy research station for studying the reproductive habits of fruit bats. In any event, the phone books and other papers provided a dandy source of fuel for a campfire, if we were going to camp.

Katie appeared by my side and took my hand. "What are we doing?" she said plaintively.

A fair question. I squatted down beside her and pushed her hood back, which then inspired me to find a comb in my purse and smooth out her damp tangles. She submitted to this while shrugging out of her dripping windbreaker. The wind was howling outside. We heard the water pelting against the hillside in violent tantrums. The light from outside dimmed as the black clouds took over. Pipe's flashlight beam was providing most, if not all, of the very small amount of light in the bunker.

Katie pulled a scruffy looking scrunchie out of her pocket and handed it to me. I gathered her hair in a ponytail and applied it. We both seemed calmer for this small grooming ritual, but our problems had not decreased.

I stood up and turned to Pipe. "Let's camp," I said.

"Excuse me?" she said.

"Camp," I said. "You know, build a fire, eat lunch, wait for the storm to pass. Camp."

Lightning flashed outside, quickly followed by a sharp clap of thunder, still dauntingly close. We all three jumped.

"Okay," she said. "But as soon as the storm clears, we've got to move on."

"Absolutely," I agreed. All the time hoping inside that the storm *would* pass and that we wouldn't be trapped in this hole forever.

"All right then," she said. "First things first—we need to secure the hatch."

The three of us trooped back to the shaft. A puddle had now formed at the bottom of the ladder. We looked up.

"It's heavy," Pipe told me, "but not that bad. I think we loosened it up some."

Since Pipe had more or less opened it from the outside the first time, we determined that she would test it again from there. Katie agreed to stay put at the foot of the ladder. Pipe climbed up and out, with me following to almost the top of the ladder. She knelt at the edge, looking down at me. She took off her hoodie and placed it half in and half out of the shaft, to (hopefully) keep the hatch from completely closing.

"Ready?" she said to me.

"Ready," I replied, though my heart was pounding in my

chest and my fingers felt weak on the rung. What if we closed it with her out there...and we couldn't get it open again? My mind went blank with horror at the thought. But we couldn't stay down in the bunker with the front door—so to speak—wide open for anyone or anything to come right in.

Pipe eased the heavy lid shut, encasing me in darkness.

Then pulled it back open, like sunlight on a grave.

"It's easy, Mad!" she said. "I think it's okay now. Do you want to try lifting it from inside?"

I nodded my acquiescence and she again lowered the lid. I can't say it was easy from my position on the ladder, but I was able to reopen it with no help from her. With the outside world visible again, I was surprised to see she had the bulldog by its collar. In her other hand, she clutched a long, slender stick.

"Where did he come from?" I exclaimed, as my head and shoulders emerged from the shaft.

"How the hell are we going to get him down is the question," said Pipe. She tossed her hoodie and the stick down to Katie, who was cavorting about down below with excitement at his reappearance. We decided Pipe would hold him in her arms and back down the ladder with me supporting her.

It was scary, but it worked. We made our way down with no mishap. She released the dog as her feet touched the concrete floor and he scampered off into the bunker with Katie in hot pursuit. Pipe then went back up to close the hatch. There was a way to lock it from the inside, so we felt sort of safe once it had clanged shut. She descended the ladder one more time and we went into the bunker. The dog was lapping noisily from the puddle of water with Katie hunkered down beside him and talking to him in a low voice. His stumpy tail was wagging full speed.

Pipe set about emptying the file cabinet of its contents, then laid it down lengthwise against a wall to create an instant bench for us. Which was good—sitting on the floor is not my thing, not even the ritziest of carpeted floors, let alone that dirty cell.

I busied myself with unpacking our meager supplies and spreading out the tarp from Pipe's backpack on top of the cabinet. I handed Pipe her lighter as she built a small fire with the available components. The storm continued its frenzy unabated outside our nest. The temperature had dropped considerably in the last hour, but it was still wasn't that cold by my standards. Certainly nowhere near Boston cold.

Pipe had the fire going. She added one of the telephone books while I watched. She was still wearing her wet John Deere T-shirt. And wearing it well. (Note to self: In the future, if the need to purchase a tractor ever arises, *definitely* get a John Deere.) I retrieved the hoodie she'd dropped down to Katie, as well as the long skinny stick and brought the garment to her.

"Thanks," she said. She stripped off her wet T-shirt in one quick motion and donned the hoodie in its place.

I went to throw the stick on the fire.

"Whoa!" Pipe grabbed my arm and pulled me around to face her. "That's not for burning."

"What's it for, then?" I asked.

She smiled and went over to the backpacks. She rooted around until she found what she wanted, then turned back to me triumphantly with a bag in her hands.

"Marshmallows," she said.

Of course. What's a campfire without marshmallows to roast?

Our discussion had not gone unnoticed by Miss Katie, who now pranced up to Pipe in hope of scoring a marshmallow or two (or twenty). Pipe was tough, however and first took the stick to draw a line in the dirt on the floor around the fire. She then informed Katie that was the line she must stay outside of at all times and gave a brief lecture on fire safety. The kid agreed without too much fuss, her mind obviously still on the marshmallows.

"Marshmallows are for dessert," Pipe declared. "What have we got for lunch there, Mad?" she asked me.

We had an apple, some crackers and some peanut butter.

My steak knife came in quite handy. First, though, I dug in my purse and came up with three moist towelettes, one for each of us. Frequent business travelers like me are all about the moist towelettes.

Pipe made all three of us share one bottle of water. I thought of all the times I'd dined in fine and not-so-fine restaurants where the waiter comes to replenish your glass of water time and time again…

I pushed those thoughts away. With luck, we'd be dining somewhere fine within twenty-four hours. We just had to get up the hill.

It was still pouring outside. And completely dark now. I didn't think our little fire would be visible from outside, not with the vegetation mostly blocking the rectangular slit. And in the dark and rain, who could see the smoke? I was hopeful the smell of smoke wouldn't give us away.

We needed the fire more for the light and the comfort. The minimal amount of heat it was giving off was welcome, nonetheless and helped to dry out our sodden clothes. The smoke drifted up and out of the rectangular slit. The small concrete space was suddenly marginally cheerful with the crackling fire and warmth. The three of us sat together on the upended file cabinet, with Henry the Eighth at our feet, watching every molecule of food as it moved from our hands to our mouths.

Katie accidentally dropped a small chunk of apple onto the dog's back, right where he couldn't get at it. Before he or I could say or do anything, she reached down and grabbed it, then popped it into her mouth.

"Wai…" I exclaimed, but too late. Katie giggled at my obvious discomfiture, chewed and swallowed. Pipe too, had to laugh at my horrified expression.

"Five second rule?" she said to me.

"Yeah…okay," I said with a rueful grin.

To Katie's delight, Pipe then mentored her in the fine art of marshmallow roasting, making sure she stayed well clear of the fire. The dog gobbled up all the burnt and/or dropped ones. I hoped he wouldn't puke them up later.

I'm not much for marshmallows, but I did eat the one nicely toasted one Katie so happily brought me. I had to laugh at myself for being so absurdly proud of her modest culinary achievement. Surely, other family's children had toasted marshmallows as adorably…but I knew I didn't believe it.

I then occupied my time by leafing through the book Pipe had foisted upon me—*A History of Bly Point*. The flickering firelight wasn't particularly conducive to serious reading, but I managed to pick up a few semi-interesting facts. A working coal mine on the bay side had been an important feature of the Point in the late nineteenth century. The top of the Point was known to this day as an excellent spot for whale watching, especially during the annual wintertime migration of gray whales heading south to Baja.

Mentions of Conrad and other Bly family members were sprinkled throughout—one chapter told the story of a competitor of Conrad's in the freight business, who had tried to build a railroad track from downtown out to the foot of the Point. That attempt had been abandoned, however, after various mysterious fires, assaults on the work crew and an overnight pillaging of the track and equipment proved to be obstacles too great to overcome.

Flipping through the pages, I came across the same picture of Conrad and his wife and daughter that Bohannon had shown me. I borrowed Pipe's flashlight to read the tiny print in the caption: "Conrad Bly, his wife Rachel Lowe Bly and their daughter, Lily."

Something in my brain finally clicked. Setting down the book, I grabbed for my purse and pulled out the "important documents" folder I'd stashed in there on Friday night—only a lifetime ago, it seemed. The flashlight beam was shaking a little as I searched for and found the document I was seeking—the marriage certificate for James and Chloe. Chloe Juliet Lowe, the small black print read. Lowe.

Could this mean Chloe—and therefore Katie—was related to Rachel Bly? And what would that mean? My mind was in a whirl.

But my research was interrupted when the marshmallow roasters closed up shop. Even Katie had had enough sugar for the moment and was showing signs of being ready for a nap. The dog actually helped by lying down for a snooze himself. Katie wanted to sleep next to him on the floor, so I folded up the tarp I'd been sitting on on the file cabinet to make a flimsy, but more or less clean, mattress for her. Babs—ever the martyr—served as a pillow and I took off my semi-dry denim jacket and laid it on top of Katie for a blanket. She drifted off to sleep almost immediately, with one little hand reached out to rest on the dog's flank.

Pipe threw the marshmallow stick on the fire, where it blackened and shriveled, then added a phone book. All of the government regulations and magazines had already fed the blaze. We still had one phone book left, but clearly the fire wouldn't last through the night. Especially a night like this, that had started at noon and would go on who knew how long... I sat back down on the file cabinet and shivered.

"Are you cold?" Pipe said quietly as she sat down next to me, our shoulders touching, backs to the cold concrete wall. She put an arm around me, her hand at my waist.

"I'm okay," I answered. Which was a better answer than the truth, for that moment. I leaned into the curve of her, savoring the body heat.

"What's this?" she asked, indicating the marriage certificate, folder and book I had strewn on the other side of me.

"Oh. Hey. I wanted to show you this—check it out." I showed her the marriage certificate, explaining how I thought Katie might somehow be related to Conrad's bride.

Pipe looked at me, her head tilted, her brows drawn together. That worried look again. "But Lowe's not that uncommon a name, right?" she said tentatively.

212

My heart sank, but at the same time my innate stubbornness rose up and would not let me back down.

"But there has to be some reason all of this is happening," I said.

"Yeah," she said. A moment passed. "What about that Daniel guy?"

The question startled me. Which made me realize I'd been assuming Daniel was as dead as Bohannon.

"You don't think he's dead?" I asked her.

"I don't know… We saw his car, Mad, but that's all. He could've pushed it down the hill himself."

"But why?" I said.

"He's after Katie. You heard him."

"Yeah, but he said he'd see me in court. And why would he attack Bohannon?"

"Well, he didn't seem too tightly wrapped to me."

I had to give her that one. Hmmph. Here I'd been constructing my whole supernatural conspiracy theory when maybe one real live crazy bastard was the problem. One was not really any better than the other, but it was well worth considering.

But what about all the weird stuff? All of that couldn't be Daniel's doing, surely. As I went over the list in my head, I realized—perhaps belatedly—that a lot of the stuff I thought was so weird could be chalked up to Mother Nature's eccentricities. The foul smell, the rotting fruit, the fog, the dead things we'd seen on the road, even the storm we were currently sitting out—a reasonable and natural explanation could no doubt be found for all of them, although I was reluctant to admit it, even to myself.

And an objective outsider could no doubt attribute a lot of the other stuff to my own stress level and lack of sleep. Scary dreams, voices in the night, a little mud on the porch steps, a little wildlife in the tub…get a grip, girl! That's what Mr. Objective Outsider would have said after dashing me in the face with some ice water.

But, no, my stubborn inner voice said. No. I knew someone or something had to be behind this chain of events. Stress level or not, no freak occurrence of nature could account for the wind chimes or the rotted baseball bat or Rachel's grave on the hill. Not to mention Bohannon's slashed tires and untimely demise.

My God, I thought, what about James's own death? My mind reeled as I tried to think about that.

Maybe I was just losing my mind. That was easier to think about and always a possibility.

Or maybe...maybe both an evil specter AND a live psycho were wreaking havoc on the Point that weekend. Boy, that would be just my luck.

All right, I told myself, slow down, Madison. Slow it down... Pipe was looking at me speculatively as I argued my way through these silent mental convolutions.

"I don't know, Pipe," I said finally. "I don't see how Daniel could have been responsible for everything that's happened."

It dawned on me then that she didn't know what "everything" was. There was a lot I hadn't shared with her.

As I brought her up to speed on the nighttime visitations, the muddy footprints and the crab, we found ourselves referring to *A History of Bly Point* for clarification and information. The book confirmed what Pipe had said about Rachel—she was buried in the family plot in Old Town. We couldn't find any explanation of the gravesite we'd seen. We did learn that she had been only fourteen when she married Conrad Bly, who was thirty-eight at the time. Poor Rachel.

A couple of pages were devoted to the history of The Curse. Bohannon hadn't gotten it entirely right, according to the book. The legend was: If you died on the Point *and* your body remained there, you were doomed to never leave and to wander within its boundaries forever.

The book went on to discuss who was buried on Shadow Point and which of those folks had died there. There were, of course, hundreds of bodies buried in San Cerros cemetery topside, but almost all of them had met their fates elsewhere. One notable exception was a local hero named Captain Newport, who'd been some kind of flying ace in World War I and a successful businessman after that. Later in life, he'd become a major philanthropist and benefactor of several local good causes. The color photo in the book showed an energetic-looking elderly gentleman with a cropped white beard and piercing blue eyes with a devil-may-care gleam in them. He had owned a sizable chunk of the peninsula in his day, including an enormous house overlooking the Pacific. Whether it was his military service or his business connections, he was one of the few people buried in San Cerros who had actually died on the Point. He still had that great view of the Pacific, I thought.

The only other veterans who had actually died on the Point and were buried in San Cerros were a handful of nineteenth century U.S. cavalry soldiers who had fought (and lost) a brief, but fierce, battle there during the Mexican-American war. The *History* explained that the soldiers had originally been buried where they fell, but the remains were later reinterred in San Cerros. A plaque marked their graves there, listing their names and regimental motto: "To honor and glory we ride!"

The book noted that there were no official civilian cemeteries on the Point, but that, of course, various souls had been buried there over the years in graves that were either unmarked to begin with or unmarked now due to the passage of time, such as Native Americans, Portuguese sailors, other early settlers of diverse nationalities and several members of the Bly contingent—most notably, Conrad himself and his little daughter, Lily.

We thought about all of that for a while. A coldness fell upon me that neither the declining flames nor Pipe's touch could keep away. I thought I was starting to see a pattern in all these puzzle pieces… A pattern that frightened me more than anything that had happened so far.

"Hey, wait," Pipe said. "If Rachel was buried off the Point, then how could those have been her muddy footprints on your steps?"

"That's the thing," I told her, struggling to keep the horror out of my voice. "I think those footprints belonged to Conrad and Lily, not Conrad and Rachel. He has his child with him. He's not looking for Katie to take his child's place—he's looking for her to take his wife's."

Chapter 30

Pipe got up and cast the last of the phone books into the fire. For Coronado and North Island, I noted remotely. Her face was in shadow as she watched it burn. I had no idea if she believed a word I'd said. She'd been awfully quiet since I'd shared my theory with her.

I felt a flicker of doubt. A flicker that threatened to become a flood. I was trusting an awful lot to this woman. It wasn't like she was keeping us down there, but... In fact, I was the one who had seen the hatch, right? Or had she led us right to the place where I would spot it? But I was the one who suggested we camp down here... And I only had her word for what had happened to Bohannon. I hadn't looked in the lighthouse, I didn't know what she saw in there... And where was she when James died?

I shook myself, mentally and physically. This was Pipe, I told myself. Pipe, who loved Katie and vice versa. Who'd shown me nothing but kindness. Whose warm bed I had slept in the night before…

She sat down next to me, still quiet. I guessed we weren't going to discuss it any further for now. The flashlight beam blinked, steadied and then blinked again. Pipe turned it off, saying we'd better save whatever was left of the batteries. We looked at each other in the dwindling light from the little fire. With all the government paper gone, it wouldn't be long before it went out.

Pipe gave me a brave smile. "Hey, it's okay," she said firmly. "I've still got my lighter. And this storm can't last forever."

We listened to the rain savaging the brush outside. The wind alternately whistling and moaning. Her hand found mine as it rested on the book in my lap. Nobody else's hand had ever felt so right.

The book.

"Hey," I asked her. "Do we still need this book?"

She considered. "I guess not," was her verdict. She rose and added it to the flames. A freshet of blue sparks shot upward as the fire bit into it. Pipe rejoined me on the filing cabinet. The bulldog snorted in his sleep and turned over, snuggling up to Katie before returning to his dreams of slow rabbits and fast can openers. The little girl slept on undisturbed.

I picked up the file, meaning to put the marriage certificate back in it, but something else slipped out instead. It was one of the airline ticket folders, with the ticket itself falling halfway out. I idly glanced at it again. It was the ticket for James, one-way to Boston, Mass. I tried to slot it back in its little folder, but it wouldn't fit. I opened it up to see what was blocking it and, lo and behold, there was the Polaroid picture Miss Patricia Klein was so eager to retrieve.

"Good God!" I exclaimed under my breath, feeling an urge to throw a hand over my eyes. I didn't really care that she wasn't a natural strawberry Blonde, but the knowledge that those freckles were ALL over was more than I needed to know. I'm selectively in favor of female nudity (if I'm doing the selecting), but having met Miss Klein in person and read her letter to my brother, it was all a bit much. I handed the photo to Pipe, who was grinning from ear to ear.

"Patsy, Patsy, Patsy," she murmured, chuckling to herself and clearly tickled to death at her foe's tacky exhibitionism. She went over by the fire to get a better look, turning the picture this way and that.

"We have to burn that, you know," I said sternly. Although Delgado would probably pay enough for it to put Katie through her first year of college.

Still quietly laughing, Pipe said, "With pleasure!" and tossed it into the fire where it immediately curled up and melted away. She came back over and settled in next to me, wiping a mirthful tear from her eye and still intermittently suffering from uncontrollable chuckles. Finally, her fit seemed to have passed. She put her arm around my shoulder and pulled me in, gently pressing her lips to my temple. We watched Katie sleep for a while, unbothered by the dancing shadows cast by the flames. She looked so small. So innocent.

"Hey, you should try and get some sleep too," Pipe said to me. "Here, you can put your head in my lap and lie down if you like. I'll take the first watch."

Her kindness had a way of unexpectedly disarming me. I blinked back sudden hot tears. I could hardly remember the last time someone had been nice to me, let alone taken care of me like this. I looked at her with an impossible feeling of love choking me, burning in my throat.

She laughed. "What does that look mean?"

And she kissed me then, so tender and slow my toes curled inside my sneakers. As our lips parted, she ran a strand of my hair through her fingertips, murmuring "Pretty hair…"

"What?" I asked, my lips brushing hers with the word.

"Your hair," she said. "That was the first thing I noticed about you, you know. I'm a sucker for pretty hair…"

Her eyes gleamed in the glow from the fire. I leaned in for

another and longer kiss, but she pushed me back with a smile.

"Not in front of the kids, eh?"

Kids. Plural. Great. How in the world did I go from being completely single and unencumbered on Friday to a child, a girlfriend and a dog by Monday afternoon? Must be some kind of record. A big yawn overtook me without warning, my jaw creaking with the effort. I lay my head down in her lap as she'd suggested. I really was so tired... As I drifted off to sleep, I felt her hand stroking my hair and heard the dog starting to snore.

Chapter 31

In the dream, I was back in James's cabin. Daylight streamed in through the open windows where the limp white drapes billowed in the breeze. I sat alone on the scratchy couch, looking out the front window. Babs, propped up next to the sickly cactus on the low bookcase, stared back at me blankly. Panic set in as I realized I didn't know where Katie was. I ran from room to room, throwing wide the doors and calling her name, but I couldn't find her. In desperation, I finally ran out on the porch and there she was, riding her red trike down the path, away from me. Relief surged through me. Everything would be okay now.

"Katie!" I called.

She stopped her trike at the end of the path, but didn't turn around. With leaden legs, I walked down to her with great effort and put my hand on her shoulder.

"Katie," I whispered.

She turned and slowly looked up at me, but there were no

eyes in her head, just gaping black pits.

Suddenly, I was at the top of the lighthouse, in the tower with all the glass broken out and the great lamp broken as well. I was staring out to sea where huge gray swells heaved and broke and spouts from whales dotted the horizon. The cold spray refreshed my face as the wind blew in my hair. An old man was coming up the spiral stairway—Captain Newport. He stood tall beside me, his cropped white hair and beard hardly ruffled by the breeze.

"Mornin', lass," he said to me.

"Good morning, Captain," I replied. "Can you help me, sir? Please?"

He eyeballed me, but didn't respond immediately. He sighed, then, saying "It's a terrible business, this."

"But she's only a little girl! We have to—"

He cut me off. "He don't care how little she is. He don't care about nothing, not that one. He's a real devil, that Bly."

"But you can help me, right?"

He looked at me again, then back out to sea. "The lads are restless, lass, but only you can call them, not I. And we'll need every last one of them to win this battle. You call them tonight, Miss Madison—and I'll take care of the rest. We'll get your wee lassie up the hill and safe in no time."

I was thrilled and he seemed pretty fired up too. But I had a question.

"But…how do I call them?"

He turned to me—almost on me—and said intensely, "You light the beam, lass. Light the beam."

I nodded like I understood, although I didn't and grabbed the railing as the wind started howling around us, threatening to blow me off.

Chapter 32

I awoke with a shudder in near total darkness. I was still flailing from my dream, but the fall from the file cabinet onto the concrete floor brought me back to total consciousness with a painful jolt.

"Ow, damnit," I said to myself. I stood up and brushed myself off. Everyone else was already awake.

"Good," said Pipe. "I was just about to wake you up. The rain's stopped and the clouds seem to be clearing a bit." She had donned her now dry T-shirt.

The fire had gone out, but I could make out my companions' outlines in the dim light of the bunker. I glanced up at the gun slit and sure enough, some daylight had definitely returned.

The dog whined. And then suddenly let loose a full-throated howl, which was as loud as it was unexpected.

Pipe shushed him, but in the distance, we heard an answering howl. Much closer, we heard yipping.

"Oh my God," I said, disbelievingly. "Wolves?"

"Coyotes," Pipe said.

Oh. Well, that was bad enough, in my book.

"Real coyotes?" I asked her as I gathered Katie to me.

She deliberated for a moment, then said judiciously, "There are real coyotes on the Point."

Which didn't really answer the question.

"We should pack it up and take advantage of the remaining daylight," she said, bending to gather various items into her backpack. Katie ran to get her pack together too. I folded up the tarp and handed it to Pipe, then put my denim jacket on. The bulldog watched us patiently, tongue out, panting quietly.

"What about him?" I said to Pipe, but she had it all worked out.

First, she climbed up the ladder and opened the hatch. I tossed the golf clubs up to her and she laid them on the ground nearby, along with her backpack. She then came back down and I was sent up with my stuff to be the lookout. I felt extremely underqualified, but brandished my golf club as menacingly as possible in case any unseen foes were watching. It was nice to be outside in the cool fresh air again, at least. Down below, Pipe had rigged up a harness of sorts with her hoodie and some clothesline. Somehow, she managed to cradle the bemused bulldog—who must have weighed at least fifty pounds—to her chest inside the harness with one arm and laboriously ascend the ladder with her legs and her other arm.

Once she was safely on top, Katie clambered up with no problem and I closed the hatch. Pipe, putting her hoodie on, was still catching her breath from her climb. The dog took the opportunity to pee on several nearby bushes, industriously scraping up the dirt with his back paws once he'd finished. He then sauntered back to us, looking quite perky and self-satisfied.

The coyote noises, thankfully, were fading over the hill toward the bayside. I sympathized with whatever small creatures they were after.

Pipe stood up, shouldering her pack. "Ready?" she said to us. We nodded. "Let's go."

Like before, we were trying to make our way to the path that would bring us out on the top of the hill near the new lighthouse. I didn't know what time it was, but it felt like about six. Not dusk yet, but getting there. Thunder still rumbled occasionally in the distance, but there was actually some blue sky above us, here and there, in the mix of white and gray cumulus. The sun was hidden behind a massive bank of clouds to the west.

The slick ground made our footing even more unpredictable than before. I slipped and fell more than once as we toiled on behind Pipe.

Time passed with no sign of the path. After a while, Pipe turned straight uphill, clearly abandoning her search for the path. As she'd warned, it felt like a nearly vertical climb. The prickly bushes grabbed at our clothes, the soil alternately gave way or threatened to suck the shoes off our feet in the muddy spots and the uphill struggle was sapping the last reserves of my strength.

My lungs were burning when Pipe finally paused. The brush seemed to open a bit ahead of her, the last rays of the setting sun illuminating the cloud cover. A long moment went by, then she turned to face us. My face and hands were scratched by brambles, my sneakers soaked and my jeans muddied. I was sweating and cold at the same time, never a good combo.

"What is it?" I said to her. I couldn't read the expression on her face.

She looked at me without speaking, then wordlessly led us into the opening in the brush. It was a natural lookout spot—a cluster of three big boulders, overlooking the Pacific. The third boulder kind of looked like...

"Bing Crosby," Pipe murmured.

"What?" I said. She was astonished, but pleased, when I pulled her in for a quick hug and a kiss that ended up more on her eyebrow than her cheek.

"Don't be so damn happy," she said to me, smiling a little

nonetheless. "We're going around in circles. It doesn't make any sense."

With a sigh, Katie sat down with her back to Bing. She looked tired and bedraggled. The dog sat down next to her and licked her face. She patted him absentmindedly. He whined, then got up and trotted off into the brush.

"Henry the Eighth!" she called after him.

Pipe dropped down next to her.

"Don't worry, sweetie—he'll be back. He just went to get himself some dinner."

"What about my dinner?" Katie said, on the verge of a whine herself.

I plopped down on the other side of her, saying "Okay, okay, let's have some dinner," hoping to head off a tantrum. "Let's see what we've got, okay?"

All the foodstuffs were now in my plastic bag. Pipe had the water bottles in her backpack. She passed one around as we examined the contents of my bag: a microwaveable cup of beef stew, a similar nuke-able single serving of macaroni and cheese, a small bag of beef jerky, crackers, peanut butter, two granola bars, a tiny box of raisins and the remaining marshmallows in their bag. And one now seriously smushed box of animal crackers.

Katie and I looked at this motley selection, looked at each other and then looked at Pipe.

"Hey, sorry," she said, trying not to laugh at our identical expressions. "I live alone, all right? I don't keep that much food in the house."

I again doled out the moist towelettes, one for Pipe and one for me and Katie to share. My supply was running low. The kid wanted the raisins, so I got her started on those. I was too anxious to be hungry. We weren't making any progress and night was almost upon us. Our meager food supplies were also running low. I was trying hard to stay cool for Katie's sake, but inside, I was close to freaking out. If we couldn't go up...and we couldn't go down...

Pipe said, "Mad." Her look told me she was sensing my anxiety. "We're gonna be fine," she said.

I nodded, wordlessly and handed her a granola bar.

"You want the stew?" she asked.

Since I was quite sure it would smell like dog food when I opened it, I declined. I ate a few crackers and some jerky instead. Katie decided she wanted to try the mac and cheese. I warned her it wouldn't be hot and she'd have to eat it with her fingers, but she was undeterred. Surprisingly to me, she wolfed it right down. I think my throat would have closed on that slimy room temperature worm-like concoction, but she acted like it was good. She topped that off with a couple marshmallows, then rummaged in her backpack to find the baby doll. Crawling back into my arms, she snuggled up for a quick catnap. Poor thing, I thought, as I brushed the hair off her forehead. We were running her ragged. She held the doll tight in her arms as she fell asleep. Its unblinking blue eyes stared fixedly into the distance.

I welcomed her checking out for a bit, though, as it would give me and Pipe some much-needed time to decide on our strategy. I couldn't stand the thought of going back into the machine gun nest, so I hoped that wasn't Pipe's plan. As soon as I was sure Katie was asleep, I said quietly to Pipe, "What are we going to do?"

"I think there's only one thing we can do, Mad. We have to go back to the cabins."

I drew in some air sharply.

"We'll be safe at my place," she said to me, coaxingly. I wanted to believe her.

"And then what?" I asked her.

"Well...tomorrow...we'll figure something out. I could maybe paddle on my surfboard down the coast to get some help. It's like four miles to Ocho, but I could make it. Or we could light a signal fire and get Topside's attention that way."

Light a fire... I liked that idea a lot better than her paddling off into oblivion and leaving me and Katie alone. Light a fire...

that brought back my dream and Captain Newport telling me to the "light the beam"…

Did he mean I had to relight the old lighthouse to summon the rest of the good guys—the non-Bly cohorts who had died and been buried on the Point? I wanted to discuss it with Pipe, but I couldn't, not after her dismissal of my theories. She thought it was Daniel who was causing all of this, but I knew—I *knew*—it wasn't.

"We can't get much farther once the sun goes down anyhow," she said.

Katie stirred in my arms and I glanced down at her. Her grip on the baby doll had loosened and it was about to fall, so I gently pried it from her grasp. Then flung it from me with a barely stifled shriek.

"What the…" Pipe exclaimed. The doll lay facedown in the dirt by her foot. She leaned forward and picked it up, then froze in shock.

Where once the doll's eyes had been, now there was nothing but two empty, staring holes.

With a shudder of revulsion, Pipe leaped to her feet and threw the doll as far as she could into the surrounding brush.

"Jesus," she said, dusting off her hands on the seat of her jeans.

But the brush was moving where she had thrown the doll. Something was coming toward us…

"Henry?" Pipe called tentatively. And was rewarded with some happy barks we thankfully recognized.

We both heaved a sigh of relief as he playfully bounded back into our circle. It was close to dark now, but that bowling ball shape was unmistakable. He growled a bit, though, as Pipe went up to him. She stopped.

"What's wrong, buddy," she said to the dog, who was continuing a low growl.

"He's got something in his mouth," she said to me. She got the flashlight from her pack and shone it on the dog, now lying on the ground a few feet away from us. And gnawing on something white and bony looking.

It was three fingers and part of a hand. One finger still wore a class ring, with a big red stone.

Pipe turned and looked at me.

"I guess it's not Daniel we gotta worry about," she said.

Chapter 33

Pipe eventually tempted him away from the fingers with the beef stew—which, let the record show, totally did smell like dog food. The rest of the beef jerky and two swipes of peanut butter seemed to fill him up. Pipe swiped her fingers in the PB, not me—never again would my hand come anywhere near that dog, I thought.

I silently handed her my last moist towelette as he lay down to lick his chops. She had used the plastic bag to gather up the body part leftovers and then bury them in a hole she'd dug with the steak knife a little ways off in the brush.

Amazingly, Katie had slept through this entire little drama. She was so drowsy when I tried to wake her to head down the hill that I ended up carrying her for the first bit. She woke up before all my vertebrae collapsed, thank goodness and demanded to be put down so she could walk. I gladly complied. She was excited to be reunited with Henry the Eighth. I was jumpy his newfound taste for human flesh might inspire him to finish her off for dessert, but Pipe pooh-poohed my fears, telling me he was completely safe and far from the man-eater I was envisioning. I kept an eye on him nonetheless. He studiously ignored me, happy to be heading downhill, stumpy tail wagging away.

Pipe and I had not further discussed the plan. I knew she was taking it for granted that we were headed back to her cabin. And we were, but only temporarily for me. Pipe's reasonable suggestions of lighting a signal fire or paddling for help sounded just that—reasonable—but the conviction was growing within me that my dream held the answer. I couldn't explain it. Hell, I couldn't explain anything that had happened to us. All I knew was I would find a way to relight the lighthouse and then we would take it from there. It wasn't like anything reasonable had worked so far anyhow.

It was completely dark when we wearily trod back into the gravel parking area in the dell, but a crescent moon cast a sliver of silvery light down upon Pipe's front porch. Nothing was moving. Everything appeared to be just as we had left it that morning.

All was quiet in Pipe's cabin as well. I got Katie to take a bath without too much brouhaha, then put her to bed in Pipe's room. As I knelt beside the futon to tuck her in, the dog wandered in and sat beside me, panting quietly with an occasional slurp to his nose.

"Madison?" Katie said sleepily. I smoothed her hair back from her forehead.

"Uh-huh." I glanced down at her.

She had Babs in her arms and those big baby blues pinned on me. "You like Pipe, huh?"

Uh-oh. Were we entering dangerous territory here? I decided to play it cool.

"I do," I assured her calmly.

"And Pipe likes you," she went on.

"Yes," I agreed. She waited for me to go on, but I wasn't about to jump into that minefield. A pregnant pause ensued.

"So, good night then," I said cheerily, leaning in to kiss her forehead, hoping to wrap it up.

"Are you going to kiss Pipe goodnight too?"

"Uh, I might just do that. Yes. Is that okay with you?"

"Is she your best friend?"

Whew, enough with the questions already. I studied her face. Considered my options. When in doubt, try sucking up.

"I think you're my new best friend, Katie."

Her face lit up and she gave me a hug, settling down with Babs for the night with no further comments or questions. Whew! I'd have to think of a good one for the next time the subject came up, I thought as I turned out the light.

The dog followed me out to the living room, where I joined Pipe on the loveseat. She handed me—what else?—a bottle of water, this one nicely chilled from the fridge. We sipped in peaceable silence for a while. I couldn't speak for her, but I was bone tired, but with that peculiar type of exhaustion that won't let you sleep. She put her arm around me like it belonged there. And it did. I felt the warm feeling of a budding relationship growing stronger.

"You're not seeing anybody else, are you?" I asked her, a sudden anxiety striking me.

"No," she assured me with a smile. "You?"

"No."

"Well, that's all right then," she said.

I leaned into her and closed my eyes for a moment.

"I saw him once," she said.

"Who?"

"Conrad."

My eyes flew open. It was hard to breathe suddenly. She glanced at me, then looked away.

"It was January or February. Near the first of the year. I'd been surfing just before sunset and I went down the path to the lighthouse to make sure Walter had locked up. He'd been working there earlier in the day. Sometimes he forgets...forgot to lock the door…"

She stopped.

"Go on," I said.

"Yeah, well, when I got to the top of the stairs, I saw there was someone sitting at the bottom. A man. He stood up and looked at me."

She shuddered. I put my hand on her arm.

"It was Conrad Bly, Madison. He looked just like his picture. I'll never forget the way he stared at me. With such hatred… burning, intense…I've never seen or felt anything like it. Like he wanted to murder me right there on the spot. It was just…evil."

My mouth was dry. I worked up some saliva and asked, "Did he say anything?"

"No. Thank God. He just gave me that look for like ten seconds, then turned and walked off behind the lighthouse."

"God, Pipe. Did you ever see him again?"

"No."

"Was Bohannon there?"

"No, it was sunset, so he'd already taken off to beat the curfew. I did sort of jokingly ask him later if he'd ever seen any ghosts out here, but he just laughed at me. Told me not to be ridiculous."

We sat there quietly for a moment. Then Pipe said, "I'll tell you something though, Mad. I asked James about it too. We didn't talk that much, but sometimes, you know, we'd say hello in passing or talk about work stuff… Anyhow, one time when Katie was in day care, I asked him if he'd ever seen Conrad."

"What did he say?" I asked breathlessly.

"He didn't say anything. But I could tell from his face. He'd seen him, all right."

"Jesus…"

We mulled that over in silence for a while.

Finally, I said what had been gnawing at me ever since I got the call from Delgado. "I just wish James would have reached out to me. Maybe I could have helped him somehow…"

Pipe looked at me with compassion, then offered me this thought. "In the end, he kind of did, right?"

I sat up. "What do you mean?" I asked her.

"Well, he put you down as next of kin, right? He must have known you would be the one they would call. In the end, you were the one he counted on."

I tried to process that and take some comfort from it. But Pipe, her face serious now, had more to say. "But what I'm trying to tell you, Mad, is I don't think this is the first run-in your family's had with Conrad Bly."

I looked at her in consternation.

She went on. "If Conrad wanted Katie...and he knew James was planning to take her away..."

"*What*?" I said. "Are you saying—"

"Yeah," Pipe told me seriously. "I think Conrad Bly might have killed your brother."

Chapter 34

I wanted to tell Pipe about my dream with Captain Newport, but I didn't. I was afraid she would try to talk me out of going to the lighthouse, or worse, try to convince me she should go instead. I was terrified, but I knew in my gut this was something I had to do myself. And alone. I obviously couldn't take Katie along, so Pipe had to stay in the cabin with her. This was between me and Conrad. McPeake vs. Bly.

Which was why, a few hours later, I was quietly letting myself out the front door into a cold, clear night. Stars sparkled above. The chill air felt clean going down, like a shot of vodka from a bottle kept in the freezer. Which made me think about the fact that I hadn't had a drink—or a smoke—for quite a while. Other things seemed more important now...

I'd checked on Katie before I left, making sure she was safe, warm and asleep in Pipe's bed. I kissed her forehead, praying I would see her again soon.

Pipe had fallen asleep on the loveseat, scrunched up in a fetal position under the chenille throw. I was afraid I'd wake her if I touched her, so I had to content myself with one last look from the door.

No, I told myself sternly. Not one last look. I'd be back. I would feel her touch again. I tried my best to believe that.

I'd left them a note on the fridge, held down by one of Pipe's magnets which was a tacky plastic rendition of the Golden Gate Bridge. Not knowing exactly what to write, I'd stood there with a pen in one hand and the flashlight in the other until the refrigerator cycled back on with a grinding noise that scared the bejasus out of me. Finally, I scribbled "Went to lighthouse—back soon," signed my name and hoped it was true.

The only hitch in my plan was the stupid dog, who insisted on accompanying me outside. We'd done a silent but intense tango by the front door, with me trying to keep him in and him determined to get out. That stuff they say about bulldogs being stubborn? They're right. In the end, he was starting to make too much noise with his wheezing, so I reluctantly let him out. I thought his only goal was to water the plants in Pipe's yard, but having done so, he then caught up with me and firmly attached himself to my side as I headed down to the lighthouse. He knew the path well, better than I did. The dirt crunched under our feet. An occasional grunt was his only comment as we made our way through the starry night.

Plan. All right, I was pretending to have a plan. That was the best I could do at the moment. Light the beam—yeah, right. Clearly, I couldn't actually turn on the big-ass light up in the lighthouse tower. I'd dug my lighter out of the depths of my purse and stashed it in my back pocket. I had some vague notion of gathering materials to build a fire in the tower. Although starting a bonfire in a small enclosed space with a ladder in the middle of it didn't really sound too safe. Let's face it—I've been known to be clumsy.

Light the beam, Mad.

236

It was frickin' dark along the path. And I was frickin' scared. So scared I was actually glad the stupid dog was with me. My mouth was dry and my pulse thudded in my ears. The flashlight wasn't helping much. I could hear the surf pounding the beach at regular intervals. We had almost reached the top of the stairs when the dog froze suddenly, a low growl emanating from his chest.

An answering rattle came from the bushes. Oh my God—had I really come this far only to die from snakebite? I grabbed the dog's collar and hauled him back a pace, thinking feverishly: What would Pipe do?

The dog sat down and looked up at me like, "Okay, it's your problem now, genius."

I let go of him and gathered up several rocks from the path, then threw them in the general direction of the rattling noise. It intensified, then stopped. I threw a couple more rocks. Nothing. I strained my ears and shone the flashlight in that direction, but saw nothing and heard only the wind and the sea…and a few twigs snapping. I hoped it was the snake slithering away. And I trusted the dog would let me know if it was safe to continue.

I took a step forward. So did he. No rattles. I took another one and he jogged on ahead unconcernedly. I followed with my heart in my throat, but we reached the stairway with no further alarums or excursions. Regrettably, the lighthouse did not look less scary at night. Shadowy, black and jagged, it loomed threateningly in the weak light of the crescent moon, looking like the worst haunted house I could ever imagine. I swallowed, steeling myself to the task ahead and told myself this was for Katie.

We cautiously descended the steps, both of us careful of our footing. Bohannon's truck was still parked near the bottom. The toolbox in the bed of the truck sparsely reflected the sliver of moon. I wondered if there was anything in there that would help me. How about a flamethrower, Bohannon? I didn't put it past the old bastard to have one of those handy.

Happily, the toolbox was unlocked. Probably he'd been using stuff from it in the lighthouse. I climbed up in the bed to investigate, the dog softly whining below. I wasn't sure if it was me being out of his sight or his recognition of his master's vehicle that was upsetting him.

"Shut up," I said under my breath, with no result.

The toolbox was well organized, with things like a hand drill, a set of screwdrivers, extension cords and lots of other stuff I didn't recognize. Nothing looked useful to me. I went to close the lid, but noticed a sturdy black plastic box bolted to the inside of the toolbox. Its yellow clasp opened easily to reveal a roadside assistance kit including...flares! Thank you, Walter. I grabbed all five flares and stuffed them in my jean pockets, then jumped down to rejoin my partner. He started to slobber on me, but then remembered he was too cool for school and turned away with a sniff. Playing hard to get.

"I know your type, buddy boy," I told him as I gently pulled his ears. At least he'd stopped the whining. I had no idea if he would follow me into the lighthouse. I hadn't forgotten what grim discovery awaited us there. But so far, so good. All I had to do now was get up in the tower and light the flares...and then see what happened.

I was having trouble with my breathing as I picked out a path with the flashlight to the lighthouse's open door. A bad smell greeted me there. I didn't really want to see what was inside and in that sense, I was grateful for the enveloping darkness within. On the other hand, I was terrified of what might be waiting in the shadows. I listened, but heard only the crashing of the waves and the labored breathing coming from both me and the dog. He began whining again, almost crying. It was heartbreaking to hear. He knew what was in there, if I didn't.

There was another slight sound in the mix, which I identified after a moment or two. The buzzing of flies. I thought of Pipe retching in the dirt earlier and was glad there wasn't much of anything in my stomach. Summoning my fearful resolve and with my sleeve held over my mouth and nose, I stepped up to the doorway and shone the flashlight around inside.

Blood. Splashes of blood on the floor, on the walls… Blood blackened as it had dried…flies dancing about a sticky patch on the ceiling. What was left of Bohannon had been dragged underneath the workbench and dumped there.

I wished I'd brought one of the golf clubs or some kind of weapon. Not that any physical kind of weapon was likely to help me against the evil thing that had done this.

The dog was pressed against my leg, shivering. I leaned down and gave him a pat. The warm furry solidity of him was reassuring somehow, despite the nightmare quality of the circumstances. I steadied the flashlight beam on the circular staircase. Almost there, Mad, I told myself. Just go up the stairs. One step at a time, like they say.

My foot was on the third stair when the heavy wooden door creaked shut behind us.

I whirled and dropped the flashlight. It rolled on the floor beneath the stairs and blinked out, leaving us in pitch black. The dog, infected by my fear, scrabbled on the narrow wooden steps, lost his footing momentarily, yelped and then grabbed my pants leg with his teeth to steady himself, which resulted in me sitting down rather hard on the second step. He launched himself into my lap and I grabbed him. He whined in my ear, then licked it.

We listened.

We listened.

Nothing. Suddenly, I felt sick of being afraid. Anger surged in my chest and that felt a lot better than fear. I set the dog down and stood up, grabbing a flare from my jeans pocket. The rough surface of the plank under our feet was sufficient to light it. I held it up in my fist. Unnatural red light bathed the interior of the lighthouse.

"Is that all you got, you bastard?" I yelled. "Is that it?"

No one answered.

The flare sputtered and burned in my hand. I got a grip and

reminded myself to continue proceeding with caution. This wasn't over yet. Carefully, I moved up another step on the spiral staircase. Then another. Making sure, each time, that the plank hadn't rotted or been removed. Slowly but surely, Henry the Eighth and I made our way up to the top. With the glass long ago broken out of the tower windows, the air was much fresher up there. I looked at the old lighthouse lamp as best I could under the conditions, but it was cracked, corroded, filthy—you name it. I didn't see any way to make it work the way it once had.

My first flare was fading a bit, but I had three more in my jeans. Should I stick them in the window frames? Attach them to the old lamp somehow? Hang out the window yelling, "Hey, sailor!"? Shit, I didn't know. And I didn't see any "Overcoming Wicked Spirits In Five Easy Steps" instruction manuals lying about. I'd have to wing it, as best I could.

The wind was pretty strong up here and gusting even stronger. The gritty surface of the cast iron stair railing, which ran around the perimeter of the tower, was even better than the floor for scraping a flare into life. One of the brackets that held the railing to the wall had come partially loose. I jammed the first flare into the space between the loose bracket and the wall, then scraped a second flare to life on the railing. It was a little late to worry about sparks from the flares unintentionally starting the bonfire I had halfway thought about. Oh, well. I put it out of my mind and hoped for the best. I crammed the second flare into a crack in the glass lens of the lighthouse lamp. The third fit into a broken window frame, with some jagged glass supporting it.

The tower was lit up pretty well now with the demonic red light from the flares. I could only imagine what it looked like from the outside. Probably a bit like Armistice Day in 1933 when it had burned. The dog was running around the tight circle of the tower, growling and snapping at stray sparks. I lit the last flare and decided I'd better keep it for myself to guide us down the ladder and out of the lighthouse. The adrenaline was pumping pretty good, to the point where I didn't feel the cold anymore.

But where was Captain Newport? I don't know if I expected him to pop out of the lamp like a genie or what. But I'd done my part—right? I'd lit the beam. What else was I supposed to do to call the lads, as he'd said?

Oh. Maybe that "Hey, sailor" thought hadn't been so far off track after all. I felt a little silly, but I stuck my head out one of the broken windows of the tower and yelled, "Lads!"

My voice sounded weak and small, the wind tearing the word from my throat as soon as I opened my mouth. I tried again, but the only answer was the wind and the waves. I wished I could remember some of their names from the book. Did the book even give their names? People buried on the Point who'd died on the Point… Native Americans, but I couldn't remember the name of the tribe. Early settlers—I didn't recall the book mentioning their names. The cavalry soldiers… Shit, I didn't remember their names either. I suck at this, I thought. Besides Captain Newport's name, the only thing I remembered was…was…the cavalry guys had a slogan. Let's Ride, Cisco. No, that wasn't it. To something the something we ride. To Honor and Glory We Ride! That was it.

The dog had run to my side when I shouted out the window and was looking up at me worriedly. I stuck my head out the window again.

"Captain Newport!" I yelled as loud as I could.

This time, there was an immediate response, but not the one I wanted. A loud wrenching noise came from downstairs, along with a harsh wordless cry that froze me with dread. The dog started barking like a maniac and ran to the top of the stairs. When I didn't move, he raced back to me, grabbed my pants leg and tugged with all his might. Clearly, he was ready to go. So was I, but there was no way out other than the spiral staircase or a thirty-foot drop out the window. I shrank from the thought of what was waiting downstairs, or worse—already on its way up. Dropping to my hands and knees, I crept to the top of the spiral staircase and peeked down. At the foot of the stairs, a single small light, like a candle flame, burned in the impenetrable darkness. Unmoving, except for the flickering of the flame, it was at about the height it would be if someone tall were holding it chest high. As I watched, it moved up a step. And then another.

My tongue was stuck to the roof of my mouth. My hands were shaking so badly I dropped the flare. The dog leaped upon it as if it were the enemy and bit the unlit end, then turned back to me and bit me on the calf. Hard. The pain snapped me out of my trance.

"Captain Newport!" I screamed. "Lads! *To honor and glory we ride*!!! You *fucker*!" (That last one was for the dog, who was cowering and whimpering now, just out of my reach.)

The candle flame wavered and then went out as the door to the lighthouse blew open with a bang. Captain Newport stood in the entrance with a blazing torch held high.

"Lass!" he shouted, looking for me within the base, then spotting me at the top of the staircase. "Come down—there's no time to waste!"

I grabbed the flare and jumped to my feet, wincing at the pain in my leg. The right leg of my jeans was shredded and bloody. The dog was trying to look remorseful, but I was having none of that. Grabbing his collar, I forced him down the stairs in front of me. We were down on the ground floor in seconds.

"The lads..." I said to the Captain.

"On their way," he replied. "And it's time for you to be too."

The objective part of me noted I was having a conversation with a ghost and not having a problem with it. In fact, I was so glad he was there I could have hugged him. He looked solid enough, but there was a sort of a shimmery quality to him as well. If I looked at him from the corner of my eye, his outline was just a little blurry. Like a photograph taken when someone was moving. The dog, in fact, had snapped at his ankles a couple times, but seemed confused when his teeth clicked together on nothing but the cool night air. I swatted the bulldog's butt and told him to knock it off. He lowered his eyes and ears demurely and took a step behind me.

"I had a dog like that once," Captain Newport told me as he hurried us toward the steps leading up the hillside. "Tore up the upholstery in a brand-new Nash Metropolitan."

Despite the minimalist moon, the landscape was now bathed in an eerie pale glow, making the Captain's white beard shine with an ethereal brilliance. I was trying to thank him for his help as we reached the foot of the stairs, but two things stopped the words in my throat. The sight of Pipe and Katie appearing at the top of the stairs—and the sight of Conrad Bly leaning against the hood of Bohannon's truck.

Chapter 35

We froze in our tracks. The Captain spoke first, his eyes pinned on Conrad.

"You go with your friends now, lass," he calmly said to me. "I'll take care of that thievin' bastard."

Conrad coolly surveyed him, then me, then moved his gaze up to where Katie stood with Pipe.

"No," I shouted, taking a step forward. "You can't have her!"

His lip curled in a sneer, he gave me a derisive look, clearly discounting me as of no importance whatsoever. He slouched against the truck as if he hadn't a care in the world, this one or the next.

"You need to go now, Miss Madison," the Captain breathed in my ear authoritatively.

"Madison!" Pipe cried from the top of the stairs, her voice tight with fear.

"Thanks," I managed to inadequately say to my ghostly

protector, then I turned and scrambled up the steps as fast I could, the dog scrabbling behind and overtaking me halfway up.

"Your leg," Pipe exclaimed as I clumsily made it to the top. She had one hand on Katie's shoulder. The other clutched a golf club. Katie seemed spellbound by what was happening below, despite the dog yelping and jumping on her.

"No time for that," I replied as I hurriedly got her and Katie turned around and headed up the path. A burst of red light and the sound of breaking glass presaged the blast of heat that knocked us down in a jumble of bodies before we'd gone three feet. Casting my eyes skyward, I saw that the lighthouse was on fire, its tower a hellish seething Medusa of red, yellow and orange flames. The flare, which I'd had in my hand all this time, rolled out of my grasp and into the brush. I hoped the rainstorm earlier meant it wasn't all dry tinder out there.

We stumbled to our feet again and struggled up the path. A glance over my shoulder and down the hill revealed half a dozen Native American guys emerging from behind the lighthouse, arrows already fitted to their bows. Their leader gave a silent nod to Captain Newport who stood with his torch held high. A couple of Portuguese sailors stood beside him, knives at the ready.

But a score of dirty, ill-kempt, rough-looking men were creeping out of the shadows behind Conrad. A few had guns, some had swords. Some had clubs or hatchets. In the distance, a horse whinnied.

"To me, lads!" Captain Newport cried.

As both sides surged forward, an arrow whistled through the eerie light to find its home in the throat of the nearest ruffian, who sank to his knees with his hands clutching the shaft, then pitched face forward to the ground. Curses, shots and screams rang out as the two sides joined the battle.

All we could do was run.

Chapter 36

We ran. Up the path as fast as we could go toward the cabins, our progress hampered by my limp and Katie's slower pace. Pipe finally picked her up, piggyback style, figuring we could make better time that way. The dog rumbled along beside us, his tongue hanging out, casting me sidelong glances. Probably trying to decide if I tasted better than Daniel, or vice versa. Original recipe or crispy. I'd deal with him later.

My foot found a rut in the path, my ankle twisting awkwardly. My feet slid out from under me entirely and I went down hard.

Pipe immediately stopped and set Katie down, then came back to where I'd fallen.

"Are you hurt?" she said.

"No," I said, heaving myself to a sitting position. "I just... ow...turned my ankle."

She held my ankle lightly, turning it to and fro ultragently. I grimaced, but it wasn't that bad. Certainly not broken.

"Take your jacket off," she said to me.

"Huh?"

"Your jacket, Mad." She helped me ease it off, swiftly and surely, then produced that ever-useful steak knife from her back pocket.

"What are you doing?" I said, fear suddenly clouding me. I pulled away from her.

"Mad," she said, chidingly. "I'm just going to cut the sleeves off your shirt to wrap up your ankle and your leg."

"Oh," I said. A moment ticked by. "Sorry. That would be good."

As she started her ad hoc home ec project, I checked out Katie, who was staring up the path toward the cabins, the dog by her side.

"Katie, come here," I said to her. Pipe was carefully wrapping up my ankle. The dog came, but Katie did not.

"Katie," I said, with emphasis. She turned dreamily and wandered over. I put my arm around her waist as Pipe worked on my other leg. The one with the rabies in it. I glared at the dog as he mooched about, sniffing at the bottoms of Pipe's shoes, eyeballing me from a safe distance. He whined, trying hard to look like butter wouldn't melt in his mouth.

Katie stiffened under my arm, still looking up the path. The dog's whine turned to a snarl.

"Hey, are you..." My voice trailed off as a faint red glow lit up the top of the path. A small figure was standing there, outlined by the light. Lily, in her red velvet dress and button-up shoes. Clutching my flare, with sparks cascading off its tip. She slowly raised the flare so we could see the lower half of her face. Smiling.

"Pipe," I said in a strangled voice, grabbing her with my other arm.

"What?" she said, as Lily turned and ran daintily up the path, the flare like an oversized sparkler in her hand.

"Jesus, was that...?"

"Yeah," I said, struggling back into my jacket. "I think we'd better get a move on."

The sounds from the struggle behind us had not diminished during this time. A sharp crack followed by a dull boom assailed our ears. Instinctively ducking, we scuttled up the path. I hoped our guys were kicking butt.

We were almost to the gravel. There seemed to be more light in the sky now—could dawn be upon us?

No, I saw, as we gained the head of the path. Lily had set the cabins on fire. The empty cabin was already fully alight, flames shooting twenty feet in the sky. Pipe's cabin was smoldering, an inferno of fire already dancing inside.

Pipe made a sound in her throat, stunned into immobility beside me. Katie was on her back, little hands clasped around Pipe's neck. We all three numbly took in the devastation—the empty cabin, Pipe's cabin and James's cabin...

Flames licked at its foundations, but I had no eyes for that. All I could see was the dead woman in her long dress, hanging from a porch beam, dangling and twisting...

A sudden movement caught my attention. Lily, darting out from the shadows and underneath James's Explorer. Where she'd gathered some brush. She bent down to apply the flare to the pile, impishly grinning out at us as she crouched under the vehicle.

"Lily, no!" I screamed, forgetting for a moment she wasn't a real child. The brush caught. It was almost as light as daylight in the dell, what with all the flames and the eerie moonlight. So I could see her face in that last instant, with the black pits for eyes...

"*No!*" I screamed, running forward. Pipe tackled me easily and the three of us again went down in a heap as the gas tank caught fire and the car exploded in an enormous, deafening kaboom. Bits and pieces of the vehicle rained down around us in a fiery downpour, but miraculously, nothing big enough to hurt struck us. Something metal and heavy came down with a crash upon the rental Jeep's windshield and hood. I was going to have one hell of a time explaining all of this to Hertz.

Acrid smoke washed over us, burning our eyes and choking us. Pipe was making sure each of us was okay, but I couldn't make out much of what she was saying due to the ringing in my ears. But clearly, she was eager for us to head topside. She yelled in my face again.

"What?" The ringing was slowly abating.

"This time, we take the road," she was saying.

I nodded. "Let's go," I said, grabbing Katie's hand.

Chapter 37

Up the hill was east. And now there was a definite lightening to the sky. It was still dark, but I could see my hand in front of my face. Both legs were feeling stiff and throbbing with pain, but we were moving along pretty well, all things considered. Katie held my hand. Pipe led the way, golf club at the ready. The pooch brought up the rear, wheezing heavily. We tacked right on one of the cutback sections of the road, then headed uphill again at a near forty-five degree angle. The footing was slippery with loose pebbles and gravel underneath, but the slowly growing light was a help. I was almost starting to think we might make it. I could see the top of the hill above us, a dark outline against the slightly lighter sky. Below us, the fires and the battle raged on, but all seemed quiet up top.

Pipe slipped and went down on one knee, but caught herself with the golf club. Unhurt, she turned to us and smiled.

"Watch your step."

Katie ran over to her and pulled her to her feet, saying, "Come on, Pipe!"

They went on ahead as I paused a moment to kick at the dirt where Pipe had slipped. Something small and round and milky white was there. Two somethings that were too perfectly round to be rocks. Not pebbles for her to slip on—just a couple of unblinking baby doll eyes. I shuddered, then kicked the dirt over them. I limped after my girls as fast I could—I couldn't wait to get off Shadow Point once and for all.

We passed Pipe's overturned truck, looking sad and crumpled, wheels to the sky. A sky that was now a delicate pale blue suffused with shades of pink. We were almost at the top of the dirt road. I could see where it ended and the asphalt began. The security kiosk was there about fifty feet north of the junction, with the administration building, the labs and the new lighthouse off to the south. My legs were killing me, but it didn't matter. Nothing mattered now except getting the three of us out of there safely.

The dog sneezed behind me. Oh, pardon me, the four of us. I still grudgingly considered him part of our little crew, but obedience school was definitely in his future. As if he could read my thoughts, he started whining again, but I paid him no mind because we had made it to the asphalt. A real road! Civilization! Four-star hotel room, here we come!

Pipe stood looking east with her hands on Katie's shoulders. I gimped up alongside and put my arm through hers. She gave me a grin and then a quick buss on the cheek.

"We made it, Mad."

The dog scampered over to sniff at the kiosk foundation. Following his nose, he disappeared around the back of the little structure as a sailor emerged from it. It was Torres, the Latina, her trusty M16 cradled in her arms. It was perhaps unkind of me to imagine that she slept with it. A sidearm was also securely strapped to her side. I idly wondered again what the Navy was so protective of out here. With the sun still low in the sky behind her, she stood in shadow in front of the kiosk.

"Torres!" Pipe called out a greeting and unhooked herself from us, then walked forward to speak with her. Torres didn't return Pipe's greeting. I didn't like it, suddenly, that her face was in shadow. Why didn't she speak? I moved Katie behind me and said, "Pipe."

She turned and looked at me inquiringly. I shook my head, once. She took a step backward, which brought Torres out of the shadows. She looked the same as always—implacable, unsmiling, emotionless—but something was different. She seemed focused on Pipe. I turned my head slightly when I caught sight of the dog coming around the side of the kiosk. He'd stopped sniffing and was looking at the back of Torres with his head cocked to one side, as if he wasn't sure what he was seeing. By turning my head, I had Torres in my peripheral vision and that's when I realized what was wrong with the picture. She was fuzzy around the outside—like a photograph taken when someone was moving.

My head snapped back toward her and she turned to look at me then. For a split second, as if a movie projector had shone an image on her, I saw not Torres, but a tall man with deep-set eyes, fierce brows and a moustache that was drooping, but not defeated. Conrad Bly.

I blinked and the picture shifted back to Torres, who was no longer cradling the gun in her arms, but pointing it at Pipe.

"Torres, no," Pipe said, hands held up as if to calm the situation. "Hey, it's me, Rosalita—Dr. Piper. Come on, you know me—don't do this."

There was a moment of stillness when Torres said nothing, Pipe took a step back and Torres's finger moved to curl around the trigger. As if in slow motion, I saw the dog slink forward, fangs exposed, then hurl himself upon the unwary woman's back, going for the neck. She screamed, the M16 went off with an earsplitting burst of gunfire and I turned and hit the ground, Katie beneath me. Horrible screaming and snarling filled the air for another few seconds, then a second, single gunshot rang out.

Silence.

Slow, measured footsteps were coming toward me. I was shaking so badly I didn't think I could control myself to look up, but I had to. I had to. For Katie.

I looked up. Pipe was walking toward us. Her steps slowed as I watched, then she faltered and sank to her knees. The left arm and shoulder of her hoodie were wet with blood.

"Oh, no. Oh, God, no. Pipe..." Katie and I ran to her and knelt by her side. I looked at her with a terrible anxiety ripping me apart inside. She sat down awkwardly, her left arm hanging down, useless. Torres lay unmoving by the guard shack, as did the dog.

"It's all right," she gasped, "It's just my arm." But her face was white as a sheet. "Check Torres," she told me.

I told Katie to stay with Pipe and she nodded, her eyes huge, her face white too. I heard Pipe trying to comfort her as I limped over to Torres and Henry the Eighth. He was dead. Torres had shot him with her sidearm as he locked onto her neck, but he'd managed to rip her throat out. There was blood all down the front of her. She lay in a puddle of it. An arterial spurt had splashed the side of the kiosk. I knelt down beside her as death rattled in what was left of her windpipe. Her eyes were open—they were his eyes for a moment. I looked deep into them. Whatever was in there slowly faded and they were her eyes again, but seeing nothing.

I turned to Henry, lying a few feet away, his furry bulk forever stilled. I sadly patted his sandy hide one last time, then wearily rose to my feet. I felt so tired.

As I half-limped, half-staggered back to Pipe and Katie, I heard sirens in the distance. Birds chirping nearby. The spell was broken. Conrad was gone—I could feel it.

I untied the shirt sleeve Pipe had so recently applied to my sprained ankle and bound up her arm as best I could, then put my jacket on her, blanket-style, to try and keep her warm. She lay in my arms, her face in my chest. Katie was bent over my back, crying, her arms wound tightly around my neck. I tried to tell her everything was going to be okay, but I couldn't get the words out.

A perfect sky stretched out above us, so blue it looked solid. From the bay to the ocean and beyond, not a cloud could be seen. It was going to be a gorgeous day, I thought disjointedly, as I watched the blood drip from Pipe's hand onto my pants leg.

The sirens were getting closer. A lot of them. Help was on the way. Pipe sagged in my arms. A Coast Guard helicopter thundered up from the bay side and hovered over us, then flew westward to investigate. I guessed they'd finally noticed all the black smoke. A Navy Jeep came barreling down the road from the administration building, then slowed when they saw the little tableau at the kiosk. I could see Delgado behind the wheel.

Cradling her in my arms, with Katie hanging on to me for dear life, I desperately told myself Pipe was going to be all right. We would all be all right. I knew what I had to do now. I would quit my job in Boston and move me and Katie to San Francisco. We'd start a new life, a new family…with Pipe too, if she would have us…

"We're gonna be fine," I murmured, half-sobbing, to whoever was listening.

Pipe shivered, either from the chill morning air or the shock or both. I pulled my Niners hat off my head and put it on her so she wouldn't lose any body heat that way.

Her face drawn with pain, she still managed to look up at me with that grin and said, "Wow—does this mean we're going steady?"

As a beautiful new day dawned over San Diego, I looked in her blue gray eyes and knew the answer was yes.

Epilogue

So, the good news was I didn't end up writing this from a prison cell. We had a *lot* of explaining to do, however, in the days and weeks that followed. And how exactly does one explain the inexplicable? Especially to the cops and Uncle Sam?

They first whisked the three of us off to the hospital with Pipe's gunshot wound being the top priority. Katie and I were looking pretty grimy and disheveled, but aside from my sprained ankle, we were both more or less physically okay once they got us cleaned up. They had a child psychologist speak with Katie too, but she was fine and passed all his tests. Kids are amazing.

But then the questions began. And I thought they might never stop.

The only bright spot was that Pipe's mom and one of her brothers swooped in and took control on the home front. They flew up from Austin immediately, as soon as they heard the news. Avis Piper was just as delightful as I had imagined, although every time she called Pipe "Alice" I had to look around to see who she was talking to. They rented a house not far from downtown, above the airport, which was great since none of us had a place to stay anymore. I also appreciated the fact that the house was inland—I was feeling pretty done with the beach for a while. While Pipe and I spent our days meeting with investigators and attorneys, Avis and Pipe's brother Ethan took care of Katie, showering her with affection, ice cream and trips to the zoo and SeaWorld. I hated not being there for her twenty-four/seven, but I think the grandmotherly attention from Avis was exactly what she needed during that difficult time.

Some of the questions we were asked were easier to answer than others. Torres, for example. Poor Torres. Her autopsy results were clear and undisputed—death due to massive blood loss due to a lacerated jugular vein due to animal attack. Obviously, we didn't kill her, the dog did. And he wasn't even our dog. The fact that Torres had shot Pipe as well as Henry the Eighth also seemed to help deflect any blame from us. Unexpected (at least to me) assistance came from Lieutenant Delgado, who told the cops Pipe was a wonderful person and apparently said I was okay too. I don't know what he told them about Torres, but there was apparently some speculation about whether the stress of her military duties had caused her to snap. There was also some speculation about the dog possibly having contracted rabies from an infected coyote or other critter, but those lab results thankfully came up clear. I felt terrible that the reputations of both Torres and Henry were being besmirched after their deaths when it was all Conrad Bly's fault, but the attorney told me in no uncertain terms to keep those thoughts to myself.

Oh, yeah, there was an attorney. A couple of them, in fact. One for the criminal stuff and one for the family court stuff. Formal charges were never actually brought against me or Pipe, thank goodness. Although we were "persons of interest" for a harrowing few weeks, neither one of us was ever taken into custody or indicted. I can't say the cops believed a word we said, but in the end, the evidence just wasn't there to show we had done anything. Well, not much of anything.

The deaths of Mr. Bohannon and Daniel from the Church of the Benevolent Fount remained a mystery. Daniel's body had been found in much the same grisly condition as Mr. Bohannon's—torn to bits by a violent attack. The same brutal force had shredded the two tires on Bohannon's truck. Although they interrogated us for days about both of those murders, they finally had to admit that neither Pipe nor I had the physical strength to commit such atrocities. Nor was there any forensic evidence to suggest we had. Neither Pipe nor I had any motive to harm Mr. Bohannon. Perhaps one could be imagined for me to want to kill Daniel, but motive alone was apparently an insufficient basis for them to charge me. I heard some of the cops wondering if rabid coyotes could tear a man apart like that, but that theory got shot down when the medical examiner said there were no bite marks on either corpse.

Shudder.

Delgado, again, unexpectedly came to our aid when he and several other Navy personnel stated they had seen and heard some strange things out on the Point. The sailors were reluctant to say much more than that, but one of the civilian employees said she had seen a mustachioed man and a little girl, both strangely dressed in old-time clothes, walking along the beach in a restricted area. When she approached them, however, they disappeared, melting into the mist.

Nobody believed the ghost story, of course, but the district attorney finally told the cops there wasn't sufficient evidence to charge us in regard to any of the deaths. Homicide by person or persons unknown, I think was how they put it. The investigation wasn't closed, but they didn't seem to have any other leads to pursue. I couldn't help them with that.

Then, of course, there was the property damage. As far as the fire in the lighthouse…well, I did actually do that one. And I told the cops all about it. Over and over and over again. But I denied having set fire to the cabins and Pipe backed me up. Without any witnesses, they couldn't pin it on me. The Navy declined to press charges on that one. I don't know if it was the lack of evidence, Pipe's standing in the Shadow Point community or the fact that all that was destroyed was three crappy cabins that were about to fall down on their own anyhow. I probably saved the government thousands in demolition costs. In any event, my attorney wheeled and dealed on the lighthouse fire and I got off with a fine and a ticket for defacing historical property or something like that. Considering the fact that it had already burned once and was in less than perfect shape, the additional harm done by my fire wasn't that significant, I guess.

Last, but far from least, was the damaged Jeep. I'm telling you, do not try messing with a rental car company! They were as relentless as the police, if not more so. In the end, the easiest solution was for me to buy the Jeep from them, thus avoiding the canceling of my car insurance. Surprisingly, after the body work was done, the heater repaired and the brake system thoroughly inspected and given a thumbs-up, the vehicle actually still worked. I gave the Jeep to Pipe, since I felt responsible for wrecking her old truck. So, that worked out okay.

Delgado came by the house to see Pipe one afternoon after she got out of the hospital. I was downtown with the attorney at the police station, but she told me about it later. Gato told her he'd been to the old lighthouse that day. The cops had finally taken down their crime scene tape and returned the jurisdiction of the property to the Navy. Delgado had stubbed his toe in the sand on something at the base of the wooden stairs. He brought the artifact to Pipe.

"What is it?" she asked him as he unwrapped it from a piece of soft cloth.

"It looks like an old Indian arrowhead. They still find those around the Point sometimes, you know."

She told me she held it in her hand. It was surprisingly lightweight, a carefully chipped piece of quartz, a dull grayish brown in color except at its sharp tip, where it was stained a reddish brown.

"So why are you bringing this to me, Gato?" she said, handing it back to him with a shiver.

"The arrowhead is old, Pipe. There's no doubt about that. But the blood looks pretty fresh, don't you think?"

She stared at him, but didn't answer.

"Don't you?" he pressed. "I could have one of the guys at the lab check it out, if you like."

"Just throw it away, Gato," she told him. "Please. Just throw it in the ocean and let it all wash away."

Most important, of course, was Katie. Her well-being and my custody of her. I did have legal custody of Katie per the paperwork from the county. Amidst the chaos and barrage of questions in the succeeding days, there was a hearing in family court where custody was again discussed. They told me they had tried to find Katie's grandparents or some other relative on Chloe's side of the family, but phones were disconnected and mail came back as undeliverable. Some Benevolent Fount guy in a dark suit was there, I remember, as was Mrs. Augustine from Child Protective Services, but it was all a bit of a blur to me. I was just about frantic those days, from the worrying about Katie to the criminal proceedings to Pipe's gunshot wound. I wasn't sleeping much. I felt like I'd been thrust from one nightmare into another, but at least this time I was fighting the living, not the dead.

Somehow, despite the cloud of suspicion hovering over me, it was determined that I was indeed the best person to have custody of my niece. This was largely due to the efforts of the attorney and Mrs. Augustine, who gave me her approval after she'd had a long chat with Katie. I think the judge looked askance at the church guy too. There was all sorts of squabbling over the legalities of

James's will and whether the church even had a say in the matter. Another hearing was scheduled for a future date, but we were safe for a while. It felt like all I'd been looking for my whole life was a safe place.

The day finally came when all the possible charges were either dropped or resolved. We were free to leave San Diego. Pipe had her new job to go to in San Francisco at the aquarium. Her arm was healing nicely. Avis and Katie were having one last surrogate grandmother fling at the stuff-your-own-teddy-bear place in the mall. Better Avis than me on that one, I thought. Pipe's brother had flown back to Austin the day before, so she and I had the house to ourselves for a few hours. We hadn't really had any time alone since we'd left the Point. Katie and I were sharing a room in the rental house, as were Pipe and her mother. With everything that had happened, we hadn't had much of a chance to talk about us and what was next for us. Was there anything next for us?

Although healing, Pipe's arm was still in a sling, her shoulder bandaged. She looked tired. We were lying on my bed together, with her good arm around me. I could see a line of strain in her forehead that hadn't been there before. I put that there, I thought. I reached out a finger to smooth it away.

"I'm so sorry, Pipe," I said. "I never meant to put you through all this."

I couldn't help it, I started to cry.

"Will you stop it?" she said, but in a kindly tone. "If this is what I had to go through to get you in my life, then it was well worth it. In case you haven't noticed, I love you, Madison."

"You love me?" I sat up. "You really...I mean, really?"

She was laughing at me now. "Yes, really, Mad. I love you." She sat up and kissed me to prove it.

"I love you too, Pipe," I murmured as her lips lightly brushed my throat.

"Just don't call me Alice," she said as she gently pushed me back down on the bedspread.

A week later, I was back in Boston at my apartment. Katie and I were there to pack it up, then we were off to San Francisco to join Pipe. A large stack of mail was waiting for me when I got back, but I'd been putting off dealing with it until the end of the week. I'd been so busy with finding movers, packing up and a thousand other things. Oh, yeah and quitting my job. I don't know who was more relieved—me or my boss.

When I had a moment to think about it, it was almost miraculous to me that I wasn't craving a smoke or a drink. Somewhere along the line, my brain had turned a corner and decided We Don't Do That Anymore. We Used To, But Not Anymore. It was all about Katie now, for me. Katie and Pipe.

The movers had come and gone that afternoon. We were going to "camp" in the now empty apartment one last night before our flight to SF took off the next morning. Katie couldn't bear to part with her new prized possession—a brand-new bicycle (that's right—two wheels!) with training wheels, so that, our suitcases and an air mattress were all that was left in the apartment. I figured I'd just buy her a new bike in California.

We'd made a habit of going to a nearby park each day that week. As she rode her bike up and down a broad expanse of sidewalk under the interlaced branches of ancient shade trees, I sat on a bench and watched. After the movers left, we went down to the park for one last ride. She looked pretty darn cute on her little pink bike with her little purple helmet, both of which she had selected herself.

The stack of mail sat next to me on the bench. With a sigh, I reached for it and removed the big rubber band holding it together. I started making two piles—one for junk, one for bills. A plain white envelope stood out from the rest. My name and address were hand printed on it. Curious, I picked it up to take a closer look. The postmark was San Diego, the date several weeks

261

back. Right before I'd left Boston, as a matter of fact. My heart began to hammer in my chest. Instinctively, I looked around for Katie, making sure she was all right. She flew past on her pink bicycle, flashing me a big smile as she passed.

"You're doing great, kiddo!" I called out encouragingly. And she was. It wouldn't be long before I'd have to ask Pipe to take off the training wheels in San Francisco.

I returned my attention to the white envelope and opened it with some trepidation. Inside was a folded multipage document and a separate single sheet of paper. A letter. From James. I recognized his handwriting although it looked rushed and agitated on the page.

Dear Madison,

I don't have much time to write this. I know you haven't heard from me in a while and I'm sorry about that. I'm sorry about a lot of things, Mad. I was wrong to turn my back on you for all those years. I know that now. Things have happened lately, things I can't explain, but they've made me realize that family is all that matters. If something should happen to me, I want you to have the enclosed copy of my will. Just in case. You and Katie are all the family I have left now. You'll always be my little sister. I love you, Mad and I know Katie will too, when you get a chance to meet her. I'll call you later if things work out.

James

Katie zipped past again, her helmet slightly askew. She skidded to a stop, adjusted it, then set off toward the next park bench some twenty feet away, our agreed upon boundary for her riding. My eyes filled with tears as I watched her.

"Look, Mad! Look, I'm doing it! I can do it!" she happily shouted over her shoulder.

All I could do was nod. The lump in my throat precluded speech. My hands were shaking as I unfolded the will, which had the same date as the letter. My eyes skimmed over the standard paragraphs of legal mumbo-jumbo, then Katie's name jumped out at me. James's new will said that, in the event of his death, sole custody of his daughter, Katherine Lily McPeake, should go to his sister, Madison... My eyes filled with tears and a sob forced its way out as I took in all the implications. Katie was safe now. *We* were safe. And James had loved me, after all...

"Mad?" Katie was perched on her bike in front of me, looking at me quizzically. "Are you okay, Mad?" she asked solemnly.

I reached over and hugged her, bike and all, telling her I was fine, just fine, everything was fine now, laughing through my tears. She wiggled her way loose as I fumbled for a tissue, patted my cheek delicately with her little hand, then pushed off for another lap.

My cell phone buzzed in my pocket. I hastily wiped my eyes so I could read the screen—it was Pipe.

"Hey," I managed to croak out.

"Hey, you," she said breezily. "Are the movers gone yet?"

"Uh..." was all I could get out before my throat closed on me. I fought for control as the tears welled up again.

"Baby, are you okay?" Pipe asked, her voice filled with concern. "Is everything all right?"

I realized that for the first time in my life, everything truly *was* all right. As the late afternoon sun broke through the branches of the tree above me, I began to tell her the news.

Publications from
Bella Books, Inc.
Women. Books. Even Better Together.

P.O. Box 10543
Tallahassee, FL 32302
Phone: 800-729-4992
www.bellabooks.com

THE GRASS WIDOW by Nanci Little. Aidan Blackstone is nineteen, unmarried and pregnant and has no reason to think that the year 1876 won't be her last. Joss Bodett has lost her family but desperately clings to their land. A richly told story of frontier survival that picks up with the generation of women where Patience and Sarah left off.
978-1-59493-189-5 $12.95

SMOKEY O by Celia Cohen. Insult "Mac" MacDonnell and insult the entire Delaware Blue Diamond team. Smokey O'Neill has just insulted Mac and then finds she's been traded to Delaware. The games are not limited to the baseball field!
978-1-59493-198-7 $12.95

WICKED GAMES by Ellen Hart. Never have mysteries and secrets been closer to home in this eighth installment of this award-winning lesbian cozy mystery series. Jane Lawless's neighbors bring puzzles and peril—and that's just the beginning.
978-1-59493-185-7 $14.95

NOT EVERY RIVER by Robbi McCoy. It's the hottest city in the U.S. and it's not just the weather that's heating up. For Kim and Randi are forced to question everything they thought they knew about themselves before they can risk their fiery hearts on the biggest gamble of all.
978-1-59493-182-6 $14.95

HOUSE OF CARDS by Nat Burns. Cards are played, but the game is gossip. Kaylen Strauder has never wanted it to be about her. But the time is fast-approaching when she must decide which she needs more: her community or Eda Byrne.
978-1-59493-203-8 $14.95

RETURN TO ISIS by Jean Stewart. The award-winning Isis sci-fi series features Jean Stewart's vision of a committed colony of women dedicated to preserving their way of life, even after the apocalypse. Mysteries have been forgotten, but survival depends on remembering. Book one in series.
978-1-59493-193-2 $12.95

1ST IMPRESSIONS by Kate Calloway. Rookie PI Cassidy James has her first case. Her investigation into the murder of Erica Trinidad's uncle isn't welcomed by the local sheriff, especially since the delicious, seductive Erica is their prime suspect. First in series. Author's augmented and expanded edition.
978-1-59493-192-5 $12.95

BEACON OF LOVE by Ann Roberts. Twenty-five years after their families put an end to a relationship that hadn't even begun, Stephanie returns to Oregon to find many things have changed...except her feelings for Paula.
978-1-59493-180-2 $14.95

ABOVE TEMPTATION by Karin Kallmaker. It's supposed to be like any other case, except this time they're chasing one of their own. As fraud investigators Tamara Sterling and Kip Barrett try to catch a thief, they realize they can have anything they want—except each other.
978-1-59493-179-6 $14.95

AN EMERGENCE OF GREEN by Katherine V. Forrest. Carolyn had no idea her new neighbor jumped the fence to enjoy her swimming pool. The discovery leads to choices she never anticipated in an intense, sensual story of discovery and risk, consequences and triumph. Originally released in 1986.
978-1-59493-217-5 $14.95

CRAZY FOR LOVING by Jaye Maiman. Officially hanging out her shingle as a private investigator, Robin Miller is getting her life on track. Just as Robin discovers it's hard to follow a dead man, she walks in. KT Bellflower, sultry and devastating... Lammy winner and second in series.
978-1-59493-195-6 $14.95

LOVE WAITS by Gerri Hill. The All-American girl and the love she left behind—it's been twenty years since Ashleigh and Gina parted and now they're back to the place where nothing was simple and love didn't wait.
978-1-59493-186-4 $14.95

HANNAH FREE: THE BOOK by Claudia Allen. Based on the film festival hit movie starring Sharon Gless. Hannah's story is funny, scathing and witty as she navigates life with aplomb—but always comes home to Rachel. 32 pages of color photographs plus bonus behind-the-scenes movie information.
978-1-59493-172-7 $19.95

END OF THE ROPE by Jackie Calhoun. Meg Klein has two enduring loves—horses and Nicky Hennessey. Nicky is there for her when she most needs help, but then an attractive vet throws Meg's carefully balanced world out of kilter.
978-1-59493-176-5 $14.95

THE LONG TRAIL by Penny Hayes. When schoolteacher Blanche Bartholomew and dance hall girl Teresa Stark meet their feelings are powerful—and completely forbidden—in Starcross Texas. In search of a safe future, they flee, daring to take a covered wagon across the forbidding prairie.
978-1-59493-196-3 $12.95

UP UP AND AWAY by Catherine Ennis. Sarah and Margaret have a video. The mob wants it. Flying for their lives, two women discover more than secrets.
978-1-59493-215-1 $12.95

CITY OF STRANGERS by Diana Rivers. A captive in a gilded cage, young Solene plots her escape, but the rulers of Hernorium have other plans for Solene—and her people. Breathless lesbian fantasy story also perfect for teen readers.
978-1-59493-183-3 $14.95

ROBBER'S WINE by Ellen Hart. Belle Dumont is the first dead of summer. Jane Lawless, Belle's old friend, suspects coldhearted murder. Lammy-winning seventh novel in critically acclaimed cozy mystery series.
978-1-59493-184-0 $14.95

APPARITION ALLEY by Katherine V. Forrest. Kate Delafield has solved hundreds of cases, but the one that baffles her most is her own shooting. Book six in series.
978-1-883523-65-7 $14.95

STERLING ROAD BLUES by Ruth Perkinson. It was a simple declaration of love. But the entire state of Virginia wants to weigh in, leaving teachers Carrie Tomlinson and Audra Malone caught in the crossfire—and with love troubles of their own.
978-1-59493-187-1 $14.95

LILY OF THE TOWER by Elizabeth Hart. Agnes Headey, taking refuge from a storm at the Netherfield estate, stumbles into dark family secrets and something more… Meticulously researched historical romance.
978-1-59493-177-2 $14.95

LETTING GO by Ann O'Leary. Kelly has decided that luscious, successful Laura should be hers. For now. Laura might even be agreeable. But where does that leave Kate?
978-1-59493-194-9 $12.95

MURDER TAKES TO THE HILLS by Jessica Thomas. Renovations, shady business deals, a stalker—and it's not even tourist season yet for PI Alex Peres and her best four-legged pal Fargo. Sixth in this cozy Provincetown-based series.
978-1-59493-178-9 $14.95